DROWNING ERIN

ELIZABETH O'ROARK

ISBN: 978-0-9898135-7-0

ERIN

The music begins. It's my turn to walk down the aisle. I clutch the bouquet of peonies and white roses and take a deep breath.

Olivia, the bride, is somewhere in the shadows behind me, surprisingly calm given how long she spent resisting the idea of marriage. I'm the one whose heart is fluttering too fast, and it has nothing to do with all the heads turning my way.

Don't look at him.

Ignore him, forget him.

I've said these things to myself a thousand times and I don't know why I bother—it's never worked once. Even now—when my maid of honor duties should be paramount and with Rob sitting somewhere in the crowd—I can't seem to stop myself. I'm not five feet down the aisle before my gaze goes straight to the one person it shouldn't: the best man.

He stands to his brother's right, watching me the way he's done often over the past few months—as if he'd eat me alive if I'd allow it. His eyes, as blue as the sea behind him, meet mine, and my heart doesn't seem to beat but *bounce* inside my chest. There's one long bounce where five or six beats should have occurred. Inside my head I begin pleading with him: *It's not too late. You can still fix this. Please, please fix this.*

～

WHEN I OPEN MY EYES, I'M STILL PLEADING WITH HIM. FOR A moment I strain to hear the cellist, and am surprised to find only normal morning sounds—running water, the whir of an electric razor. My heart is still bouncing in my chest as I roll toward the nightstand and slip on my engagement ring. I can't believe I'm still having that dream after so many years have passed. I can't believe I'm having that dream about someone who never deserved a moment of my time in the first place.

The therapist I saw told me it was cold feet and that it happens to everyone. God I hope she was right.

Rob emerges from the bathroom clad only in a towel. "Sorry," he says, frowning. "I was trying to be quiet. Go back to sleep."

"I made you shortribs last night," I say, yawning.

He runs a hand through his hair. "Sorry hon. It was just a stupid client thing. I didn't think it would take as long as it did."

It's hard to get mad at him when I know he only got a few hours of sleep. It's also hard to be mad when I'm lying here, fresh from a sexually charged dream about someone else. I flinch at the memory of it, wishing I could drown that dream until it's too water-logged to ever surface again.

Rob grabs boxers and drops the towel, revealing a perfect body, honed by long hours in the gym. It's a pleasure to watch him dress, even this early in the day.

"You know, we're both awake and in the same place at the same time, for once," I suggest. "I can think of something I'd rather do than sleep."

His shoulders fall and there's an apology in his eyes. I already knew he was going to turn me down. I don't know why I even suggested it. "They're eight hours ahead in Amsterdam, hon," he replies. "I've really got to get going. But I'll be home early."

For the dinner. The dinner I desperately don't want to attend.

"Don't remind me," I groan.

Rob arches a brow. "Come on, Erin. Brendan's been gone for four years. You can live through a single meal with him. You're about to be godparents together, right?"

Caroline, Olivia's second child, is the most beautiful baby I've ever laid eyes on, with eyes exactly like her uncle's. He may be a menace to about fifty percent of the population, but no man alive has eyes like Brendan's—a pale, translucent blue, the color of beach glass.

I *used* to love beach glass. Not anymore.

"Yes and seeing him at the baptism will be more than enough interaction, I assure you."

"You promised you'd be nice," he warns.

"I only promised to be civil. Which is more than I'll get from him in return, I'm sure."

He sighs, pulling on his jacket. "I don't understand why you hate him so much."

It's nothing I've ever been able to explain. Hatred for Brendan is like some underground water source—you think you've got it all out in the open, but it just keeps coming.

Except when I'm dreaming about him. I don't seem to hate him much then.

⚜ 2 ⚜

ERIN

A file floats gently through the air, landing in front of me. I glance up to the top of the cubicle wall to find my office-mate, Harper, staring down at me. "I just added something new to your Pinterest board," she says. "The bouquet is calla lilies, tied with this orange ribbon that matches the sash on the bridesmaids' dresses."

Harper's obsession with my future wedding never fails to amuse me, given her own disdain for commitment. "The sash on *what* bridesmaids' dresses?" I ask. "We haven't even set a date yet."

She jumps down and comes around to my desk, moving several files to the floor before she sits on it. "Because you're quote unquote 'too busy'. At a job you hate, I should add," she says with a sigh. "So anyway, what did Rob say about the money?"

I arch a brow. "*What* money?"

"The money you loaned your brother," she says. "I heard you on the phone yesterday."

I laugh and groan at the same time. I do love Harper, but she has no understanding of the concept of boundaries. "I know we can hear each other's conversations," I reply, "but we're supposed to at least pretend we aren't actively listening."

She nods, but only to acknowledge that I've spoken and not to acknowledge that I'm *right*. "You're avoiding the question, which means you either didn't tell him or he was really pissed."

I shrug. "I was asleep when he got home last night. And besides, it's my money. I don't need his permission to lend it to a family member."

"A family member who's a drug addict," she says.

"A recovering addict," I counter.

She raises a brow at that, and for good reason. Sean's been off the wagon more than he's been on it during the years since Harper and I began working together.

We both hear our boss's tuneless whistling in the hallway. I tip my chin at Harper to go back to her own cubicle, but she just crosses her legs and swings them insouciantly. Unlike the rest of us, Harper does not give a flying fuck about Timothy's opinion. Sometimes I think she *wants* to get fired, and I can't entirely blame her. He's singlehandedly made East Colorado University, my alma mater, a terrible place to work.

Timothy's thin lips press tight as he walks over to us. "Erin's cubicle isn't a water cooler, Harper," he says. "Don't you have someplace to be?"

She shrugs. "It's after four-thirty, Tim-O. I'm off the clock."

"There *is* no clock, because you are salaried," he says. "So if you are truly done for the day, which I *doubt*, please move along and let the rest of my employees get their jobs done."

She, naturally, doesn't move a muscle, just stares at him until he walks away.

"You know what I dream about sometimes?" she asks. "Working in a factory. Some job where you just push a button or something every three minutes."

I picture it. A job where I only push a button, and where there is no Tim around to suggest ways I could push the button better, or waxing poetic about what it *means* to push the button. I sigh. "That does sound nice."

"And there'd be this hot factory guy who spends the entire day saying dirty shit in my ear," she continues dreamily. "So I push the button and then leave right on time to do unspeakable things with him."

I laugh but feel a stab of envy. Sex, for Harper, is like some kind of ultimate amusement park—a ride that just keeps getting better every time she hops on.

"If I had that factory job, I'd probably just spend more time asleep."

"Then Rob's doing something wrong," she counters. "You haven't been with him *that* long. It should still be exciting."

I don't expect her to understand because she didn't grow up like I did. But I'm not looking for excitement. I simply aspire to the absence of pain. And therefore, I have exactly what I want.

ERIN

As we drive to the restaurant to meet Brendan, my stomach swims...the way it would preceding any unpleasant event. I've barely seen him since he left for Italy four years ago, and I'm sure it will be fine, but I can't get rid of this feeling—nerves, dread, anticipation.

I should use this time to tell Rob about the money I lent my brother, but I'm too tense about the hours ahead. Too resentful of them as well.

In theory, tonight will be a double date, though I'm not sure *date* is really an accurate way to describe Brendan's relationship with any female.

"Is he actually bringing someone he knows," I ask as Rob parks in front of the restaurant, "or is this is some girl he slept with last night and can't shake off?"

"Erin," Rob says with a raised brow. "Give him a chance."

Right. As if Brendan will give *me* a chance. As little as I like him, he likes me even less: I've lost count of the number of times he's tried to convince Rob to dump me.

We step onto the large patio, and I hear it: Brendan's laugh, a sound I'd know anywhere. It's deeper than Rob's, a husky, low chuckle that resides somewhere toward the bottom of his chest. I'm pretty sure he could get laid on the basis of that laugh alone, sight unseen.

I turn toward the sound, and my heart stutters.

He's in a chair by the fireplace, sitting with his legs spread, his hands behind his head—looking for all the world like a guy who's about to get his third blow job of the day. Knowing him, it might not be that far from the truth.

And he's changed. He still has that indecently soft mouth, but the boyish side of him is gone. He's broader, his hair is shaved close, and there was a softness to his face that's now absent. Brendan was always capable of making my breath come short, but this new, harder version of him makes me feel like I might have no oxygen at all.

His head turns, and his eyes lock directly on mine. For a moment I see something there, but by the time he stands it's gone.

When we reach him, he punches Rob in the shoulder and then turns and pulls me against him. Rob is hardly a small guy, but I feel dwarfed by Brendan, as if he could crush me by accident were he not careful enough. My face presses to his fleece, and I get a brief whiff of soap and him—something endlessly familiar, though I wish it wasn't.

I pull back and turn toward the pretty redhead standing beside him. I know I came into this wanting to hate her, but she makes it easy, smiling at Brendan as if he's the celebrity crush she just won a date with. She tells me her name is Joie, making sure to spell it for me as if we're going to be penpals after this. We won't. Brendan's never with the same girl twice anyway.

"I guess congratulations are in order," Brendan says. "When's the big day?"

"We haven't gotten that far," Rob replies, "because *one* of us won't set a date." He tries to sound as if he's joking, but I hear displeasure there too.

Brendan eases back in his chair. "You know, in Europe it's pretty common to just get engaged and leave it at that."

"Did you hear that, babe?" I ask Rob. "I'm just being European about it."

"Except I don't want a European girl. I want my Irish girl from New Jersey," Rob says, pushing my hair behind my ear with an affectionate smile. "And I *do* want a wedding."

Brendan watches us with a look I can't quite name. It's disdainful, yet distant, as if we're animals in a cage he's forced to observe. I guess it makes sense. He's only had one relationship that I know of—a girl in Italy—and it didn't last.

Joie smiles and says something vacuous about how nice it is. I'm not sure if she's referring to our wedding or simply the fact that Rob wants one. I could assure her right now that if she's hoping to get married herself at any point, she's barking up the wrong tree with Brendan.

"So what about you?" Rob asks. "You said something about a bike tour company. What's the plan?"

"I'm still looking for office space, but hopefully we'll open up in June," he says.

"You sure you want to blow all your savings on a business?" Rob asks. "A huge percentage of new businesses fold in their first year."

Brendan's smile fades. "I'm investing in something that will make me happy every day. What else am I going to do with it?"

"You could sock it away," Rob counters. There's a hint of condescension in his tone that sets my teeth on edge. As much as I dislike Brendan, I'm tired of watching people piss on his dreams, and this is the exact kind of crap his brother says to him too. "Every penny you save will have grown exponentially between now and retirement. Worry about what makes you happy after you have what you need to survive."

Brendan's eyes darken slightly. "Look," he says, "there are guys who want to do the same bland shit every day when they go into work. They're the same guys too scared to ski black diamonds or surf a decent wave. They like a nice, hummable tune during their forty-five-minute commute home, but they never jump in the mosh pit. That's not living. That's watching life from a distance, like it's a television show. And to me, that sounds like a death sentence."

"My 'death sentence'," Rob replies evenly, "might be looking pretty good to you in thirty years."

"Then I'll plan on living in your basement when I retire," Brendan says.

Rob grins and the moment of tension evaporates. It's always been like that with them, though. They're so different it's hard to imagine how they became friends in the first place, but their shared past, it would seem, is all the common ground they need.

"You're still staying with your mom?" Rob asks. "That's a hell of a daily commute."

Brendan shrugs. "It's just until I know where the office will be. Then I'll get a place closer in."

"Stay with us," says Rob. "We've got the whole pool house sitting empty. I'm going out of town anyway."

My jaw falls open. Brendan is the last person I want staying in this state, much less my home, a fact that Rob is well aware of. And just because *he's* going out of town doesn't mean *I* am.

Rob doesn't seem to notice my reaction but Brendan certainly does. His eyes shift to mine, a quick, menacing glance, accompanied by a smirk that makes my teeth grind.

"You're sure that's okay with your partner over there?" Brendan asks Rob, nodding at me.

"Of course it's okay," Rob says. "Isn't it honey? Then you'll have someone around while I'm gone."

He's put me in an impossible position. I can't say I don't want Brendan there without looking like a total asshole. "I'm just not sure he'll be comfortable," I suggest. "It's so small. And you're only gone a week. I think I can manage."

"A week?" Brendan asks, sounding surprised, as if he'd heard something else.

"Possibly longer," amends Rob.

The "possibly longer" part is new information to me, but before I can ask him about it, the waiter comes to take our order, which is when Brendan's dumb date takes hold of the conversation, grilling the waiter about the menu because of her many food sensitivities. He suggests the steak and she tells him she can't. "Too much gluten," she says.

"There's gluten in steak?" I ask once the waiter leaves.

"Well if the cows have been eating grain, you're eating it too," she says. "This is kind of my specialty."

I glance from her to Brendan. *This is going to be good.*

"Oh?" I ask. "What is it you do?"

She sips off her wine and gives me a tight smile. "I'm a doctor."

"A *doctor?*" I ask, choking on my drink. Rob kicks my foot and I ignore him. It's not *just* that she's an idiot. It's also that I find her lack of specificity highly suspect. "What *kind* of doctor?"

"I'm a doctor of energy medicine," she says. "Illness is just the result of the loss of our soul parts. I commune with beings from other realms, and they guide me to those lost parts."

Brendan's smug, gloating, punchable face dims slightly. Apparently this is news to him too.

Rob's foot lands on mine but it's too late. I can't stop myself.

"Ohhhhh," I say, directing my widest smile at Brendan. "How interesting. I thought you meant you were a *real* doctor."

She sits up a little straighter. "I've cured things no one with a medical degree would touch. Heart disease, terminal cancer. You'd be amazed by how much conventional medicine doesn't know. About humans and animals both."

I smile at Brendan. "Gosh," I say, "so your brother just wasted all that time in med school like a chump."

Rob kicks me again and I go to the bathroom, texting Olivia as I walk.

Will's medical degree is useless, I write. **Brendan's date can cure cancer by COMMUNING WITH BEINGS FROM OTHER REALMS.**

I reapply my lipstick and resolve to be better behaved when I go out. It's not Joie's fault she's an idiot, and the truth is that she's not the one I have a problem with. It's Brendan, with his consistent preference for looks over substance, who irks me.

I walk out of the bathroom and jerk to a halt. Standing partly in shadow, his face lit by the neon exit sign, Brendan waits. He looks almost sculptural, chiseled, his hard jaw leading to the perfection of his soft mouth.

Ugh. Why can't I even notice him without sounding like I'm narrating porn?

"That wasn't very nice, Erin," he says.

"I'm no *doctor*," I reply, "but I'm guessing it went over her head."

"Are you going to be like this every time I have someone over, *roomie?*"

I narrow my eyes. He knows I don't want him in the guest house. It's probably the only reason he's agreeing to it.

"I don't know," I reply. "Will they all be 'doctors' or do you think you'll branch out a little? Maybe an astrologist? A psychic?"

He steps into the light. There's this weird little gleam to his eyes that wasn't there earlier. A charge. It unnerves me.

"No," he says, "but I might try to find one who can pull that stick out of your ass."

He's too close. I'm finding it hard to think clearly. "If that's your way of suggesting a threesome, I'm gonna pass."

That charge between us grows. His eyes fall, so fast I almost miss it, to my mouth.

And suddenly I'm remembering another time like this. Where one minute we were bickering, just as we are now, and the next his mouth was on mine and his hands were inside my shirt.

I'm not scared, I realize. I'm *excited.*

I hate that Brendan is capable of eliciting any feeling from me. But I especially hate that it's that one.

I return to the table, but I find I don't have much of an appetite once our food arrives. I sense Brendan's gaze on me but refuse to meet it.

Why did he have to come home? Why couldn't he have just stayed away?

And how much worse are things going to get until he leaves again?

~

"I CANNOT BELIEVE YOU DID THAT," I TELL ROB ONCE WE'RE back in the car.

"Come on, hon. We have this huge place, and the pool house is detached. It's not like he'll even be living here. It'll be more like having a neighbor."

"Which is great if I wanted Brendan as a neighbor," I reply. "As I'm sure you can imagine, I *don't*."

"He's nice enough to you," Rob sighs. "I don't get why you have such a problem with him."

"My *problem* is that I have a full-time job, and I don't feel like coming home every night to discover he's turned our house into the Playboy Mansion. You'd better make sure he knows I'm not dealing with him having threesomes in the hot tub—or whatever else it is he'll inevitably do."

Rob sighs. "You know, when Harper has a threesome or hooks up with a stranger, you can't wait to tell me about it. But Brendan does it, and you're ready to perform an exorcism."

Yes. Because it's totally different when it's Brendan. "He's just...a bad influence."

"A bad influence on whom, Erin?" he asks. "I'm not even home half the time."

That's probably a good question.

~

IT'S MUCH LATER WHEN MY FATHER CALLS. HE'S SLURRING, BUT that's nothing new. And he sounds desperate, distraught, but that's nothing new either. Thank God Rob is a sound sleeper. I don't think these calls have ever woken him, and that's a godsend because there's a whole lot about me and my life I don't want him to know.

"Hi, Daddy," I whisper, walking out of the bedroom and curling up on the living room sofa. "Where are you?"

He mumbles something that sounds like Anson Street, and I ask him if he's called a cab.

"Don't need a cab," he slurs. "M' fine. But I can't find my car."

"Dad, I need you to promise you won't drive, okay? Give me the name of the bar."

He argues, of course, but he doesn't argue for long. He's too exhausted and drunk for that. I put him on speaker while we wait for the car to come, and as always, his anger at the cards he's been dealt in life turns to tears. He says the things he always says: that he never got a break, that he failed, that he should have been a better father.

It hurts, listening to him. It hurts to know that he wanted so much and fell so far short of it. I'm twenty-six, but right now it's as if I'm back in high school, juggling all the unhappiness afloat in my household to keep it from crashing down on us. And just like I did back then, I wait until he's safe before I let myself cry too.

≈ 4 ≈

BRENDAN
Four Years Earlier

I don't understand why anyone buys a fucking bread maker.
You know how much good bread you could buy for $150? A
lot. A lot of really, really amazing bread. Bread of every color
and taste and variety, without lifting a fucking finger.

Bread makers are like relationships. I don't know why anyone
would give up all that freedom, all that variety, to be with only one
girl, and for a far heavier price than any bread maker—remembering holidays, visiting her family, listening to some long-winded
story about what Friend A said to Friend B. And you can't even
bank on getting laid once you've put in all the work. I've seen it
play out with my friends again and again: the amazing high of
those first few weeks, followed by months and months of lame shit
like farmer's markets and playing Pictionary, the sex getting a little
duller, a little more infrequent with each week that passes.

My buddies all express dismay when this happens, as if it's
somehow *surprising* that it's gone down that way. That's when they
laud my ability to stay single, which also makes little sense. Relationships are remarkably easy to avoid if you know what you're

doing: don't take a girl out who isn't going to sleep with you, and don't sleep with girls who will expect a call the next day. It's that simple.

Everyone knows these are my rules, so I laugh when my brother tells me to stay away from Erin Doyle, his fiancée's best friend. In fact, he goes so far as to make it a condition of getting me a job with his old tour company.

"Erin?" I scoff. "You really think you have to warn me to stay away from *Erin?*"

She's exactly the kind of girl I avoid—the sort who will want to hold hands for six months first, who gets a subscription to *Brides* magazine right after your first date. I've only met her a few times, but I know the type.

"Do us both a favor," Will says, "and stop pretending you're not attracted to her."

"You couldn't pay me to go out with that girl," I tell him. Just contemplating it makes me feel suffocated. "Not if she were the last woman alive."

THAT, OF COURSE, WAS BEFORE I STARTED THE JOB. BUT WHEN I walk in for my first day of work and see Erin again, in person, I hesitate. She looks different. Will could have at least mentioned how fucking pretty she'd gotten. And I also forgot about those lips of hers—I'm not sure how—but it makes no difference. She smiles at me with her heart in her eyes, and I know immediately she's still the same girl, the type who wants a relationship straight out of 1955, complete with promise rings and corsages and chastity.

I've nearly saved enough to get out of this place, and I'm not letting any female—even one who looks like her—change my plans.

She grins as she hops on the sign-up desk, swinging legs that are much longer and leaner than I remember. I guess I've never seen her in shorts before. "Hello, fellow summer hire. You want a tour?"

I shake my head. "I've seen it before. Where's Mike?"

Her smile falters a little. I know I'm being a dick, but something about her brings it out in me.

"He's in the back office working on next week's schedule. I think he meant for you to just use today to get oriented. You want me to call him?"

I walk past her. "I'm a big boy. I can find him all by myself."

I sidle through the rows of bikes to Mike's office. I know him fairly well through Will, who worked here almost two years before moving to Seattle.

Mike raises a brow. "Surprised to see you back here," he says. "I thought Erin would give you a tour."

"She offered," I say. "But I've been here enough. You want me to get started on something?"

"So I just gave you the chance to hang out with one of the hottest girls who's ever set foot in this building, and you want to work instead? I thought I was hooking you up."

I shrug. "I just don't feel like hanging out with Erin any more than I have to."

"Shit," he says with a sigh. "Did she dump you or something? Is this going to be a thing all summer?"

I can't believe his first thought is that *she* dumped *me*. Clearly, he doesn't know me as well as I thought.

"We've never dated," I reply. "I just find her irritating."

His reaction, like Will's, is disbelief. And that makes me like her even less.

❦ 5 ❦

ERIN

Olivia can't stop cackling. "I hear you're getting a new roommate!" she says. Then she starts laughing again.

I sigh. "I should have known you'd enjoy this situation a little too much."

"You want to know what *I* would do if Will invited someone to live with us without asking me first?"

No, not really. Olivia's solutions always involve objects I should shove up someone's ass, and any time Rob upsets me, she insists it's time I "cut him loose."

"You talk a good game, but we both know you wouldn't do anything," I tell her. "You can't stay mad at Will for two seconds."

"Okay, maybe. But I sure as shit wouldn't have *agreed*. I thought you hated Brendan."

"I don't *hate* him," I say. *Okay, yes, I totally hate him.* But I'm adult enough to lie about it. "I just don't need him smoking pot or having threesomes in my hot tub."

Her voice softens. "He's changed a lot, Erin. That girl in Italy really messed him up. I don't think you have to worry about it."

I feel a pang in my chest at the mere mention of it. I've always been inexplicably bitter about Gabi, the girl he dated in Italy. And I really shouldn't be, after all this time.

"I thought Brendan never wanted anything serious with anyone," I mutter.

"I guess she was the exception," Olivia says. "And it definitely changed him."

A piece of me is glad someone broke his heart. He deserves it after all the damage he's wrought. But mostly I'm just wondering what this girl had that I did not.

THAT NIGHT, I MEET ROB AT THE OPENING FOR A BAR HIS investment group has dumped some money into. I'm still annoyed that he invited Brendan to stay with us, and that he forgot to tell me his trip to Amsterdam would be a month rather than a week, but it all falls away when I walk into the bar and his face lights up. My family vacillates between resenting me and blaming me, asking me to fix things and being upset when I fall short, but Rob...he's always been the one person who just wants to have me by his side. And seems proud that I'm there.

"Thanks for coming," he says, giving me a quick kiss. "You know I hate these things."

I don't think he hates them as much as he claims, given that they're hardly mandatory and he attends every one of them, but I just smile and lean into him for a moment. He orders me a gin and tonic and then pulls me through the room, shaking hands with the other investors. They ask, as always, about the wedding, and then make some joke, as always, about how Rob had better hurry up and lock me down—a joke that's grown somewhat awkward over the course of our lengthy engagement. Sometimes they try to remember what I do for a living, and then fail badly until I remind them, at which point their eyes glaze over. I don't fault them for that. I like what I do, but college marketing isn't the most lucrative or interesting job.

When we've made our circuit and finished our drinks, Rob squeezes my hand. "You ready?" he asks, lifting a brow.

I nod, hoping his eagerness to leave means we'll be tearing off clothes fifteen minutes from now—though to be fair, we really don't have a *tearing off clothes* sort of relationship—and follow him to the exit.

Just as we reach the door, one of his colleagues walks in and Rob stiffens.

"Erin, you remember Brad, right?" he asks.

Brad hugs me before punching Rob's shoulder. "That was crazy the other night, huh? How long did you guys stay out?"

"Not long," Rob replies. Under normal circumstances I probably would have tuned this conversation out by now, but there is something about Rob that has me on alert. His posture, his voice —they strive for normalcy but don't quite achieve it.

"Christina was plastered," Brad says. "Did someone get her home?"

Mic drop.

Christina? The same Christina who hits on him constantly? The one who, at last year's holiday party, unbuttoned her shirt and asked if my boyfriend was ready for a change of scenery? It wasn't even what she said that night that bothered me, though. It was what Rob didn't say. He didn't say *no.* He didn't say *I'm engaged.*

He said *I'm sure the view is magnificent.*

We had a fight over it on the way home that night, and I suspect we may be about to have another right now.

Once we are out the door I walk fast, trying to gain control of my thoughts before I ask about it, but my heart is drumming too fast in my chest for any kind of restraint.

"Erin," Rob says from behind me.

I round on him. "*When?*" I demand. "When exactly did this magical night with Christina take place?"

He groans. "That client thing on Tuesday. She's the head of M&A, hon. It's not like it was a date."

My head is spinning. He told me he was going to cut out early that night. I made him braised short ribs and mashed potatoes and I'd actually felt *sorry* for him when he said he was stuck with clients. "So Christina was the reason," I reply, "that I wasted two hours cooking a dinner you didn't bother to come home for."

"Of course she wasn't!" He doesn't shout, but his voice is raised, something that rarely happens with Rob. "There were like ten people there, half of them clients, and there was no way I could extract myself."

My laugh is bitter. "Just like there was no way you could tell her you were engaged when she hit on you last winter."

He closes his eyes. "She already knows I'm engaged. We've gone over this. She says crazy shit that she doesn't mean when she's drinking. Do you understand how awkward it would be if I made a big deal of it every time she says something inappropriate?"

It's the same rationale he used the last time, and I eventually claimed that I got it. But this time he knew, and he went out with her anyway.

"What I understand is that you blew me off to stay out with a woman we've already had one major fight over. And failed to mention she was there."

He sighs, as if I'm being tiresome. "I don't always get to decide when I'm going out or who it's with," he argues. "And I'm very well-compensated for that fact. This is how business works. You have to live with the downside sometimes if you want the upside too."

We ride home in silence. I know there's a point to what he said, but I'm still angry, and it's so unusual for me to be angry at Rob that neither of us is even sure how to proceed. Olivia thinks the fact that we rarely argue is a bad thing. She says it means we never dive below the surface with each other, and perhaps she's right, but I'm okay with that. Things under my surface are dark, much darker than Rob—with his storybook childhood and perfect parents—could ever understand. I like the fact that when Rob sees me, he sees the girl I might have been instead of the one I actually am.

"I don't want to fight with you," he says with a sigh as we walk in the house. "We finally have some time to ourselves. Can we please put it behind us?"

His arms go around me, and I press my face to his chest, though all I can smell is the starch of his shirt. His hands slide from my waist to my ass. "Let's go to bed."

I agree in part because I hate arguing, but mostly because we've only had sex once in the past month, which may have as much to do with my foul mood right now as anything else.

I tell him to give me two minutes and take the world's fastest shower—the water still isn't quite hot by the time I'm done. I don't bother wasting time on lingerie. Rob would barely notice anyhow.

And then I walk into our bedroom to find the lights off and him on his back, snoring loudly. My disappointment turns to resignation as I climb in beside him. It's not his fault. I doubt he got more than four hours of sleep last night. The past month isn't his fault either.

But as I settle into bed, I'm still thinking about sex, and when I fall asleep I dream about it. That makes sense, under the circumstances.

What doesn't make sense is that it's Brendan I dream about.

6

ERIN

Wednesday, Rob's last full day in the States, comes too fast. It really isn't a big deal that he's leaving, so it's hard for me to explain the sense of impending doom I feel whenever I think about it.

He calls just after lunch. This in and of itself is unusual, because Rob never calls while I'm at work. But it's his voice I find most alarming—flat, without inflection or apology, telling me he thinks he might work late.

"Rob," I sigh. "This is the last time I'm seeing you for a month. I'd think just this once you could tell your boss no."

"Yes, and I'd think that just once you might be able to tell your brother no, but apparently you decided to give him all of your money instead," he shoots back.

Oh. Fuck. "Did Sean call you?" I ask.

"Yeah," Rob says with a bitter laugh. "He wanted to thank me for being so 'cool' about you paying his tuition."

"I meant to tell you," I say weakly. "You've just been gone so much."

"Don't you think you should have discussed it with me *first*? I thought we were a team, Erin."

There's nothing I can say to defend myself. I *should* have discussed it with him. There's only one reason I didn't: because I knew I'd pay Sean's tuition whether Rob agreed or not, and I knew he wouldn't agree.

"Sean was going to work at a bar instead," I reply. "But he just got out of rehab. It was asking for trouble."

"That's not the point," he snaps. "We're supposed to discuss these things. We're *engaged*. Or have you forgotten?"

My eyes widen at the sheer bitterness in his voice. This isn't just about the money. "What's that supposed to mean?" I ask.

"It means we've been engaged for eighteen months, and you haven't moved one millimeter toward picking a date or anything else," he says. "You keep claiming you're too busy, but when you do something like this, I have to wonder if that's all it is."

He makes an excuse about a meeting and ends the call, leaving me with my head in my hands. I had no idea he was this upset about my failure to plan the wedding. And I can't begin to explain to him why I haven't. There are just too many things about me and my family I'd rather he not know.

I make dinner for us but it's cold by the time he gets home. I'm mad, but my grounds for anger are so minimal compared to his that I push it down deep.

"There's food on the stove if you're hungry," I say quietly. "You'll just need to heat it up."

"I met Brendan and got something at the bar," he replies, throwing his jacket on the chair.

I close my eyes to keep from rolling them. Being late is bad enough. Being late because he was hanging out with *Brendan*, however, is really doubling down.

"Let me guess," I say. "He told you to dump me for the hundredth time?"

Rob sighs. "No. He said I should get clear on what bothers me before we have a conversation because you're a fixer, and you can't fix this until you know what the problem is."

My jaw falls open. "Has the world stopped spinning on its axis? *Brendan* actually paid me a compliment?"

Rob smiles. "Not exactly. He said he hates fixers. But anyway, he meant well."

I hold my arms across my chest. "Any other sage advice from the guy who's never had a relationship?"

"Yeah, he said I should go home and get laid."

That sounds more like Brendan.

Rob leans forward, resting his elbows on his knees. "Look, I'm not happy about it, Erin, but I don't want to fight with you tonight. So can we just table all this for a time when it's not my last few hours with my beautiful fiancée?"

I agree with relief, and he throws his tie next to his jacket. "Then it seems to me you're wearing too many clothes."

"I'm only wearing a tank top and shorts."

He grins. "Like I said. Too many clothes."

We walk into the bedroom. I don't think we've ever once had sex anywhere else. Harper calls it boring, but there are far worse things than a boyfriend who's a tiny bit predictable. His shirt comes off, his pants follow, and he slides into bed, pulling me against him.

"I can't believe I'm going to have to go without for a whole month," he says against my mouth.

I nod in agreement, although we've only slept together a few times since he started work on this merger, so I'm not sure a month apart is really going to feel all that different.

He rolls me on my back and I try to focus on his face. *I won't think about Brendan tonight. I won't.*

"Jesus," he groans, already hard, pressed against my stomach. "It's been so long. This is going to be over before it starts."

I tell myself I don't mind, but my thoughts flicker briefly to Brendan, and then to Harper's imaginary hot factory guy. I bet sometimes it's over with them before it starts too.

7

BRENDAN
Four Years Earlier

I'm on the floor fixing a broken bike chain during my second week at work when Erin walks up. I expend a lot of effort avoiding her, so it's annoying when she seeks me out. For just a moment, all I see are bare legs, long and starting to tan though summer hasn't quite begun. She's got her hair down, wearing no makeup. There's something about that bare, full mouth that I'd like to look at one moment longer, and it bothers me that I'd want to.

"Yeah?" I ask irritably.

"You don't have to be a dick," she says. "You don't even know what I'm going to ask."

"No, but I'm anticipating that it'll piss me off," I reply.

Hurt flashes over her face for a moment, and I feel bad about it, but not for long. It's best that we get clear right now that I don't want her around. Her presence is a constant irritant, like a pebble in my shoe or an itch I can't reach.

She closes her eyes for a moment and then continues in her

professional voice. "AJ called in sick. Can you lead an extra tour this afternoon?"

"Sure," I say, returning my gaze to the bike as I answer.

"There. Was that so hard?" she asks.

Yeah. It sort of was. That one tiny interaction is enough to ruin my afternoon.

I CALL WILL. OLIVIA ANSWERS AND ASKS IF I'M BEING NICE TO Erin. I assure her I am, though I'm not, and then Will takes the phone with a very different question.

"You're leaving her alone, right?" he asks.

I roll my eyes. "You have nothing to worry about. She annoys the living shit out of me."

"*Erin?*" he says, with a startled laugh. "Why?"

I tense. I can't put my finger on precisely what I find annoying. It's just everything. Each day when I walk into the tour office and find her there, I feel my irritation ticking upward like a thermometer on a hot day.

"She just does."

"Name one thing she does that's annoying," he says. "I dare you."

"The baking," I reply. "Every day she's bringing some homemade shit into the office."

Will laughs. "Yeah, wow, she sounds terrible."

I pinch the bridge of my nose. He just doesn't get it. He doesn't know what it's like to be in there with her, day in and day out.

"And she's too fucking cheerful," I add. "Morning to night with that big smile on her face."

"What a nightmare," he says dryly. "I don't know how you stand it."

I'm not sure either. But every day she bothers me more.

8

ERIN

'm still at the office when Rob calls at the end of our first
week apart. It's two in the morning in Amsterdam, and he's
just getting in, which has been the case most of the nights
he's been there. The eight-hour time difference has made
connecting hard—one of us is always just getting up, just going to
bed, or at work.

But what's also hard is that he seems to be having the time of
his life, while I am not. I've come back to an empty house for
months, so it's not as if things are so different with him gone, it's
just that when he was here, it felt temporary, and now it's not.
There's just me, with no one to talk to all weekend, and five week-
days spent at a job that makes me miserable.

Tonight he tells me first about dinner with the team in an old
pirate radio station, and then he details the bar crawl that ensued
afterward.

I shouldn't be jealous, but I've been at work for nine hours and
have big plans for a night in with Mr. Tibbles, Rob's cat, and
possibly a delicious bowl of cereal for dinner. My unhappiness isn't
Rob's fault, but knowing that doesn't seem to puncture the small

bubble of resentment in my chest, a bubble that swells every time he tells me yet another story about fancy dinners and wild nights he's enjoying without me.

I make appropriate sounds of interest about the meal and the bars and the shots he did. When the conversation lags, he asks if I've had a chance to look at reception sites, and I make weak excuses that we both know aren't true.

"I meant to," I tell him. "I was just so busy."

"Okay," he says, the affection in his tone now absent. "Well, I should probably get to sleep. Love you."

I start to tell him I love him too, and that I'm sorry I haven't done more work on the wedding, but he's already hung up the phone.

I go home, wanting something, without a clue what it is. I go to sleep, hating that there'll be no warm body beside me in the morning. And wondering when, exactly, my life turned so empty that a warm body would be the only thing to look forward to in the first place.

ON SATURDAY MORNING, I'M STARING AT A MACHINE I HAVE NO idea how to operate when Brendan strolls into the yard. I've seen signs of his presence over the past few days, but I'd prefer to see no sign of him now. Rob's weird insistence on doing his own yard has never annoyed me more, and Brendan's just going to worsen my mood.

I ignore the way his khaki shorts hang loose, and I particularly ignore that his T-shirt is just fitted enough to make clear that he is all muscle beneath it.

"Aerating the yard?" he asks with that ever-present smirk. "What an amazing way to spend a Saturday. Marriage looks so awesome."

"We're not married." My voice is clipped, tense, precise. I promised Rob I'd be nice, but already it's taking all of my effort just to be civil. I crouch down to look at the engine, hoping he'll be gone when I stand.

He sighs. "Staring at that thing isn't going to make it turn on."

I roll my eyes. "Thanks, farmer boy. I knew you'd prove helpful."

"Why the hell are you trying to aerate the yard anyway?" he asks. "Leave it for Rob when he gets home."

I take a quick, calming breath. "Rob must have rented this thing before he knew the dates of his trip," I reply. "They just delivered it this morning and I can't get our money back."

He pulls the handle away from me. "Go sit in the shade and look pretty. I'll do it."

I put a hand on my hip. I've gone through too much in life to be condescended to by some douchebag who will never grow up. "I'll have you know that I am perfectly capable of—"

He places a finger over my lips. "Shhhhh," he says. "You know I grew up on a farm, right? And you grew up in an apartment in New Jersey?"

"Yes, but—"

The finger rests on my lips again. "Go sit, sweetheart."

Part of me feels like I should tell him to fuck off. The bigger part of me doesn't want to aerate a lawn.

"Fine, smart guy," I reply, walking away. "I'll go relax, and you can show me how it's done. There's a bunch of laundry inside. Maybe you can show me how good you are at that next."

I go to the front door but glance back at him once, just as he's pulling off his shirt. My hand tightens around the doorknob. It's irritating, how pretty he is. It's irritating that he does everything so confidently, that he's managing to make aerating a yard look sexy. Ridiculous. Harper would pay for footage of this.

I turn and go inside, resolving to stay there until he's done. When you've only had sex once recently and it only lasted two minutes, being anywhere near Brendan Langstrom's perfect, exposed abs is just inviting trouble.

❧ 9 ❧

BRENDAN
Four Years Earlier

Being stuck in the office with Erin is no longer merely irritating—it's my private, existential hell.

First, there's the humming. When she's in the back, sorting helmets and counting oars, she's humming the entire fucking time, if not outright singing to whatever comes up on the playlist.

The humming is just one of a thousand irritating habits—there's also the way she sits, for instance, with her legs all tangled as if she's made of Silly Putty, as if there's too much of her to possibly go straight. Or the way her teeth sink into her lower lip when she's uncertain, or the fact that she doesn't realize her old high school track team T-shirt is now way too small through the chest. And then there's the little groan she makes when she smells Thai food, the way she bounces out of her seat when her favorite song comes on. The way her hips sway when she's wearing heels, and the way every guy in the office is riveted by the sight of it.

But tonight we're all out drinking and she's blissfully absent, which means for once I can escape the judgmental little smirk she gets on her face whenever the girl I'm with says something stupid. I'll admit *that* happens more than I'd like it to.

The guys are all talking about this huge rafting trip we led over the weekend during a thunderstorm. I hear my name, but I'm not really listening because—though I'm happy Erin is absent—I keep wondering why that is. Yes, I've gone out of my way to be a dick so she won't want to come out with us, but until tonight, I was failing miserably. So where the fuck is she?

I finish my first beer and start on my second, while this pressure builds in my head.

"What's the matter, babe?" asks the girl beside me.

Her name is Anya, I think, but I'm not entirely certain. All I know is she's wearing the shortest shorts I've ever seen, and in about an hour, I plan to remove them.

I open my mouth to suggest we leave, and something entirely different emerges.

"Where's Erin?" I ask Pierce, the assistant manager. Anya shifts unhappily beside me.

"What do you care?" he asks. "You act like you hate her most of the time."

I shrug. I'm not willing to say I hate her, necessarily. Hate seems like something that should be confined to the truly awful, like Hitler, or smooth jazz. But it annoys me that everyone *other* than me loves Erin. It's tedious the way she charms people, with the big smile and the eagerness to help. It's as if she never got the memo that she's smart and good-looking and doesn't need to work so hard for everyone's approval. Pierce in particular seems to love her a little too much. If I catch him looking down her shirt again, he and I are going to have an issue.

He nods toward the door. "There she is right now. So you can proceed with acting like you're irritated."

My head swivels to see her moving toward us, wearing sky-high heels and a little skirt with a pristine white button-down—the outfit she wears on Mondays and Thursdays, when she goes to her internship. It's hot as fuck, and it pisses me off that she didn't change before she got here.

"The naughty librarian look," Pierce says under his breath, grinning at me. I don't smile back.

He stands and pulls out the chair next to him when she gets to the table, while I pretend not to notice she's even arrived. To my chagrin, she's now also sitting beside my date, who looked just fine here on her own, but now, next to Erin, looks like she's trying way too hard.

"Well, well, well, look at Miss Corporate America," I say to her. "How was a day spent selling your soul to the man?"

I see a flash of anger in her eyes. She largely ignores me now; sometimes that flash of anger is all I can get.

"Laugh all you want," she says. "When you're fifty and living in Will's basement, I'll be laughing too."

"Maybe you can visit me there when you're finally ready to lose your virginity," I reply.

To my unhappy surprise, she smirks. "Unless you've devised a time machine—and let's face it, you're unlikely to exert the effort—that ship has sailed."

I spend the rest of the night feeling bitter. I don't even like her, so why I am pissed off that I'll never be her first?

꒰ 10 ꒱

ERIN

We're only five minutes into Friday's staff meeting, and Timothy has already used the word *synergy* fifteen times by my count. I have trouble staying awake during these meetings under the best of circumstances, but after another late night dealing with my dad, it feels almost impossible. He's called twice this week, which means he's on another downward spiral. I'm sure my mother hoped—though she would never say it—that the move here, away from his friends and past, would give him a clean start. Instead he's lonely, and my father's solution to every unhappy feeling is to make it go away with booze.

I feel my cell buzzing in my lap—it's Rob, and I can't take the call because I need to hear my boss say *synergy* several more times. I picture winging the phone at Tim's head. I imagine the clunk it would make on impact, the shock on his face. It's small consolation for being stuck here.

When the meeting's over, I go outside to call Rob back, as Harper won't hesitate to shout commentary over our shared cubicle wall if she's around.

He answers, and I hear rustling in the background, which forewarns me that he's busy and about to rush me off the phone for another of his big nights out.

"I've got to run here because people are waiting," he says. "But I wanted to let you know, it looks like we're not getting out of here until July."

"July," I repeat blankly.

It's April. He was supposed to be home the first week of May, and that was bad enough, but *July?*

"They're bringing in new staff to replace some of the people here, and we can't even begin the transition until that's done. None of us are happy about it but..."

He continues to speak, but I've stopped listening. I don't want him to justify this to me. Does he really think I care deeply whether or not the transition is a success? I don't. All I'm thinking is this: July is more than two months away.

"What about Olivia's race?" I ask, my voice devoid of inflection, barely a whisper.

We already have our plane tickets. We were going to fly into Reno and spend a day in Tahoe before we drove up.

"I think the tickets are refundable, but you should still go," he says. His tone is encouraging, as if he's being *kind* somehow when he's actually bailing on our first trip together in a year. "It'll still be fun."

Yeah, nothing like a trip to Tahoe alone, Rob.

I dig my nails into my hands as he continues to justify the decision, telling me what a big deal this is for the company. Only two weeks have passed, and I'm already going crazy. How the hell am I going to stomach three *months?*

I stew about it all day, and I'm still at work and still not over it when Harper emerges from the office bathroom early in the evening, clad in five-inch black heels and a *tiny* black dress.

"Wow, Harper. I don't know who this guy is, but I guarantee he's going to like that outfit."

She grins wickedly, winking at me. "As long as he doesn't make me wear it for long."

I laugh, but feel a squeeze of envy. I miss that—the excitement, the anticipation, the way just getting ready felt like foreplay. Sex with Rob is now like a shortcut through the woods, everything trampled down by repetition to make it easy, straight to the point. I guess that's a good thing. It's just that sometimes, when I see Harper heading toward a destination she can't begin to predict, I feel like I'm missing out on something I shouldn't be.

WHEN I GET HOME, THERE'S A FEDEX ENVELOPE ON THE FRONT step waiting for Brendan. If it weren't about to rain, I'd be tempted to leave it. Instead, with vast reluctance, I go out back and tap on his door. Three crisp knocks: my civic duty and not a shred more.

He has thirty seconds to answer before I throw it and walk. I've counted to twenty-five when he opens the door.

"This was at my place for you," I say, thrusting the envelope toward him.

He takes it from my hand, studying me a little too carefully, and steps aside for me to enter. I really don't want to go in, given that I suspect he's made our pool house smell like sex and bad decisions, but I can't come up with a reason to demur.

My eyes are drawn to the center of the room. My jaw drops. "You hung a *hammock* in the living room?"

"I checked with Rob first."

"But...*why?* You already have a bed."

He shrugs. "I like to mix things up."

My chest tightens. "Are you talking about sleeping in the hammock or something else?"

He gets this secretive smile on his face. "Hammocks are good for a lot of things, Erin."

I flinch as I picture it. Brendan has an ease in his body most men don't, a natural athleticism. If anyone could manage sex in a hammock, he could.

My arms fold. "Our liability insurance isn't going to cover it when you fall out and crush the poor girl to death."

He gives me a crooked grin, a little light in his eyes that wasn't there a moment earlier. "Haven't had an accident yet. Maybe I'm a little more agile than the guys you know."

I make some noise that sounds an awful lot like "harrumph," which is something only portly old men in Dickens' novels say. But this information sits poorly, right on the heels of Rob's announcement that he's not coming home.

I'm not asking for that much. I don't need some stranger eagerly removing my little black dress. I don't need hours of sex in hammocks with men whose agility is almost unfathomable to me. But I need something more than I have, which is nothing at the moment.

He frowns, watching my face. "I can take the hammock down if it really bothers you."

I bite my lip and feel an unexpected urge to cry, though I have no idea why, and I'll be damned if I'm going to do it in front of Brendan. He'd enjoy it too much.

"It's fine. The hammock's fine."

He steps closer, and his proximity makes me feel fluttery and unsettled. "You talked to Rob?"

"Yes." I swallow. The urge to cry grows. Maybe Brendan knew about Rob's trip getting extended before I did, and that bothers me too. "I guess you heard he's staying longer."

He nods as his eyes roam over my face, and for once there's no smirk. It's possible I even see concern there, as unlikely as that is. The old Brendan would have made a joke, no matter how inappropriate the circumstances. The new version of Brendan seems to understand grief a little better. Maybe Olivia wasn't entirely wrong about him. "I'm sorry," he says.

"It's fine," I reply, but my voice catches a little. "I have no reason to be upset."

"Aren't you supposed to be upset? He's your fiancé."

"I just..." I don't know why I'm discussing this with him. We aren't friends. It's going to turn into something he uses against me later. "It's not like I see that much of him when he's home."

"So what's different then?" he asks.

It's the question I've asked myself a hundred times. "He filled just enough of my hours when he was home that I felt like I had a purpose," I reply. "And I've suddenly discovered I don't."

A muscle ticks in Brendan's jaw, and for a millisecond he seems angry, making me regret every word I just said. I'm sure he's somehow turning this into one more piece of evidence that Rob should have dumped me long ago.

"Never mind."

I turn to leave but he stops me just as my hand reaches the doorknob. "You should figure that out before Rob gets back," he says.

I shoot him the nastiest look I can muster. "Yes, Brendan, thank you. I'm well aware of all the ways you think I'm not good enough for Rob. I'll add this to the list."

His frown deepens. "Who ever said I thought you weren't good enough for him?" he asks.

I laugh unhappily. "You did, every time you ever tried to talk him out of dating me."

"Sometimes people just aren't a good fit," he argues. "It doesn't mean one of you isn't good enough."

I roll my eyes and reach for the door. "Give me a break, Brendan. You told him he was making a mistake a thousand times. It's pretty clear why you said it."

He starts to argue, but then his jaw snaps shut. "You understand a lot less than you think you do."

I open the door and let it slam behind me. I've heard enough of Brendan's bullshit to last me the rest of my life.

11

BRENDAN
Four Years Earlier

I t begins with a mosquito bite.

A bite on Erin's ankle, one she bends over to scratch approximately once a minute, her shorts riding perilously high as she does it. There isn't a tour leader or male client in this room who hasn't noticed. If Mike were a better manager, he'd realize how unproductive this is and stop her. He doesn't say a word, of course. Probably because he's too busy enjoying the show. And I know, as I watch, that I'm going to be thinking about her bending over like that tonight, and the next night too.

"Leave that bite alone," I finally snarl.

She looks up at me, surprised, hurt by my tone. I feel like I've just slapped a young child, and for a moment I'm desperate to fix it. It's a relief when her hurt turns to anger. Anger is something I can handle.

"You need Prozac," she replies, eyes narrowed. "A bucket of it."

"No can do," I reply. "It causes sexual dysfunction."

She smirks. "And you've already got enough sexual dysfunction."

I lean back in my chair, grinning at her in that way I know she loathes. "I assure you, all my parts work just fine. I can prove it, if you'd like."

"I'll pass," she replies. "If I'm going to have hate sex, it'll be with someone less likely to carry disease."

The moment she says it, I can see it—hate sex, not disease. I can imagine the thousand ways I'd like to punish her for being such a pain in the ass, for making my summer so fucking endless in the worst possible way. I feel a shot of excitement that begins in my stomach and seems to pulse through my limbs, as if I'm suddenly electrified.

That night, with someone else, I picture it again and finish seconds later. There are no words for how much I hate that I'm thinking of Erin during sex now. And the fact that it seems like I always might.

❧ 12 ❧

ERIN

The call that comes just after two AM is the worst kind I get. My mother is crying so hard she's almost unintelligible, and I already know what she's going to say: that my father never came home from work and won't answer his phone. I already know I'll be awake most of the night looking for him, and panicking at every car accident I pass on the way. It hasn't been him yet, but one day it will be. It's only a matter of time.

I've learned way too much about my parents' marriage from these nights when my dad doesn't come home. "He didn't want to settle down," my mother would tell me, weeping, even when I was too small to understand. "I should have listened." It's perhaps the only lesson I've learned well: if someone says they don't want a relationship, you take them at their word.

"I don't know what to do," she says now, again and again. She said it when I was little too, and even then I felt the burden of those words. Someone had to fix it, and if it wasn't her, it needed to be me.

I tell her I'll take care of it, and dress quickly.

Sleep dazed, I open the garage door...and shriek when I see a large male walking up my driveway.

"It's just me," says Brendan, stepping into the light.

"Jesus Christ," I gasp. "You scared the shit out of me."

"Where you going, blondie?" he asks.

I've never wanted Rob to know about these trips, so I don't want Brendan to know either. He won't hesitate to run and tell Rob everything.

I swallow. "Nowhere."

He raises a brow. "You're going *nowhere* in the middle of the night?"

Every bone in my body wants to lie to him, yet my brain is blank, without a single plausible excuse. Maybe I'm just too tired to lie, exhausted not just from tonight but from all of the past years, all the lies I've told and the effort it takes.

I just don't feel capable of lying even one more time.

"My dad had a little too much to drink. He needs a ride home."

"Isn't he in Denver?" Brendan asks. "Can't he just take a cab?"

"We don't actually know where he is," I mumble.

I see understanding dawn on his face. "Does he do this a lot?"

"No, of course not. I think he just had a bad day." My answer is too hasty and too defensive. I sound like I'm lying. Which, obviously, I am. "But can you...can you not mention this to Rob?"

I can't imagine why I'm throwing myself at his mercy here. Brendan doesn't like me. He has no reason to show me any kindness, and I've never gotten so much as a hint that he'd be willing to.

"Okay," he says, putting a hand on the small of my back. "But I'm driving. You're half asleep, and my face is way too pretty to wind up smashed into a tree."

I stiffen. "You don't need to come with me."

"You're not going alone." His voice is firm. In it, I hear the subtext: he's coming, or he's telling Rob.

I don't want him coming with me. Particularly given how ugly it can get when my dad has *a little too much.* "You're not going to get any sleep," I argue.

He swallows, and his tongue darts out to his lower lip. "My dad used to drink a lot too," he says quietly.

I'm torn. I can see how everything he learns tonight will eventually be offered up on a platter to Rob, in a file titled *See? I told you I was right about her.* But his face is open and honest and serious in a way it isn't normally.

He leads me to his car. I don't resist.

WE ARE SILENT AS HE TAKES BACK ROADS TO THE INTERSTATE. I don't know how to be around him anymore unless I'm being spiteful or guarded, which I don't entirely understand. It's not like I'm cruel by nature. Why is it so hard with him?

He yawns. "Okay, blondie, you've got to keep me awake here. Tell me something."

My hands twist. "Like what?"

"Tell me something no one knows about you, not even Rob. Other than this."

I wouldn't normally engage in this kind of game with him—or any game, really—but I've already handed him one of my worst secrets. The rest seem minor by contrast.

"Every time I go to Denver to visit my parents, I stop by the Ducati dealership and test drive one."

He laughs. "Bullshit."

I shrug and stare out the window. I'm not sure if I'm insulted or just relieved that he doesn't believe me. Both, perhaps.

"You were *serious?*" he asks. "You, Erin Doyle, ride motorcycles."

I frown at him, folding my arms across my chest. "Is it really that unthinkable? You're making it sound like I'm Queen Elizabeth."

He laughs again. "Come on, Erin... I mean, you're not exactly the type. Perky little blondes in marketing don't drive Ducatis. They drive something sensible, like a Prius."

I sigh. He's probably right. It's not who I ever aspired to be, but I'm well on my way to it if I'm not there already. "Well Rob agrees with you, so please don't say anything."

"Why wouldn't you tell him?" he asks. "There's nothing wrong with driving a motorcycle."

"There's nothing wrong with lots of stuff," I reply. "It doesn't mean you want the whole world knowing."

He glances at me. "Except Rob's not the whole world. He's your fiancé. And that isn't something you should have to hide."

I say nothing, but the truth is this: Rob is a big part of my world, and he would not accept this or so many other things if he knew.

The rest of the ride is silent. We arrive in Denver less than an hour after we left, and with shame rising in my chest, I direct him to a particularly rough section of the city, a section neither of us would choose to enter under normal circumstances.

"Let's try Slaney's first," I say, sounding, unfortunately, like someone who's made this desperate search before. "You can wait here, and I'll run in."

He scowls. "Are you high? I'm not letting you go in there at this hour alone."

I argue that I'll be fine and he ignores me—no surprises there.

We walk in together and the bartender waves to me like an old friend. "Sorry," he says. "Didn't see him in here tonight."

"Still want to claim this doesn't happen a lot?" Brendan asks under his breath as we walk out.

"You're going to tell Rob aren't you?" I ask. "You've been gunning for me ever since..."

His head tilts. "Ever since...?"

Ever since you kissed me at the wedding.

"Ever since Rob and I got together," I reply.

He runs a hand over his head. "I told you I wouldn't say

anything and I won't. But this is a big secret to be keeping from someone who's supposed to know you best."

After three bars and twenty minutes of searching, we find my dad, slumped in the corner of a booth while the staff cleans up around him.

"It's Erin, right?" the manager asks.

I avoid Brendan's eye. "Yeah. I'm sorry about this."

"Write down your number for us," he suggests. "That way we can call you the next time."

I nod while my stomach sinks.

Sometimes I feel like a sandbag with a pinhole leak. I've spent my entire life trying to erase the small trail of debris, evidence, I've left behind. Tonight that leak has become a full-fledged tear, and it's as if I'm hemorrhaging now. I wonder how much more I'll prove unable to contain.

We load my father into the passenger's seat with some difficulty, and I direct Brendan to my parents' neighborhood. Their standard of living dropped a fair amount after my dad lost his job in New Jersey. It's not as if Brendan grew up with a ton of money, but I'm embarrassed anyway—by how they live, by my mother's tears and by the way she reacts when she realizes I'm not alone.

"I didn't know you were bringing company," she says, as if this is a social call. She wipes her face on the inside of her robe. "You could have warned me. I'm not even dressed."

I've broken the cardinal Doyle family rule: don't let outsiders see the ugly underbelly. People who've met my parents generally rave about them. Back when my dad was still doing okay, my parents would fly out for cross country meets, take me and my friends to dinner. My dad was the life of the party. *"You're so lucky,"* everyone would tell me afterward. "Your dad is so much *fun.*" Never realizing that I'd cut the night short at the precise moment I saw my dad teetering on the edge, about to descend from fun and irreverent to sloppy and irresponsible.

"He's not company," I say through my teeth. "We're not staying."

Brendan helps my dad to his bed and then, taking one look at the tension between me and my mom, gracefully departs, telling me he'll wait outside.

"What an awful thing to let a stranger see," my mother says after he leaves. "What's he going to think of us?"

I know what she's doing. She wants me to apologize, to agree that tonight is all my fault. It *has* to be my fault, the whole evening, because if it's not mine, it's my father's, and we can't have that. But I don't have it in me to apologize or play this game right now. I pretend too much. I lie too much. I've been caught at it tonight, again and again, and I'm just too damn tired to keep going, to lie and pretend for her sake or my own.

"He's probably going to think Dad's sick, and that you and I are pathetic and broken," I tell her. "And I'm not going to apologize, because it's all true."

I walk out, shutting the door behind me. I'll pay for that comment later, but right now I don't care.

"Everything okay?" Brendan asks.

I nod, too choked up to speak. It's not unusual to feel this way. When one of my familial crises ends, I often find I've been holding my grief at bay until there is room for it. But that's not all it is tonight. I think what's making me tear up right now is Brendan. Beautiful, reckless, irresponsible, hateful Brendan—who I've loathed for so long—has been kinder to me tonight than anyone I can think of, ever.

I handed him my secrets—things I've never trusted to anyone —and though I don't want to admit it, I know he will guard them as if they are his own. Brendan, who I wanted to believe was cruel, is actually kind. And Brendan, who I thought could not be trusted, is someone I trust implicitly.

I want to continue hating him, and the fact that I won't be able to anymore terrifies me.

～

BRENDAN PARKS ON THE STREET, AND WE WALK TOWARD THE house together. "I won't tell Rob, but I have one condition," he says. "I want you to call me any time you have to go deal with your dad."

"I've been making some version of that trip for a long time, Brendan." There's no sense pretending at this point that tonight was a one-off. "I'll be fine."

"You know who says things will be *fine*?" he demands. "Every person who insisted they weren't too tired to drive and then wrapped a car around a tree. Every woman who has ever been raped after figuring it was safe to walk home. Your belief that you will be *fine* is meaningless."

A day ago, I'd have expressed some surprise over the fact that he cares whether I'm injured, that he actually seems *angry* at the possibility. It's disconcerting, once again, to think I may have misjudged him. It's even more disconcerting to think I did so intentionally.

"What do you want me to do?" I ask. "You're barely ever home."

"Just text me."

Right. As if I'm going to yank him out of some stranger's bed every time I have to go to Denver. The whole thing is embarrassing enough without that. "I appreciate the offer but—"

"Perhaps I didn't make myself clear," he cuts in, his eyes darkening. "You *will* text me the next time you make that trip, or I will tell Rob."

My jaw drops. "Only you would somehow turn an offer of assistance into blackmail," I fume.

He opens the door to the house and shoos me inside.

"I'm gonna take that as a compliment."

"It wasn't!" I shout, but he's already closed the door.

13

ERIN

I call Olivia the next afternoon on the way home from work. Despite my lack of sleep, the pressing matter of Brendan is my first priority. I don't know what all that was last night, but I know I don't like feeling indebted to him.

"I need to get Brendan a thank-you gift," I tell her. "What would he want?"

"Thank him for what?" she asks. "You hate him, remember? And you're already letting him live with you for free."

I'm struck once more by the odd discomfort of knowing I've been maligning someone for years, perhaps without cause, and a big piece of me wants to keep doing it.

"He's been helping with some stuff around the house," I reply. "Do you know what he'd want?"

"He'd love some of those coconut almond bars you make. The last time he visited us, he took the entire container, the bastard."

I roll my eyes. "He must not have known I made them."

She clucks her tongue. "Of course he did. I know you don't believe me, Erin, but he doesn't hate you."

I sigh, rubbing my eyes. "Sure. He just thinks I'm not good enough for Rob."

"Has it ever occurred to you that maybe he thinks Rob's not good enough for *you*?" she asks.

I ignore her. Olivia doesn't know about the kiss at her wedding, doesn't know that Brendan has irrefutable proof I'm not worthy of his friend. Or that he's getting more proof every day.

In the end, I decide to make him the bars, and I actually enjoy the process. I used to bake all the time, and tonight it fills me with a sort of contentment I haven't felt in forever. I leave them in a box outside Brendan's door, feeling oddly satisfied—a sensation that lasts only until I tell Rob about it.

"Why'd you do that?" he asks.

My heart rate picks up. Why did I have to bring this up?

"Oh," I stammer, "he's...been helping out. He aerated the yard."

"Sugar, fat, and flour. The white menace," says Rob. "You're sure you aren't just trying to kill him?"

I've heard Rob's spiel about this before. I'd like to say it's never annoyed me until now, but I think it has. This gnawing irritation with him feels far too familiar. I suppose it's why I stopped baking, even though it used to be one of my favorite things to do.

"You just dismantled a company and laid off thirty percent of its work force," I reply, "but I'm the bad guy for making someone dessert?"

"Jesus, Erin. It was a joke," he says. "You've got no sense of humor these days."

When we end the call, I sit staring at the phone. I gave up baking to keep the peace, I realize. I gave up a *lot* of things to keep the peace. And I'm pretty sure Rob cannot claim to have done the same.

14

ERIN

"I'm worried about you," says Harper, hopping onto my file cabinet. "When's the last time you got laid?"

I laugh and shake my head. "That's not as big a deal for everyone as it is for you."

"Come out with me this weekend," she says.

She's suggested this many times in the past. I usually say no, since Harper tends to go home with a random guy twenty minutes after we've paid our cover, but the truth is I'm feeling a little desperate right now. I'm not sure I'm capable of staying in to watch any more TV, and I'm about one step away from dressing Mr. Tibbles up in a miniature North Face pullover and taking him out to dinner with me.

"I'm not looking to get laid," I reply, "but I'll be your wingman."

She claps her hands together and hops off the file cabinet. "And do me a favor," she calls walking away. "Try not to dress like we're heading to tea or an American Girl doll party, okay?"

I flip her off, though she's already walked away.

"And stop flipping me off," she adds.

~

I MEET HER ON FRIDAY NIGHT AT A BAR WHERE SOME BAND SHE loves is playing. I'm wearing a tank and skinny jeans, which looks a little tame next to her micromini and thigh-high boots but appears to suffice.

While we wait for our drinks, Harper assesses the quality of the men around us.

"How many minutes do I have before you're pulling some guy into the bathroom?" I ask.

"I'm not that bad," she replies.

I laugh. "You did it the last time we went out."

"Well, I'm not doing it tonight, but... Wow..." She stops midstream, and my eyes follow hers to the guy at the far end of the room: very tall, broad shoulders, nice ass. He isn't facing us, but I'd know those shoulders anywhere.

"Fuck," I sigh. "It's Brendan."

He's too far away to have heard us, but he turns, his gaze breezing past Harper and landing directly on me.

Harper is already reaching for her lip gloss. "I'm gonna do things to that man you don't even know can be done," she says under her breath.

I feel an odd sort of panic, something fluttering and desperate. I want to distract her from him like a child, offer her candy or a balloon in his place. "You don't want to do that," I tell her.

Her mouth curves upward. "Why? Because you want him for yourself?"

"No! Of course not!" I exclaim as he puts down his pool stick and moves toward us. I'm engaged. I don't want him for myself. I just don't want her to have him either, which she definitely will, because all men love Harper.

She smirks. "You sure about that, Erin? Last chance to admit it before I make my move."

I feel like I'm holding my breath as he reaches us, bracing for the way he'll look at her—that gleam he'll get in his eye, the cocky way his mouth will curve up to one side when they talk.

Except he doesn't even seem to *see* her.

"What are you doing here?" he demands, looking only at me. "You never go out." He doesn't even try to hide the displeasure in his tone.

"I'm not *stalking* you, asshole," I reply. "We came to see the band."

His gaze drifts to the hint of cleavage visible beneath my tank top. "And why are you dressed like that?"

I groan. Does he think he's my watchdog while Rob's gone? "Why? Does this not meet your high standards?"

He shakes his head, the action so minute I get the feeling it wasn't intended for me. "You just...normally you're all covered up. With sweaters and shit."

"Brendan, it's the first warm night in nine months. I'm not wearing a sweater."

"Yeah," he says, flinching, running a hand over his shorn scalp. "I noticed. It's fine. Just...be careful."

My mouth falls open. Harper's wearing a quarter of the clothing I am. So are most of the girls here. "Be careful of *what?*"

His eyes meet mine. I feel certain there's something he wants to say, but instead he clenches his jaw and sets his empty glass on the bar with a thud.

"Never mind," he says. "Do whatever you want."

He walks away without even glancing at Harper, which I'm fairly certain hasn't happened to her since she hit puberty.

"Are you sleeping with him?" she asks. There's no judgment in her voice, just curiosity.

"Of course not," I reply. "We hate each other."

Her mouth twitches. "If you say so."

~

WHEN THE BAND BEGINS, I DRAG HARPER TOWARD THE STAGE. They're good, but I'm mostly doing it to escape Brendan's watchful, resentful eyes. He's spent the twenty minutes since he left us glancing over, as if he's convinced I'm going to mount the first guy who approaches.

Eventually I manage to forget about him. The band mostly plays covers, and I find myself singing along, dancing...and happy.

What strikes me most about it is how unfamiliar it feels. I guess I'm not happy very often these days, and that wasn't always the case.

"Thanks for convincing me to come," I tell her when the band finishes their set. "This was great."

"Your bodyguard didn't seem to enjoy it much," she says, nodding over her shoulder. I follow her gaze to see Brendan ten feet behind us, glowering at me with his arms crossed.

"Has he been there the entire time?" I ask, stupefied.

"The entire time," she says. "You're sure you're not sleeping with him?"

"What?! No! I'm engaged, remember?"

She glances back at him. "Sure, I remember," she says. "Not sure he does, though."

I'M JUST WALKING INTO THE HOUSE WHEN ROB CALLS, AND FOR the first time in a while I finally have something worth reporting.

"I'm glad I caught you," he says. "I was worried you might be in bed."

"I'm just walking in," I reply. "I went to a show with Harper."

"A show?" he asks. His voice is flat. I don't blame him for being surprised, but what bothers me is that he also sounds displeased. "Where?" There's a hint of accusation in his voice, as if I'd promised to stay home and pine for him but broke our deal.

"Is something wrong?" I ask.

He says no in a tone that implies otherwise, and I'm not sure how to get around it, or if I even want to get around it. I've spent three weeks hearing about the restaurants and clubs he's gone to, but when I finally go out and find something I enjoy, he can't bring himself to even pretend to be interested?

He tells me, halfheartedly, some story about work, and I listen just as halfheartedly, putting the phone on speaker and walking into the closet to get my pajamas at one point. More and more, our calls are like this: one or both of us irritated, forced to maintain a conversation neither of us cares to have.

"So if you're going out with Harper," he finally says, "I suppose you haven't had time to look at reception sites." The words are flat, utterly emotionless.

I knew he'd come out with it eventually.

"Seriously, Rob?" I explode. "I go out *one* night and you're on me about this?"

"Just don't bother telling me you're too busy anymore, okay?" he snaps. "Let's at least be honest about it. You've got no interest in getting married."

"And you apparently have no interest in any part of my life that doesn't involve you. Good to know."

I'm not sure who hangs up first. I only know that we aren't people who fight, and we aren't people who hang up on each other, and lately it seems that's all we do.

❧ 15 ❧

BRENDAN
Four Years Earlier

By midsummer everything about Erin has turned gold—her hair, her skin. Her mouth is pink like a rose in bloom. Sometimes I catch myself just staring at her face.

This metamorphosis of hers is a complete pain in the ass for me. It means every time she walks through a bar, she's getting checked out, and every time she walks away from our table at night, some guy will stop her with the world's lamest excuse to strike up a conversation—like the guy stopping her at this very moment, over near the bathrooms.

My need to get involved in these situations hasn't escaped anyone's notice either. As I jump to my feet, a few guys at my end of the table start laughing.

"Let me guess," says Kirk with a smug little smile. "You really hate Erin, yet you're gonna go tell that guy to beat it."

I narrow my eyes. "Someone has to. I don't see any of you assholes taking care of it."

"Yeah," he says, "because that's not something normal people do. She's twenty-two, not twelve. She's allowed to talk to boys. Why don't you just admit you like her?"

"I don't *like* her," I say with disgust. "She's practically family."

"Cool," he says, eyeing me. "Then you don't mind if I ask her out?"

Everyone privy to this conversation is watching the two of us like it's a tennis match. I swallow. Why do I care if she goes out with Kirk? I don't. And anyway, I know she won't say yes. For some bizarre reason, Erin still likes me. Every time she walks in the room I catch a glimpse of it before she tucks it away. It's as if she forgets, for just a moment, what a dick I've been each minute of this summer.

She makes it back to the table on her own, without my intervention. We spend the next hour bickering, as we always do. She's as irritating as ever, but when she rises to leave, I find myself wishing she would stay.

I wait until she's out the door before I follow. People still think of Colorado Springs as a small town, but bad shit happens everywhere, and it happens disproportionately to women. She's standing by her piece-of-shit car, fumbling around in her purse for her keys. That's when I notice the guy who spoke to her earlier crossing the parking lot and heading her way. She doesn't even see him, and if I have anything to say about it, it'll stay that way. I step in his path.

"Hey, buddy," I say, folding my arms across my chest.

"I'm not your buddy," he says. "Get out of my way."

His haste confirms my suspicion that he was heading toward her—to talk or worse. "What's your rush?"

He glances beyond my shoulder at Erin, and tries to sidestep me. I step in his path again and he takes a swing, which makes my night. Because I was dying to punch this motherfucker from the moment he spoke to her, and he just made it legal.

❧ 16 ❧

ERIN

T en-mile runs suck. Running intervals sucks. Combining them, though? That's a whole new level of suck.

Were it not for Olivia asking me to run a small portion of her hundred-mile race with her, now only weeks away, there's not a chance I'd be doing this. Even when we ran college cross country together, enduring grueling two-a-day workouts, she was so much faster than me that it looked like I was walking by contrast. And in the years since we graduated, her training has only increased, whereas mine has dwindled to a few casual runs each week. I wanted to say no when she asked, but it's impossible to tell a woman who has just given birth that you don't think you can run one-tenth of a race with her. My pride won't allow it.

By the time I get home it's dark, and I'm so drained I barely have the energy to climb the stairs to my door. I shower quickly and slide into the hot tub, already so stiff I'm wondering how I'll climb back out.

I close my eyes and lean back against the headrest. Rob and I practically lived in the hot tub when we first moved in, but I don't think he's been out here once in the past year. I understood it, because he had so little free time, but he sure seems to have plenty of free time *now*. Just this past weekend, he and a few colleagues went to Brussels, while I can't remember the last time he didn't work a weekend while he was home. That shouldn't annoy me as much as it does.

I shut him out of my mind and begin to drift off. I might hate long runs, but this is one of my favorite things—the way exhaustion plus hot water lulls you to sleep.

"Hello, roomie." My eyes fly open, catching on the tattoo on Brendan's right shoulder and the definition of his chest before I drag them away.

"Shouldn't you be out?" I ask.

"It's nine PM. That's early for most people in our demographic. Not you, obviously. I'm shocked you're not already in pajamas, talking to Mr. Tibbles."

I stiffen, wondering if he's actually been looking in the window at night. I do, quite often, talk to Mr. Tibbles. "I just finished a long run. Olivia wants me to do part of her race with her."

He looks like he's considering something, and then sighs. "I rented a car if you need a ride to Squaw Valley," he says, "since we're on the same flight."

"We *are*?" My chagrin borders on despair. I didn't realize Brendan was going at all, much less a day early like me. Even in another freaking *state* I can't get away from him.

He raises a brow. "Rob gave me his ticket to Reno. I thought he told you."

My molars grind so hard I can hear them over the sound of the Jacuzzi jets. How could Rob not have mentioned this? As if it's not bad enough that I have to live with this guy, I now have to sit right next to him for an entire flight?

"He didn't mention that," I reply between my teeth.

I'm no longer enjoying the hot tub. I only remain because I don't want to give Brendan the satisfaction of knowing he's driven me off. He barely restrains a smile, leaning his head back and stretching out his arms. "This is one hell of a set-up you've landed," he says. "Big house, pool, hot tub. Rob's quite the provider. I can't believe you didn't get all this shit locked down the minute he proposed."

Rage gives me a sudden burst of energy. "Fuck you, Brendan. You've known me for way too long to sit there and pretend you think I'm a gold digger."

He's quiet for a moment. "You're right," he admits. "I'm sorry." His eyes close, as if this sudden burst of honesty has exhausted him. "It was my shitty way of asking why you're dragging your feet."

"Who says I'm dragging my feet?"

He laughs quietly. "Everyone. Everyone alive thinks you're dragging your feet. I'm not judging you. I just want to know why."

I shouldn't answer. He just accused me of being a gold digger, and he's definitely not on my side here. It's insane to hand him more information about anything. But he's also the only person who knows about my dad outside of my family, which makes him the only person to whom I can tell the truth. And I suppose I want just one other person alive to know how I feel.

"It's my dad," I admit. "I think the stress of the wedding will set him off, and he's been doing poorly since they moved out here as it is. He'll drink at the ceremony, even if I ask him not to, and my mother will make an ass of herself trying to cover it up. And he'll drink at everything leading up to it—any party, the rehearsal dinner. There are so many things that can go wrong, and I'm just...tired." My voice catches a little, as I realize how true that is.

I *am* tired. I'm *so* tired of those calls at night and the worry and the sense that I have to be on my guard every moment of the day to keep the world from falling in on us all. Rob's family is kind but judgmental, and I just can't stand the idea of them all looking askance when my father shows his ass. I can't stand the idea of Rob doing it the most.

I clear my throat. "It feels like too much right now."

He gives me that careful, assessing look I've seen far too often.

I sometimes get the sense that he hears ten extra words for every one I speak, drawing my secrets from me without my consent.

"And you've never told Rob any of this."

I sigh. "No. He won't understand. He won't respect it. He won't respect that my father has so little self-control. He won't understand why I coddle him by going to Denver."

"You spend so much time hiding shit from him," Brendan says. "Wouldn't it just be better to let him know who you are?"

I flinch. His voice is gentle and it doesn't sound like an accusation, yet it is one, and I can't even blame him for it. His oldest friend is about to marry the biggest liar who ever lived.

"If I don't like who I am and what my family is, how can I expect Rob to like those things?"

"You've got nothing to be ashamed of," he insists. "And you shouldn't be with someone who doesn't feel the same way. Olivia thinks that's why you haven't planned the wedding. Because you know something's wrong."

"I can't believe Olivia thought *you* were the best person with whom to have that conversation," I say.

He shrugs. "She's worried."

"Yeah, so worried that she told the guy who doesn't want Rob to marry me all about it. That's extremely helpful."

The corner of his mouth tips upward. "She hates me slightly less than you do, so she's not inclined to think the worst."

I swallow. "I don't hate you."

"You just pretend to," he says softly, holding my eye.

He's being serious, and there's something in his tone that draws goose bumps to the surface of my skin. The moment he says it, I know he's right. I am pretending. I have been forever.

"It's too warm. I'm done," I say, jumping to my feet. I glance up to find that he is not smirking, but staring at me as the water slides over my skin.

He looks away, and I'm out of the tub when I hear him speak.

"Don't worry, Erin," he says quietly. "I'm just pretending to hate you too."

17

BRENDAN
Four Years Earlier

Although I'm staying on to lead tours in the fall, most of the staff takes off at the end of the summer—either because they're returning to school or because they've acquired a real job. Erin, who got a full-time offer out of her internship, is among them.

Mike hosts an end-of-summer party, and some girl from high school is in my lap when Erin shows. Ponytail, work T-shirt, and no makeup, but she's tan, and her hair looks like spun gold, and I wish the world would freeze so I could stare at her perfect, annoying face.

She flushes as our eyes meet, taking a quick glance at the girl in my lap and turning the other direction. I watch her walk away. And then I continue to watch, while the girl in my lap drones on about some *Real Housewives* bullshit I can't begin to be interested in.

When Erin heads inside, out of view, Kirk gets this big, shit-eating grin on his face and cocks a brow at me. "You know who else is inside?" he asks.

"Who?"

"Taz," he says.

We hate Taz. The guy thinks he's a fucking celebrity because he was on the pro cycling circuit for a few years and ostensibly is friends with Lance Armstrong. He's also the kind of guy who will be all over Erin like a rash.

"Who the fuck invited him anyway?" I ask. "He's not on staff."

Kirk laughs. "Dude, Erin's a big girl. She can walk away if she wants to."

Less gracefully than I should, I remove the girl from my lap and march inside. Sure enough, Taz has Erin cornered in the kitchen. She appears to be fascinated by what he's saying, which annoys me even further. The last thing that guy needs is encouragement.

I go over to them. "Can I speak to you for a minute?" I ask her.

Taz looks at me. "We're in the middle of a conversation."

"Go tell someone else about the time you met Lance Armstrong, douchebag," I say, walking her away with my hand at the small of her back. I've got four inches on the guy—he knows better than to complain.

"What do you want?" Erin asks with a weary sigh. "Were you worried I might be experiencing a moment of happiness?"

What do I want? I don't even know. I just don't want her going home with anyone.

"That guy's a jackass," I reply. "Why are you even here? Shouldn't you be out doing whatever people in marketing do? Which I guess is sleep."

She taps her lips with her index finger, and for a moment I'm unable to look away from her mouth.

"Hmmm," she says. "I'm trying to figure out what's going on here. Because it sounds like you're jealous, and I don't know if you're jealous of that guy because *you* never got to hang with Lance Armstrong, or if you're jealous of me because I've acquired this mystical thing known as *full-time employment*—which I realize is a foreign concept to you, but something you should probably look into eventually."

I take a step closer, drawn to that flash of anger in her eyes, and then I take another one, until I can feel the heat of her skin.

"One day," I tell her, "I'm going to bend you over my knee and spank that smirk off your face."

"I think you're just looking for an excuse to get your hand on my ass," she replies, meeting my gaze.

"I don't hear you arguing against it." We're so close now. I can feel the uneven huff of her breath against my chest as I speak. "I'd spank you so hard you wouldn't be able to walk the next day."

"Promises, promises," she says as if bored. "We both know you don't have it in you."

I press her to the wall. Something inside me, something taut and tense that I've barely controlled, has finally snapped, and I'm not sure if I want to kill her or fuck her—I'll figure it out later on. I capture her mouth—that sweet, willing mouth that's driven me crazy all summer long. She tastes like sugar and vanilla, the way I knew she would, and to my surprise I am not in this alone. She meets me move for move, her tongue sliding against mine as my hands wrap tight in her hair.

I want so many things from her in this moment that it feels impossible to pick just one. It will take me all night, possibly all year, before I'm sated. I move farther into the darkness, slide my hand into her shirt, teasing her through the lace of her bra with my fingers, and when she groans in my mouth, I'm done for. I lift her up and wrap her legs around me, pressing against her, but it's not enough. I need all of her, spread out in front of me. I need time.

I pull back just enough to tell her we're going to my apartment. Her eyes are closed, her mouth swollen. I don't think I've ever wanted to be inside someone so badly in my entire life.

But then her eyes open. And I see lust there, but I also see hope—and hope is the exact fucking thing I never want to see on any girl's face. The job in Italy is all set up and I'm not changing the plan.

She's not a one-night-stand girl, and I've known this all along.

Maybe I could talk her into it, but I don't want to be the guy who does that. Not to her.

I set her down abruptly. "We shouldn't be doing this."

She looks hurt, which I hate, but which also tells me I've absolutely made the right decision.

"You started it," she whispers, her voice raspy.

"I'm sorry," I tell her. "I shouldn't have."

18

ERIN

I drive to Denver on Saturday to have breakfast with my parents. There have been two calls from my father during the week, which means he's getting worse. I know this pattern: he will continue his downward slide until something big happens— a DUI, a fight in a bar, a lost job—and then he will straighten up, sort of, briefly. Of course no one ever refers to the event as a "wake-up call." In our family lore it's just another piece of bad luck handed to him. I'm not sure a visit will do any good, but I have to try.

Rob never comes on these trips because I'm scared the truth will slip out. His disgust when my brother relapses has proven, time and again, that he just won't understand that you can love people in spite of their flaws.

My dad is hung over, but he rallies because I'm there, with help from that disgusting instant coffee he prefers and a Bloody Mary that is way too pale an orange to contain the correct ratio of tomato juice to vodka.

He asks how everything is going and I tell him it's great. My dad gets a glossy, soft-focus version of my life, always, because I'm never sure which of my life's bumps and bruises will require a tequila chaser for him.

"So when are you and Rob setting a date?" he asks.

"Soon," I reply, as always. "When he gets back from Europe."

"There's a nice Catholic church down the street," my mother suggests.

Inwardly I groan. Neither Rob nor I are religious. There's no way he'd agree to a one-hour nuptial mass at my parents' church. "I don't know if we're planning to have a church wedding."

"If you're not married in the church, you're not married in the eyes of God," my dad thunders. "It won't count otherwise."

If any other person alive were to say this to me, I would roll my eyes. But I don't rock the boat in my parents' house. "Rob's not Catholic," I remind him, and it's not until I see the shock on my parents' faces that I realize this is new information.

"Well, you're both supposed to be Catholic to get married in the church," my mother says, her voice growing high and thin, the way it does when she's worried. "But we can talk to Father Duncan. He'll make an exception. He might even let us do the reception in the parish hall."

I groan internally. God, I wish this topic had never come up. I wish I'd just lied, right from the start. Or maybe my lies are the issue. How is it that I haven't mentioned Rob's lack of religion in four years? How is it that they're still under the impression we'd drive to *Denver* to hold our wedding? I don't want to, but this needs to be corrected right now before it goes any further.

"Mom, we live near Colorado Springs. That's where our friends are. We'll probably just do the whole thing someplace like the Broadmoor."

"The *Broadmoor*?" my mother asks. "That'd cost a fortune!"

"Rob and I will pay for it," I assure her. "He does really well. You guys don't need to worry about a thing."

There's a shadow over my father's face, and then my mother's. *Stupid, stupid, stupid.* My father is about to lose his job, and he's taking Rob's success as some kind of slight against his ability to provide. I look at him, and then my mother, and I feel lost. I feel the way I always felt as a child, as if we stand on a sinking ship in the middle of an empty sea. We're always doomed, no matter what I do. It's just a matter of time.

~

It's well after two AM when my phone rings, as I expected it would. Except it's not my dad on the phone but my mom, which means I have a decision to make.

Brendan told me to call him. Well, actually he *threatened* me, *blackmailed* me. But I do not want to involve him again. Not because he wasn't a godsend the last time—he was, in a thousand ways. But this is my family's problem, my family's secret, and I resent that he's forcing me to share it. I peer out at the street and don't see his car. After a moment of internal debate, I dress quickly and then text him:

Going to Denver. I'll be fine. Don't need help but thanks.

I'm not even down the stairs when he texts back to tell me he's on his way, and five minutes later he's outside with the Jeep running. I'm so mired in resentment and shame that I have no idea what to say. How do you approach someone who's being kind to you and making you miserable simultaneously?

"You really didn't need to do this. I've done it on my own for a long time."

He exhales unhappily. His untucked shirt makes me suspect my text interrupted something, so I understand his irritation, but I'm not the one blackmailing people.

"Look, it's bad enough that I had to tell you about this without you acting annoyed that you're here," I say.

"That's not why I'm annoyed," he replies. "Lots of people have a parent who drinks too much. I did. But it's completely fucked up that your mother is asking *you* to drive to Denver when she's right there."

Possibly. But this is the way we've done things for a long time.

Even in high school, I was the one in charge of my father. "She isn't making me do it. She falls apart and is completely helpless when anything goes wrong."

His hands clench the steering wheel. "So you've got a helpless mother, an alcoholic dad, and a brother who's a cokehead. And every fucking one of them turns to you when they need help."

And I'm the liar who's kept most of this from his best friend. "This isn't going to impact Rob if that's what you're worried about," I reply. "I'd never expect him to deal with this or help pull their weight."

"Of course you wouldn't!" he shouts. "He doesn't even fucking know it's happening."

I lean my head against the window, wishing I was anywhere but this car. I don't need a guilt trip from him on top of everything else. "If you agree that it won't be a problem for Rob, why do you care?"

A muscle in his jaw flickers. "I've known you for six years, Erin. I'm allowed to worry about you too."

There's a small ache in my chest once more. He's always worried about me. He thinks I don't know that he used to make sure I got to my car safely that summer we worked together. Or that for every shitty thing he'd said, he'd done something sweet— reporting the assistant manager for hitting on me, changing the radio to my favorite station when I came into work. He'd even washed my car one day, although when I'd tried to thank him, he'd insisted it got wet "accidentally" when he was cleaning off the kayaks. It was those small things that kept me clinging to the idea of him, even when I wished it would stop. And I find myself wanting to cling again, which is a dangerous prospect, given that I'm engaged to someone else.

We arrive in Denver and repeat our adventure from a few weeks prior. My father is again at the third bar we visit, and my mother is again livid that I've exposed our family in this way. This time, she chooses not to speak to me at all, not a single word. My father grabs my hand as I go, slurring an apology, telling me he's going to do better.

He's told me this so many times before. I know he'll try. I just know better than to hope it will last.

I walk out of their condo feeling exhausted and hopeless. There are times, like right now, when I sort of wish it would all end. Not just the drinking, or Sean's problems, but all of it. I can't abandon them, but sometimes I wish I could shut my eyes and have all four of us cease to exist.

Tears are going to come whether I want them to or not. I turn my head toward the window, hoping Brendan won't see. It doesn't work.

"Is this about your dad or something else?" he asks quietly.

I dry my eyes on the inside of my T-shirt and clear my throat. "I feel," I begin, my voice rasping, "like everything is falling apart with Rob gone. Not just my family, but me too. I don't even know what I want to do in my *leisure* time. I'm not sure I like anything, which is the most depressing thought of all."

"You?" he asks. "You love tons of stuff. You love to bake. You love to bike. And go on road trips. Remember when you drove to Portland to see that band because you liked *one* of their songs?"

I'm a little surprised he remembers *anything* about me, much less all this. Even Rob would have struggled to come up with that list.

"Life changes after college," I reply quietly. "I've got no one to bake for, and everything else—those were college things. I mean, who am I going to bike or kayak with? Who's going to roadtrip to Portland now? We all have jobs."

He frowns. "All I'm saying is that you used to like plenty of shit. I'm not sure why you're not doing any of it, but the problem isn't that there's nothing you enjoy."

I guess he's right. My life changed and narrowed when I got out of college, but it wasn't because I stopped having interests. It's just that there somehow didn't seem to be space for them. What else have I let go of since then? And is there any way to get a little of it back?

We get home faster than I expected. He stops the car, but neither of us gets out.

"So, are we, like, friends now or something?" I ask. If this is only a temporary cease-fire I'd like to know.

He hesitates, glancing at me and looking away. His jaw is knife-sharp, silhouetted by moonlight. "We can try," he says.

I sigh. "I didn't ask you to climb Everest. I just asked if we could be friends."

"Yeah, I know," he says. "I know."

I get the feeling he'd rather climb Everest.

19

ERIN

The next evening I'm struggling to keep my eyes open when Brendan taps on the door and walks in. He's tan from a day in the sun and wearing a navy blue fleece that makes his eyes look unreal. I'm so tired I can barely see my hands in front of my face, but I can't stop noticing him.

He thrusts a Diet Coke and a pint of Cherry Garcia at me. "As I recall, you like Diet Coke with your ice cream, which is completely illogical, by the way. Why the fuck would you drink diet soda with ice cream?"

It's so weird that he's here, and that he remembers yet another obscure thing about me. "What's this for?"

He shrugs. "You wanted to be friends. I'm attempting it. No promises though."

My chest feels warm and fluttery. "If it lasts for thirty minutes, I'll be shocked," I assure him.

He suggests ordering Thai. I'm not sure if I agree because I'm craving it or if I'm simply stunned by Brendan's 180-degree turn. I'd forgotten he could even be like this—pleasant, sweet, thoughtful. I'd forgotten he was like this most of the time, to everyone but me. And that on one occasion—many years ago—he was like this with me too.

When the food arrives, he spreads it all out on the coffee table, sliding the red curry chicken over to me.

I groan as I take my first bite. "It's so good."

For a fraction of a moment, something shifts in his face—his gaze hazy, his lips parting. And then it's gone.

For lack of any other neutral topic, I ask him about his tour business. Because his friend Caleb invested, he tells me, he now has enough capital to run heli-skiing tours over the winter to keep the business afloat. He has an actual business plan, cost and profit projections. He certainly doesn't sound like the lovable ne'er-do-well Rob always made him out to be.

"So that's me," Brendan says. "But what about you?"

"What about me?" I ask, pushing the chicken around on my plate.

"You need a life, Erin."

I stiffen, regretting the things I told him last night. "I have a life. It's just on hold."

"Having Rob's life isn't the same as having your own," he says, his face earnest. "And you seemed to be doing pretty well before he ever came into the picture. Where'd that girl go?"

I shrug. Last night, change seemed possible. Today I've acknowledged how unlikely it is. "People grow up, Brendan. Was I going to keep mountain biking and snowboarding into my seventies?"

"Possibly. I see people older than that doing both. But more to the point, you're not seventy. You're twenty-six. And you've given up everything you used to love. I'd be depressed as fuck too if I was coming home to some big, empty house every night with nothing to look forward to but more of a job I hate."

For some reason the words make my eyes sting. It's one thing to think you're in a temporary bad spot; it's another thing entirely to have someone sum up for you just how bleak every waking moment of your day is. I don't want to cry in front of him again, but I think it's inevitable. I close my eyes and bury my face in my hands.

"Aw, babe," he sighs. "I didn't mean to make you cry. Come here."

When I don't move, I find myself pulled into his chest, my body half lying on the couch and half lying on him.

"Erin," he whispers, his breath against my hair. "Don't cry, hon. I'm sorry. I was being a dick."

"No," I whisper. "You were just being honest. And you're right."

For a single moment I allow myself this—Brendan's warmth and his firm chest beneath my head and the smell of him, like soap and sand and clean air—before I pull away.

I laugh. "I think I've cried more in front of you than I've ever cried in front of Rob."

"Yeah," he says, "because he has no idea what makes you sad. He doesn't even know you *are* sad. So what are you going to do about it?"

I shrug, returning to the conclusion I came to earlier in the day. "Just wait it out, I guess. I mean, I could throw myself into stuff now, but I'd just have to give it all up when he comes home. Nothing I like is going to fit with our life. Rob works long hours and when he's not working, he just wants to chill."

"So let Rob stay in by himself," says Brendan. "'Let there be spaces in your togetherness'. Isn't that the quote?"

I laugh. "Holy shit, did Brendan Langstrom, the biggest whore in the state, the man who hates relationships, just quote Kahlil Gibran to me?"

"Those who can't do, teach," he says with a sheepish smile. "But seriously. You're allowed to have things you love. You're allowed to have space for yourself in this thing. You need it. Otherwise, you lose who you were in the first place. Come biking with me this weekend. Let's figure out what you love."

I feel another tug on my heart as Brendan walks into the kitchen. He certainly has no interest in biking with me, and he probably has no interest in being here. Yet he is. With my family, with Rob, even with Olivia, I've always been the fixer, the person who does whatever is necessary to make sure everyone's happy. I can't think of a time in my life, until now, when someone tried to fix things for me.

He returns with the Cherry Garcia, already shoveling the most enormous spoonful I've ever seen into his mouth.

"I know what you're thinking," he says as he hands the container to me and pulls his fleece over his head. I catch a glimpse of tan stomach, abs that curve in perfectly symmetrical hills and valleys. "Why can't *all* men be as charming as me?"

I laugh, but later on, I realize he was right.

That's exactly what I was thinking.

20

ERIN

I don't know how Brendan convinced me to bike down the Encinitas Trail with him, when I haven't been on a bike in years. But I imagine there are a whole lot of women in the world wondering how Brendan convinced them to do one thing or another, so I probably should have expected I'd get my turn.

The Encinitas Trail is not for neophytes or people who haven't biked in ages. It's steep and dangerous, with hairpin turns and insane descents. It's positively deadly, and as I fly down at breakneck speed, I don't think I've ever been happier. Brendan isn't a cautious biker, and neither am I. We don't talk—trying to hold a conversation during a ride like this would be like trying to hold a thoughtful conversation during sex: if it's possible, you're not doing it right.

"I'd forgotten how much I love this," I tell him when we reach our turnaround point. "It's been ages since I was on a bike."

He grabs his water bottle and chugs, and I can't help but watch. There's something so unequivocally *male* about him, his throat, as he swallows.

"Let me guess," he says. "Because Rob doesn't bike?"

I make a face. "That's just how relationships are. It's a process of attrition. You look for common ground, and sometimes that means shaving away at the hard edges."

"Seems to me," he says, "that you shaved down too much."

I'd like to argue, but I can't. I've spent so much time trying to make sure Rob is happy that maybe I forgot to ask if I was too.

BRENDAN'S DOWNSTAIRS AT THE STOVE WHEN I GET OUT OF THE shower after our ride. I didn't realize he'd still be here, didn't brace myself for it. And I really needed to brace for *this*: him shirtless, standing there in nothing but bike shorts, his broad shoulders tapering to narrow hips. My stomach tightens.

"I'm making breakfast burritos," he says. "Are you hungry?"

"Sure," I say weakly. "Want me to take over so you can shower?"

He turns, and his eyes flicker downward, almost unconsciously, from my wet hair to my bare legs. He swallows. "Okay." He hands me the spatula as he leaves, his bare chest brushing my arm. There's a millisecond in which I'm only aware of his skin, of the precise point where we meet. It seems as if the entire world stops moving forward and there is only this, a thing that is happening and should not be. Images flood my mind and leave me momentarily rooted in place, feeling robbed of air.

I take a deep breath and begin crumbling sausage in the pan. I'm not a cheater. In four years with Rob it's never occurred to me, even in times when he was barely home, times when we hadn't sex in so long I'd lost track. I don't know if it's Brendan's presence or Rob's absence at the root of this issue, but it sort of doesn't matter: I'm engaged, and it shouldn't be happening in either case.

"How's it coming?" he asks when he returns, peeking over my shoulder.

I can feel his whole body pressed against my back, solid in ways the average male is not. I could bounce a quarter off that chest. I allow myself a heady moment to breathe him in, imagine how this might proceed if we were very different people.

"Almost done," I reply. I sound breathless, and he hears it. I can tell by the way he grows absolutely still for a moment before moving away.

He starts coffee. "So if you hate your job so much, why do you stay?"

I shrug. "I'd love my job if it weren't for my boss. But it's not really the time to be switching jobs anyway. I gave Sean all of my savings, and if I left now, I'd have nothing to fall back on."

He glances around the house, from the six-burner Wolff range to the custom light fixtures in the foyer. "No offense, but it doesn't look like money is an issue around here."

I should just agree and let the conversation end. I'm not sure why I don't, except the truth feels like a balloon expanding inside me, and it's such a relief to let some of the air out.

"Sean's been to rehab too many times to count. It costs a lot, and my parents don't have the money. My father can't keep a job and I've had to cover their mortgage twice since last August. Rob's not going to put his income toward that, and I'd never ask him to. So I'm always going to need something of my own."

He grabs two coffee mugs. "I don't understand why you're with someone who doesn't even know you," he says. "Name one thing that makes having to lie all the time worthwhile."

I think about the aspects of a relationship that would appeal to Brendan. Sex is the big one, and I guarantee he's getting a lot more of it outside a relationship than I am in one. He hands me a cup of coffee, and I hand him the first burrito.

"Teamwork," I reply. "Like this. Working as a team makes everything easier, makes it more enjoyable."

He shakes his head. "How can that possibly be worth everything you're giving up?"

"I don't get you," I say with a sigh. "Your mom and Peter are blissfully happy. So are Will and Olivia. Why are you so convinced a relationship is a terrible thing? Because you can't imagine only wanting one girl?"

"No," he says, glancing at me before he turns away. "I can imagine only wanting one girl."

I'm sure it's my imagination, but for one heady moment, I wonder if the girl he's referring to is me.

BRENDAN
Three and a Half Years Earlier

Fall arrives, and the tour office is almost empty. I expected Erin's absence to feel like a relief, but it's sort of like that mosquito bite she wouldn't leave alone. I'd gotten used to scratching it. I'm not sure what to do in her absence, and everything feels empty. I'll see her again at Will and Olivia's engagement party, and I know it won't be enough.

I miss her.

The realization hits me suddenly and sharply, and once it's there, I can't be aware of anything outside it.

I miss the smell of her hair when she walks by. I miss the way she rubs her bottom lip when she's listening to someone, the way her fingers tap any available surface when she's annoyed. I miss the feel of her against me, the way she kissed, the way she yielded. It feels like I'm homesick, with this longing for a girl I never wanted around.

Except I still want to see the world. I'm not ready to get tied down, and Erin is someone who will settle for nothing less. I know

I did the right thing ending that kiss, but it doesn't stop me from counting the days until I see her again.

❧

THE PARTY IS HELD ON A RARE WARM NIGHT AT THE END OF September, out at the farm where I was raised. My mother and her husband have put the place on the market, which means this will probably be the last event held here. I'd expected that to make me a little nostalgic, but as it turns out, I really don't care. I just want to see Erin.

My mother positions me behind the grill with way more steak than I'm interested in being responsible for. My closest childhood friend, Rob, stands beside me, fresh out of his MBA program and a summer internship at Lehman Brothers.

Anyone who knows both of us might struggle to understand how we became friends. We no longer have a whole lot in common, but we've always had each other's backs, and he's a part of almost every memory I have of high school. We met as scrawny thirteen-year-olds, getting our asses kicked by the older kids. That kind of bond remains, no matter how different you become.

He's telling me about his new job when he suddenly stops and lets out a low whistle.

"Holy shit," he says, setting his plate down. "Who's *that*?"

I look up to see Erin walking toward my mom. She's wearing a fitted yellow dress and heels. For a moment all I can see are legs and hair, and I feel my stomach bottoming out. I think about kissing her, about the smooth skin under her shirt, the sounds she made when my hands slid over her for the first time.

"Erin," I say quietly. I want to stare at her until the end of time. Jesus I've missed seeing that face.

"The one you hate?" he asks in astonishment.

"I never said I hated her," I argue. "I said she was annoying." I smell burning steak, but I'm still watching her, unable to look away.

"A girl who looks like that can be as annoying as she wants," says Rob. "Introduce me."

"Not a chance. That's not how I want to spend my afternoon." More to the point, that's not how I want Rob to spend *his* afternoon.

"Fine," he says. "I'll introduce myself."

And with that he walks away, and my stomach drops. Rob, unlike every other guy I scared off this summer, is not a douchebag. In truth, he's far better for her than I could ever be. And now he's got his Harvard MBA and his brand-new job with a salary so high I thought he was joking when he told me.

It feels as if my life is still coming together, as if I have all the time in the world to go after the things I want for myself. But as I watch Rob introduce himself to Erin, it occurs to me for the first time that maybe she's one of those things. And maybe it's already too late.

✣ 2 2 ✣

ERIN

It's been only four days since my bike ride with Brendan, but it feels as if something has shifted inside me. Like hearing a song from high school and being catapulted back in time, I'm beginning to remember who I once was, the person I left behind in the process of becoming the person Rob wanted me to be. I'm angry at myself for letting that version of me slip away, and I'm secretly hoping Brendan will help me find her again.

Harper is sitting on my desk, eating the cookies I brought in and offering a far-too-detailed description of her date last night with a guy who hadn't shaved (*"He went down on me, and it was like someone was scrubbing my vagina with fucking sandpaper"*). When Brendan texts, asking if I want to bike this weekend, her story comes to a sudden halt and she reads over my shoulder, having no concerns with privacy—her own or anyone else's.

"Texting the new boyfriend, huh?" she asks with a smirk.

"He is *not* my boyfriend. As you know."

"Oops. I meant to say 'texting the guy who you've masturbated to thoughts of for the past month'. Oh, wait, maybe that was just me."

I bury my face in my hands. "I went to Catholic school, Harper. I'm still not ready for ninety percent of what comes out of your mouth."

"Speaking of people who need to get laid, you're still coming out with me Saturday, right?" Harper has somehow scored an invite to a private party for a bunch of the Broncos, which I honestly have no desire to attend.

My arms fold over my chest. "I'm not going out with you to get laid."

"Obviously," she says, as if offended. "I was referring to myself."

I sigh. I had a really good time with her the night we went out and I know I need to start doing more things. But I just don't see the appeal of this party. "Since when do you like football, anyway?"

"I don't have to like football to enjoy a guy with a perfect ass and a big dick," she replies.

So it's going to be that kind of night. At least I know it'll be a short one.

ON SATURDAY MORNING I BIKE WITH BRENDAN AGAIN. WE STOP at a restaurant for brunch on the way back. I'm not sure which of us suggests it, but I know I'm relieved. I'm fine with Brendan in public. It's in private that my mind starts to go haywire.

"So what's the plan for tonight?" he asks. "Romantic dinner, just you and Mr. Tibbles?"

I smile, relishing the fact that I can put him in his place for once. "I'm going out, I'll have you know."

He spears a home fry off my plate. "I didn't know the library extended its hours."

I laugh. "To a *bar*, asshole. A bar with men in it. *Broncos*, to be more precise. Harper got us an invite."

His cocky smile dims, then disappears entirely. "It's good that you're going out but, you know...baby steps."

I push my plate toward him, knowing he wants to finish my

meal. "I'm not bringing one of them *home*. I'm just attending something."

"I just..." he trails off, frowning. "There are a lot of guys out there who have a way of getting what they want."

I roll my eyes. "You'd know, wouldn't you?"

"I don't mean getting what they want by *persuasion*, Erin," he says, a muscle twitching in his temple. "I mean they get a girl into a situation where it's hard to say no or where it won't matter if she says no. Just...be careful, okay? Don't drink anything you don't watch being made by the bartender. And don't leave by yourself. Make your friend walk you to your car. Or a bouncer. Or call me."

I raise a brow. "*You're* going to drive downtown in the middle of the night and walk me to my car?"

"A, it had better not be the middle of the night when you're going home, and B, yes, without a single snide comment, I will drive down there. Promise me, Erin."

He's annoying, but it's also sweet. So sweet. But still annoying.

"Why do you care all of a sudden?" I ask with an exasperated laugh. "You didn't even like me until a few weeks ago."

He looks at me, suddenly serious, and his mouth opens as if he plans to argue before he stops himself. "Maybe you won me over with the coconut bars," he says.

It's not what he was going to say, and I really wish, just this once, he'd have told me the truth.

❦ 23 ❦

BRENDAN
Three and a Half Years Earlier

I'm standing at the altar with Will beside me. He's nervous as fuck, but I would be too if my fiancée had gotten cold feet as many times as Olivia has. There's a twenty-five percent chance she's catching a cab to the airport right now.

I'm nervous too, sick with it. I haven't seen Erin since the engagement party, nearly a month ago, and there's this hunger for the sight of her that I never dreamed possible. I know she and Rob have gone out. I didn't ask for details, and I've cut him off each time he's tried to share them anyway, but based on the expectant, excited look on his face as he waits for her to appear, I assume it's going well.

She arrives at the other end of the aisle, and the itchy, desperate thing in my chest goes away. I could stare at her all day, every day. I want to. I want to hear her hum as she works; I want to watch her face light up when she gets that first bite of Cherry Garcia. I want to hear her groan in my mouth when I kiss her, the way she did at Mike's house, and I want to hear it every fucking night.

She walks down the aisle and stands across from me as Will and Olivia say their vows. It's impossible not to stare at her as I admit something I should have figured out long ago, something I think I sort of already knew: she never annoyed me. I was annoyed that I wanted her. I was annoyed by the way my stomach would tighten every time she walked in the room.

The prospect of unlimited girls no longer appeals to me—why would it, when I'm just going to be picturing her face each time? I want only her, and I'll visit her family and go to farmer's markets every fucking day if that's what she wants. It feels like a stunningly small price to pay for what I'd get in exchange. I'm still leaving for Italy, but it's not forever. We can travel back and forth until I'm home again. We can figure something out.

Olivia and Will are pronounced man and wife. As it happens, I glance at Erin. She's got tears in her eyes, but she smiles at me, and I smile back. *I'm not ready yet*, I think, *but one day I think that might be us up there.*

It's a shitty thing to do to Rob, and odds are if he likes her as much as I think he does, it's going to ruin our friendship, but I'm telling her tonight. Maybe I'm too late, but I won't be able to live with myself if I don't at least try.

We are immediately dragged to the beach for photos, and I know it's my chance—to at least tell her I want to talk to her before Rob is hovering a foot away. But I've never been this guy before, the one who wants something real, the one scared of being shot down.

The moment passes, and then Rob is there, asking if he can take the flowers for her. It didn't even occur to me to offer. I don't know how to be *that* guy and I'm going to have to learn fast.

For the next few hours, all I can do is wait. I stand off to the side of the dance floor, staring at her in a manner I'm sure anyone would find creepy, wondering if she'll even hear me out if I get her alone, given that I was such a dick to her all summer. I'm not sure I'd listen in her place. The hotel's clueless wedding coordinator stands beside me, suggesting we go check out the penthouse and refusing to move on, no matter what I do to discourage her.

When Rob finally walks away, I cross the floor to Erin.

"Let's dance," I say. There's so much urgency in my voice I sound almost angry.

She frowns. "I'm only agreeing for one reason," she says.

"Because this is your favorite song?"

"Did you know that?" she asks. "Or are you guessing?"

"I knew," I tell her. Of course I fucking knew—that's why it's played on repeat in my car for months.

I lead her to the dance floor and place my hands on her hips. She feels perfect under my palms, fragile and thrilling. I trace the bare skin of her back, press the pads of my fingers tighter. She looks up as if she knows what I'm doing, as if she wants me to do more, and I can no longer stand to wait.

"Come here," I say, grabbing her hand, pulling her through the crowd to the darkness at the building's side.

"Why are we here?" she asks.

"For this," I say. I press her to the wall, placing my palms on either side of her face, and I kiss her. For a moment she softens beneath me, her body pliant, her mouth opening in response to mine. It's perfect. It's what we should have been doing all along.

And then she jerks away. "Stop."

"Why?" I demand. "Because of *Rob?*"

"No," she says. "Because you don't get to treat me like shit the whole time we work together and then suddenly decide you're interested the minute your friend asks me out."

Her voice is raspy, as if she's on the cusp of tears. It makes me hate myself. How could I have realized everything so late? I've completely fucked this up.

"That's not what this is..." I begin, just as the deejay announces that Will and Olivia are getting ready to leave.

"I have to go," she says, pulling away. "I need to help Olivia get ready."

"Erin, you've got to give me a chance to explain," I plead.

"Meet me back here after Will and Olivia take off." I pull her to me before she can object and kiss her once more—hard, a silent plea: *please give me a chance; please believe me.*

I take her stunned silence for agreement. It's only later, when she never returns, when I receive a text from Rob saying he's finally gotten Erin into his room, that I realize she wasn't agreeing at all. She was walking away for good.

24

ERIN

I've done my hair and makeup by the time Harper arrives on Saturday night. I'm wearing the same tank and skinny jeans I wore the last time we went out, but her loud groan tells me she does not approve.

"No," she says, taking one look at me before heading straight for my closet.

"No to what?" I ask.

"All of it. You're in your twenties, Erin. Stop dressing like the only stores you know of are Ann Taylor and Lady Footlocker. And you're wearing *daytime* makeup."

"There's a difference between daytime and nighttime makeup?" I ask.

"Oh, my sad little butterfly," she says, patting my head. "You still have so much to learn."

When we arrive at the club an hour later, I'm wearing more makeup than I've ever worn in my life, along with the inside layer of a black dress, which Harper is making me wear alone with my highest heels. I'm not sure if I feel pretty or cheap. Perhaps a little of both.

It's my first VIP line, and the club itself is the kind of place with which I have little experience: low lighting, club music, bass reverberating off the walls. The moment we're inside, Harper starts dragging me toward the cordoned-off section of the room, where the men stand a foot taller and a foot wider than normal human beings.

"Not ready for that," I object. "I haven't spoken to a guy who isn't Rob or a client in four years."

"You seem to talk to Brendan all the time," she says with a brow raised. Ever since she saw us together at that show a while back, she's been like a dog with a bone.

"He doesn't count." I sigh. "I need a drink first, at least."

"How does Brendan not count?" she asks, waving a twenty at the bartender.

I think about him, about his sharp cheekbones and the way that hollow beneath them seems to throb sometimes when he's thinking. About his miles of smooth skin, his broad back in those bike shorts, everything I noticed contained *within* those bike shorts when he turned around.

I swallow. "It's just not like that."

She slides a shot in front of me. "Keep telling yourself that. It doesn't make it true."

Twenty minutes later, I'm holding a drink I didn't ask for—one that *didn't* come straight from the bartender as Brendan required, because you can't go through life assuming everyone is a rapist—and I'm talking to some guy named Jason. I assume he's a football player, based on his size, but it hasn't come up, and so far I've been pleasantly surprised. My only experiences with football players, prior to this, were with the conceited dicks at ECU who fought us constantly for space on the track, but Jason is nice enough. He's telling me all about the house he's trying to renovate in Beaver Creek, which is something I can discuss at length, since

I directed most of the rehab of Rob's place too. I wonder, sporadically, if I should tell this guy I'm not single. I suppose I should have worn my engagement ring, but it's been sitting on my nightstand since Rob left town. I've just never felt comfortable with it on. Three karats are for Kardashians, not girls who save mascara for a special occasion.

Jason and I are debating the merits of a glass-front refrigerator when a proprietary hand wraps tight around my hip, and a voice I'd know anywhere brushes my ear, followed by his lips. "Sorry I'm late, babe."

Brendan. Who is warm and familiar and smells amazing, and is looking at Jason in a way that doesn't bode well.

Jason politely excuses himself, and I jerk away from Brendan. "What the hell? Are you so convinced I'm going to cheat on Rob that you had to come keep me away from men?"

He lifts a shoulder, and the seams of his shirt strain a little at the motion. He's wearing a button-down, which I haven't seen him do in ages. Is there anything he doesn't look amazing in? "Of course I don't think you'll cheat. But that guy was bad news."

"Yeah, it was *super* threatening the way he quietly walked off when you showed up—I really dodged a bullet," I reply. "Why are you here? And how'd you get into the VIP area?"

"Friends in high places," he says. "And I'm here because you didn't answer my texts. I thought I'd better come check on you."

I sigh and smile at the same time. Good lord, Brendan can be sweet. And also a pain in the ass. "I wasn't checking my phone because I was getting ready, and then because I was here, doing what *you've* been telling me to do for weeks."

He pinches the bridge of his nose—the same thing his brother does every time Olivia's frustrating him. "I'm pretty sure I didn't tell you to dress like you want to get laid and go nestle up to the first football player you find," he says, his words bitten off and unhappy.

I swallow hard. "I can't believe you just said that." I feel tears closing in and turn, walking rapidly down the stairs and toward the exit. But before I can get there, his hands are on my hips, and he's pulling me against his chest.

"Please, Erin. I'm sorry. I'm so fucking sorry. It came out worse than I meant it to."

I shrug him off. "Whatever, Brendan. It's fine. I'm going home, though, so you've done what you came to do."

"No," he says. "Don't do that. You look really good, okay? You sort of look too good. And it pissed me off because I'd been worrying about you already, and then I show up here and you look like that and that guy was looking at you like... Whatever. I just got pissed off. And I'm sorry."

A small thrill shoots up my spine. Brendan's opinion shouldn't matter to me, but it always has, and I think it always will.

"Come on," he says, pulling me toward the bar.

A part of me wants to resist, but he got dressed up just to come here and make sure I was okay. Which is...a lot. More than Rob would have done in the same situation. "If we're staying, we should probably go back up to the VIP section with Harper."

He sighs, his eyes closing for a moment. "You look hot, Erin. I don't mind throwing a few elbows, but I'm not in the mood to fight off an entire professional football team." He orders my drink, knowing what I want without asking, and then hands it to me, looking me over from head to toe. "Jesus. Don't let Harper dress you anymore."

"I'm right on the cusp of being offended again, just so you know."

"I'm not saying you're doing anything wrong. I just don't like worrying about people, and if you're out dressed like that, I'm gonna worry."

Stupid overprotective alpha male, acting like I'm fragile somehow and in need of his care. I don't know why I like it so much, why it makes me feel like my heart is swelling in my chest.

He nods at my drink. "Slam it and we'll dance."

I shake my head. I can't remember the last time I really danced

—it's on the long list of things Rob just refuses to do. "It's been so long I don't remember how."

"I've seen you dance," he says, cutting me off. "You dance like someone who does it for a living."

I smile a little. "Are you saying I dance like a stripper?"

"I'm saying you dance like a dancer. One who'd potentially be a fucking awesome stripper." And with that he pulls me into the crowd.

For the first few seconds I feel awkward, my limbs stiff and unnatural, as if this is something I'm no longer supposed to do. But the crowd pushes us close, and under the throb of the bass, his hips guiding mine, it all comes back to me. I find myself moving— so in sync with him you'd think we'd been doing it all of our lives. It reminds me of another time, a time when things still felt possible, when it seemed like all was right with the world and only getting better.

Dancing, I realize, is another of the many things I loved, and gave up for Rob. It's beginning to seem like I didn't just tone myself down for him, but killed myself off entirely.

The song changes into something slower, with more bass. Brendan's hands land on my hips, and with them comes the memory of those hands as we danced at Olivia's wedding. It's perhaps the most dangerous memory I have.

I remember the way he pulled me against him—a way that felt decisive, almost aggressive.

"Put your arms around my neck," he'd said, his voice rough and low, still watching my face as if it were the last time he'd ever see it. That's when his hands slid to my hips, hands so impossibly large I was certain he could wrap them around me if he really tried. Things with Rob were new then, and I couldn't even remember who he was when Brendan looked at me that way.

And I'm finding it hard to remember Rob right now, nearly four years later. All I can see is the stubble on Brendan's jaw, the tiny, beautiful scar at the top of his right cheekbone, and the look in his eyes as they brush over my face.

"I think the last time I danced was with *you*," I tell him. "At Will and Olivia's wedding."

His eyes hold mine, a question there I can't quite read. "I thought you'd forgotten."

I'm not sure how he thinks I could have forgotten. That was the night he ruined everything, the night I gave up on him for good and decided to move on.

I thought I'd never forgive him for it either, but here I am.

He pulls me closer, and I realize neither of us is breathing normally. His eyes flicker to my mouth and hold there.

Yes, Brendan, do it. I think it for only a moment, and my mouth parts as if being directed by someone other than me while his hands tighten on my hips.

It's so much like the last time, except I suddenly remember how that time ended, how Brendan broke my heart. And I remember it was Rob who put me back together.

I pull away, unable to think of a single word I can use to explain or justify what I very nearly did.

"I should go," I whisper. He nods and the two of us walk out in silence. His eyes hold mine as he opens my car door. I climb in, struck by a realization that sickens me: I didn't give up on him after Olivia's wedding.

No matter what happens, no matter what he does, Brendan will always be the one I want most.

25

ERIN

On Monday morning, I stumble in a little late. I've spent the past thirty-six hours stressed out about Brendan, wondering if we just destroyed our fledgling attempt at friendship. I haven't seen him since we left the bar Saturday and I'm worried that's intentional on his part.

Harper pops her heard over the cubicle wall. "I heard Timothy got reamed out by the chancellor last night," she whispers. "I guess there was an error in something."

I sigh heavily and rest my head against the back of my chair. There are so many bad parts about my job, but this is the worst: one tiny error in a brochure, and you may have just ruined a ten-thousand-dollar print job. One tiny error means it's possible you'll be fired, and it's *certain* you'll never hear the end of it.

Even though Timothy and the client both have to approve any project before it goes to print, blame is like water. It will trickle down until there's no place left for it to go, and that place is me. I'm senior project manager here. Almost everything comes through me before it goes out.

"Do you know which piece it was?" I ask.

"Does it matter?" she counters.

No, it doesn't. No matter who wrote it, I'm the one who should have caught the error in the end.

"He can't fire you," she says. "You do his job better than he does."

It's true, but I suspect that's the reason he dislikes me the most.

Timothy remains holed up in his office all morning, and by the time he finally emerges midday, there isn't a single person here who hasn't started pulling his or her resume together.

"Erin, can I see you in my office?" he asks.

Fuck. I've never been fired before. *What's going to happen if my parents need help and I'm unemployed? What if Sean needs to go to rehab again?*

"I suppose you know why you're here," he says, after I take the seat in front of him.

The first law of being caught at anything—speeding, cheating, murder—is to never admit your crime. Fairly easy in this case, since I have no freaking clue.

"No, I don't."

He raises a brow. "Really, Erin? The counseling center brochure?" he asks, sliding it across the desk.

Relief washes over me, turning the fine layer of sweat I'd broken into cold. "That's not my project. Edie did it and never asked me to review it." Which doesn't surprise me. Edie thinks sunshine blows out of her ass. She *never* thinks her work needs editing. If she can bypass me, she will.

His nostrils flare. "I'm not trying to create a witch hunt. But you need to take responsibility for your actions. Write a letter detailing what went wrong and how it won't happen again, and it'll be fine."

And that's when it all becomes clear: *he* didn't have me review it. It's his job to look for my initials on every project we submit, which means he either failed to check, or he reviewed it himself. If

I don't take the fall, he does, because nothing can leave this office without my okay or his.

I sit up straighter. "The final mock-up will be on file with a supervisor's signature on it. I'd start there."

"I don't *need* to start there," he says between his teeth. "I know I didn't sign off on it, which means you did."

Normally I keep the peace, somehow allow him to save face. But today I don't.

"When you can prove that," I tell him, rising from my chair, "let me know."

My hands are shaking. I've never really stood up to him before. I'm not sure if I'm thrilled or terrified, but I know the one person I want to discuss it with is Brendan. Is there a way for us to be friends without everything else that exists between us? I desperately wish that there were.

I leave work early and drive home, hoping he's there and wondering what I'll say. I come to a dead stop when I walk into the kitchen. The key to the pool house is on the table, with a Post-it note that just says "thanks".

I sink into a chair, feeling sick. When Rob calls a little later, I don't want to answer, but I do. Eventually, I tell him Brendan's gone.

"See?" he asks. "I told you it wouldn't last forever."

The problem is I'd begun to wish it would.

26

BRENDAN
Three and a Half Years Earlier

Three weeks after Will's wedding, I moved to Italy. I wasn't supposed to arrive until March, but shit happens. I've been here a month now, leading bike tours. I'm not sure how long it'll take for Florence to seem mundane, but I was raised on a farm in the middle of nowhere...so maybe never.

The only time the streets outside my window are quiet is the middle of the night, and even then, there are cars and the sound of doors slamming, the occasional shout echoing in the darkness. I like that, though. The air is muggy in the morning, stained with the scent of coffee and exhaust fumes by the time I rise. I like that, too.

The other Americans I work with, Brad and Sully, are homesick. They talk about the things they miss—decent Mexican food, burgers, people who understand the concept of sidewalk space— but I miss none of it. There's only one thing I miss, and it's the very thing I was certain for so long I didn't want.

My mother begged me not to run off, but it felt like I had no choice. It was either leave or watch Rob and Erin together, suffer Rob's daily reminders that I fucked up, that I waited too long, though he'd have no idea he was reminding me of anything at all.

I don't know why I thought Erin would hear me out. Why she'd choose me over Rob with his degrees and his job and his two-thousand-dollar suits. I really did, though. And while a part of me hates her for her decision, the rational part of me says she made the better choice.

ONCE THE HOLIDAYS END, WORK SLOWS AND BOTH BRAD AND Sully leave, which means I'm the only non-Italian at Bike Tuscany. The local guys are cool, but they've got their own shit going on. It's still better than being in Colorado, though.

I'm reminded of this almost daily—every time I see a couple walk by with that same besotted look Rob and Erin had before I left, anytime I see a couple kissing.

Or when Rob calls to tell me he just bought a five-bedroom house.

"Why the fuck do you need five bedrooms, Hugh Hefner?" I ask.

"Well, it's not always going to be just me here," he says. "And I don't know about Erin, but I want a lot of kids."

"*Kids?* You're not even married yet."

"It's all down the pike, though," he says. "Sooner rather than later, I hope."

I tug at my hair. "Don't you think you're moving a little fast? I mean, fuck, you just started dating her last fall." I know I sound pissed off. I don't give a shit.

"She's not moving in yet. She thinks we should wait until next summer. I'm not worried. Eventually, with Erin, I always get my way." He laughs, and there's a dirty edge to it that makes me wish I could reach through the phone and punch him.

When we hang up, I go for a long run, even though I biked fifty miles earlier in the day. I'm not sure if I'm trying to punish myself or exhaust myself until I'm beyond caring, but either way, it doesn't work.

❧ 27 ❧

ERIN

For the next two days, Timothy makes my life hell. He
dumps more work on me than he does the rest of the
office combined, demanding copy within hours of
assigning it. On Wednesday, he sees me leaving two hours after
everyone else and throws another job on my desk, telling me it's
due first thing in the morning.

He's trying to punish me for not taking the fall, and the parallels between him and my mother surprise me. How is it that I've
allowed so many people into my life who want to throw me under
the bus the second problems arise?

In a way I don't mind though. At least it gives me something
other than Brendan to think about.

I call Olivia on the way home. She tells me to quit, which is
what she always says.

"Or plant a bomb in his car," she suggests. "It's so easy. One can
of gunpowder and five rocket igniters."

"I knew I could come to you for advice," I say with a quiet
laugh, though the truth is that I didn't call her to talk about work

at all. "Have you heard from Brendan? I was just wondering how his new place is."

And how he is.

And if he's dating anyone, and if he misses me.

If he wishes he'd kissed me that night on the dance floor, or if he looks back on it like some kind of bizarre aberration, which I'm certain is how he looks back on the times he actually *did* kiss me.

"I didn't even know he'd moved," she muses. "I bet you're relieved, huh?"

I tell her I am. And of all the lies I've ever told, this is perhaps the biggest.

On Thursday night I'm up late, writing more last-minute copy for Timothy, when the doorbell rings.

As many times as I've thought of Brendan in the last hour, I half-wonder if I'm not imagining him when I open the door. But if I were imagining him, he wouldn't look like he does at this moment. He and Will both have the kind of face that looks etched, carved in stone, when upset. As he moves into the living room, I begin running through a list of reasons he might be here, and they are all bad. He sinks into the couch, leaning forward, his hands clasped between his knees, his body tense.

"I'm sorry," he says. "I shouldn't have come so late."

"You're freaking me out. Is everything okay?"

He stares at the floor. "My mom called tonight. She's having a lumpectomy tomorrow. I guess it's kind of like a mastectomy, but less invasive."

I freeze in place, still standing across from him. That can't be right. His mother, Dorothy, is young and energetic, and he and Will have already lost their father. It seems too unfair to be true— as if anything has ever led me to believe life would be otherwise.

"Oh God," I finally manage. "I'm sorry. I didn't even know she had cancer." I move beside him and grab his hand.

"I didn't either," he says. "No one did. She's kept it to herself for weeks. I think she only called tonight because Peter forced her to in case something..." He stops, swallowing hard, composing himself. "In case something goes wrong tomorrow."

"Nothing will go wrong," I tell him. I would give anything right now to be able to swear that, but I guess I can't.

"You know what I did when she told me?" he asks quietly. "I went to a bar. Not five minutes after she told me, I fucking drove to a bar. And I'm sitting there with this drink I don't want, about to go home with some girl I don't even like, when it hits me how fucking ashamed my mother would be if she could see me. I'm twenty-eight years old, and the minute I get some bad news, I run off like a coward and try to pretend it didn't happen."

I squeeze his hand. "Brendan, handling bad news poorly doesn't make you evil. It just means you handle bad news poorly. Did you talk to Will and Olivia?"

He sighs. "My mom doesn't want them to know. She's worried it'll throw Olivia off before the race."

That is just like Dorothy to be more worried about Olivia's race than her own health. She will sacrifice anything for her kids. I've always wondered what it would be like to have a parent like that.

"So I guess you're heading to Boulder in the morning?" I ask.

He looks excruciatingly defeated. "She needs Will there, not me. He's always handled the catastrophes in our family. What if I make it worse somehow?"

I hate that he's even suggesting it. In the Langstrom family, Brendan was long ago given the role of loveable fuck-up, and he's never seemed to mind. But right now I can see how damaging it's been. He actually believes it.

"You won't," I insist. "Of course you won't. Your mom needs at least one of her boys there, and she loves you every bit as much as she loves Will."

He glances at me and then back at the floor. "Is there any chance...you could come with me?"

I think fleetingly of the article Timothy demanded be on his desk tomorrow morning and decide I don't give a fuck. If I could give negative fucks, I would. "Of course, if it would help."

"Yes," he says with palpable relief. "It would totally help."

I scoot closer, and he immediately pulls me against his chest. It feels natural, like something we've done a thousand times. I know I'm enjoying this whole situation far too much. The smell of him beneath my nose: soap and fabric softener and a hint of alcohol. His warmth and his size.

"I don't know what to do," he whispers.

I know that feeling so well. Every time my father can't be found, every time Sean sounds like he's using again, every time my mother cries to me because of some way she's been hurt, I feel suffused by my own helplessness.

"There's nothing you can do," I reply, "except try to survive it."

WHEN I WAKE, I'M HALF STREWN OVER BRENDAN, WHO'S holding me tight to his chest. He has one long leg over the edge of the couch and the other on the floor. It looks horribly uncomfortable, but he's awake and seems in no rush to leave.

"Erin?" he whispers, "you were the only one I wanted to talk to last night. Even if I could have spoken to Will and Olivia, you'd still have been the one I wanted to tell."

I feel my eyes welling over. I've been so busy ruing my own loneliness—but mine is temporary, and Brendan's is not.

"I'm glad you did."

He pulls me closer. "I don't know why, but this just makes everything feel better."

I don't tell him, but lying like this makes everything better for me too.

DOROTHY'S SURGERY IS SCHEDULED FOR EIGHT, SO WE LEAVE FOR the hospital a short time later. I email Timothy on the way and tell him I'm sick. In four years of working there, I've only taken sick leave once, yet I guarantee he'll be pissed.

When we arrive at the hospital, we're ushered back to Dorothy's room. She and Peter both grow animated when we enter, but it's a false, panicked excitement, the kind you see when a mother is assuring her child that the broken bone jutting out of his skin is going to be just fine. They speak too fast, they laugh too loud, and when Dorothy squeezes my hand and thanks me for coming, her eyes brim with tears.

We've only been here a few minutes when the nurse comes in to take her back. Brendan is frozen—not willing to let his mother leave, not willing to say so aloud. He looks at me, panicked and lost, and I twine my fingers through his as if he's Olivia's three-year-old son, Matthew, nervous as we step onto the teacups at the fair. I pull him to Dorothy's side, leaning down to kiss her forehead. He squeezes the life out of my hand as he does the same. Then they wheel her out of the room, Peter following them down the long hallway.

"What do you need right now?" I ask Brendan once we get to the waiting room. He's sitting there with his shoulders hunched and his hands clenched. The sight of it breaks my heart.

"Nothing," he says, but he slides me closer to him, wrapping an arm around my shoulders. I rest my head against his chest and feel his relieved exhale against my hair. "Just you."

IT'S NEARLY TWO HOURS BEFORE THEY TELL US THE SURGERY IS over, and another hour before they allow Peter to go back. When he comes out, I try to send Brendan in, but he refuses, grabbing my hand again.

"No," he says. "I want you there."

Seeing Dorothy is a shock. I'd never say so to Brendan, but she looks bad—her skin so pale it has a bluish cast, papery thin and dry. They've taken all but one line out, but she has bruises and bandages covering her at multiple points. If I'd been told she was dying, I wouldn't have expected her to look any worse than she does.

She pats Brendan's hand. "I'm fine," she whispers. "You should go home. I'm just going to sleep all day anyway. But I'd like to chat with Erin for a moment if I could."

Brendan hesitates, glancing at me, and when I nod he walks out of the room with Peter, shutting the door behind them.

I step next to her bed and she grabs my hand. "Thank you for coming out here like this. It would have been so much harder on Brendan without you."

"It was nothing. I'm glad I could help."

"No, it wasn't nothing. He needs someone to lean on, even if he doesn't think so. Ever since Gabi, he just refuses to try," she says. "I'm not sure he's ever going to be serious about anyone again."

Gabi, the ex-girlfriend with whom it ended so badly. I feel a moment of blistering jealousy for this girl who held his heart, something I was never capable of.

"People recover from all sorts of things," I reply. "He may surprise you."

"Maybe," she says without conviction, leaving me to wonder just how bad something has to end for people to assume you'll never enter a relationship again.

❧ 28 ❧

BRENDAN
Three Years Earlier

For several months, Italy stops living up to the hype. Whoever coined it "sunny Italy" must have come from the Pacific Northwest, because we get one day of sun here for every seven I'd have gotten in Colorado. Business slows to a trickle, and my ample downtime is spent at bars with the guys from work. I rarely leave alone, but it's empty. All the things I thought I wanted, when I was so determined to steer clear of Erin, turn out to mean nothing to me.

I've begun to contemplate a move to Bali by the time the weather starts to improve and business picks up. That's also when we get some new staff, including another American, Gabrielle, also from Colorado. Sully set it up, assuring me by email that the girl was "smoking hot"—which is a little fucked up, given that she's his cousin.

Seb, the owner, asks me to come in on my day off to take her around. He tells me I'll thank him after I see her. And when I get to the office on Monday morning and find her waiting on the front steps, I have to admit that Sully was right. Italy is full of hot girls, but this one blows them all out of the water: black hair swinging halfway down her back, perfect pouty mouth, almond-shaped eyes.

I don't sleep with co-workers, but that rule was a little easier to follow when all my coworkers were dudes. When she smiles, it lights up her entire face, and I know that rule has officially reached its end.

The clouds part and the street is suddenly bathed in gold. It feels like a sign. She hasn't said a word, but for the first time in the six months since the wedding, I feel hopeful. Maybe she's what will make me forget about all the things I've been trying, without success, to leave behind.

❧ 29 ❧

ERIN

I discover multiple missed calls from both Rob and Timothy after I get home from Boulder. I can't say I really want to talk to either of them. My desire to avoid Timothy makes sense. My desire to avoid Rob, though...I can't quite put my finger on.

I suppose it's just that it was a hard day, but I have a sneaking suspicion Rob's going to want to tell me all about his fun night out regardless.

I force myself to call, hoping I'll get his voicemail. It's one AM there, which is when he usually seems to be out doing shots and eating caviar or however the hell he spends his nights.

He answers on the first ring.

"Where the fuck have you been?" he snaps. "I've been calling you since this morning."

My jaw falls open. Does he think I'm supposed to remain at home on a leash, awaiting his calls all day? "With the number of my calls you've let go to voice mail since you left," I say through my teeth, "do you actually think I'm going to be okay with you unloading on me when I do the same?"

"You didn't answer your cell, so I called your office and they said you were sick," he says. "I was fucking worried, Erin."

I close my eyes and decide to let it go. Maybe his attitude makes sense. Maybe that's what happens when people worry about you. It's still a somewhat novel experience for me. "I went to Boulder with Brendan," I tell him. "Dorothy has breast cancer and she had a procedure this morning. He was pretty stressed out."

"Are you telling me," he says tightly, "that *you*, of all people, took a day of sick leave to comfort *Brendan?*"

For the second time in less than three minutes, my jaw falls open. "Are you serious right now?" I ask. "I just told you a woman you've known since you were thirteen has cancer, and your concern is my use of *sick leave?* You're not even going to ask me how she is?"

"Of course I want to know how she is. I also want to know what the hell is going on, because when we talk on the phone, it's like I don't even know you."

"Yeah, Rob, that makes sense," I reply as I hang up. "I'm pretty sure you don't."

EVENTUALLY ROB CALLS AGAIN, AND I FORCE MYSELF TO PICK UP. We both apologize, but neither of us sounds sorry. There's a forced civility to our conversations now, as if they are held between two warring countries negotiating a treaty. It's a relief to end the call. I do my best not to examine that too closely.

Brendan texts Sunday on his way back from Boulder to see if I want to come over for dinner. Although he's been texting me with updates on his mother since we got home from the hospital, I haven't seen him in person. I know it should probably stay that way, but I can't say no. Even though the margins around Dorothy's tumor were clear, it's still been hard on him. I know he could use a friend.

Even if he didn't, though, I'd probably be too weak to resist.

~

HIS PLACE IS IN THE HEART OF MANITOU SPRINGS, NEAR HIS new office. He lives in the upper half of a subdivided row house— just two rooms badly in need of updating, yet way more to my taste than Rob's shiny McMansion. This place has character: the kind of moldings they don't put into homes anymore, gorgeous hardwood floors worn just the right amount.

He smirks as I look around. "I'm sure you're wondering where the guest suite and billiards rooms are."

"It'll be adorable once you paint," I reply, flipping him off. "I'm just relieved you took down that stupid hammock." For many reasons.

"I didn't," he replies. "It's in the bedroom."

I feel sick and excited at the same time. And why on Earth would I be excited? It's not like *I'm* going to be trying out the hammock, for God's sake.

He pours me a glass of red wine and goes outside to the grill while I work on a salad. I tend to hum when I cook, so I'm in my own little world when he comes back in, not realizing he's there until I feel his hands on my hips. His hands, just like they are, have inspired a hundred different thoughts I never should have had.

"You ready?" he asks.

His voice is a quiet rumble, not his normal voice. His breath is against my neck, so warm and close I swear that if I leaned back only a fraction of an inch, I'd feel the press of his lips. The fine hairs on the back of my arms stand on end.

I still haven't even found the words to respond when reaches overhead to grab a plate. That's when I realize he was asking about the food and his hands on my waist were nothing more than him maneuvering around me in a small kitchen. Jesus. He can't even touch me in the process of getting a dish without me turning it into something dirty. One more reason I shouldn't be here.

I carry the salad to the table and he meets me there with the steaks. Over dinner we talk about his mom's recovery. Dorothy is still planning to travel to Squaw Valley for Olivia's race next week, which seems ambitious, given that she just got out of surgery.

"She says she'll never forgive herself if Olivia wins and she's not there to see it," Brendan says. "I guess she knows what she's doing. Thank God she'll have Peter there to help. I didn't realize until all this happened how lucky we are that she has him."

"See? There are some benefits to being in a relationship," I chide.

He quirks a brow at me. "Really? That's the best argument you've got? That I'll have someone to take care of me if I get breast cancer?"

I sigh wearily. "Fine, Brendan. I'll try to appeal to the only thing you care about: you could get laid all the time." *Not that he isn't already getting laid all the time.*

He makes a face. "Please never mention that again when we're talking about my mom and Peter. That's a pretty piss-poor argument anyway. I'm getting laid a lot more often than you are."

I stare at my plate. He's right, of course, but Rob and I are hardly typical.

"His promotion changed things. I'm sure it won't be like this forever."

"His *promotion?*" he asks. "He got that promotion *last* summer. I was just talking about you being on different continents for the past few weeks."

Brendan's surprise provides me a moment of clarity. I'm still young, and for the past year, an important part of my life has been pretty much non-existent. One more item on the long list of things I've given up for Rob. I'm beginning to wonder if that list is *too* long.

WHEN I GET IN, I CALL ROB, FEELING A RELUCTANCE I CAN'T entirely explain. He tells me he's sorry he didn't call earlier, but they were all out late, and he passed out when he got in. I didn't even *notice*, but I keep that to myself. He starts telling me about some shot contest they attended, and I yawn, trying to wrestle off my jeans while I hold the phone with my left hand.

"Christina had to be——" he begins, and then his voice stops and starts, "uh, carried out."

Christina is a common name. Just because there's a girl there named Christina does not mean it's the same Christina we fought about. Surely it cannot be the same Christina, because he couldn't possibly have failed to mention it to me for six *weeks*.

"Not Christina from Denver." It's not a question, it's a fucking warning, because it had *better* not be Christina from Denver.

"Well, yeah," he stammers. "I mean, she's a key player in the merger."

I say nothing, because honestly, I just can't believe he's managed to keep this fact to himself for so long.

Can. Not. Believe. It.

Right now, an empty space is carved out in my chest. But I can already hear the rumble of rage that's about to fill it.

"Erin..." he begins.

"Has she been there the whole time?" I ask the question already knowing I won't get a straight answer. Already knowing he'll come back with a litany of excuses and conclude with a patronizing little comment like *you just don't understand how the business world works*.

"Well, we needed to have her here for——"

"I did not ask you, Rob, what her *role* is there. I don't give a *fuck* what her role is there. I asked you if she's been there the whole goddamn time."

He huffs in irritation. "And I was trying to tell you. Yes. We needed her here because——"

"So Christina, the little whore who's hit on you in front of me more times than I can count, is among this group of people you're wining and dining every night, and it's taken you six *weeks* to share that with me."

"It isn't a big deal," he says with a groan. "I'm shocked you care. You don't even act like you miss me half the time.

"Did she go to Belgium with you?" I remember him telling me only a few of them went, and how oddly vague he was about the entire thing. It was the first time he was ever more interested in hearing about my weekend than telling me about his.

"Erin—" he begins, and that's really all I need to hear.

I cut him off before he can offer me more unnecessary explanations about why it's perfectly reasonable that she's there and traveling with him. Or why he's been lying about it.

"Tell me nothing has taken place with Christina since you left." My voice is like ice. "Absolutely nothing."

He is silent, and in that moment of silence I realize a whole world of possibilities exists in a place where I believed there was only one. I've believed so thoroughly in his loyalty that it never once occurred to me there was another option. He was the person who would always do the right thing and wouldn't ever hurt me the way Brendan had. And it was an illusion.

"One night we kissed," he says on an exhale. "I was drunk, but I stopped it, and that was it."

I have no idea anymore if he's telling the truth. I still feel certain he wouldn't cheat, and yet I also felt certain he wouldn't kiss someone else. And I felt certain he wouldn't lie to me about who was with him for six weeks. He failed me on both counts.

"I don't even know what to say," I finally whisper. "I really don't."

"Look," he says, "the distance has been hard on us both. I'm gonna come home sometime for a visit over the next few weeks and—"

"Vist? Why would you visit? You're due home in early July."

He sighs. "They're saying late August now. But we need to see each other. I'll come back for the weekend and—"

"*No.*"

The word bursts from my mouth with six weeks of rage behind

it. *No, Rob. No, no, no, no, no to all of it. To your stupid job and your three more months with Christina, to all of it.*

"You don't want me to visit?" he asks.

"Five *months*, Rob. It'll be five months by the time you get back," I reply, feeling very certain and very stunned all at once. I gave up myself for him. I gave up the things I loved. I hid and scurried to present him with the version of me he'd find most palatable. And this is what I get in return. "You never once asked me if I was okay with it."

"You never acted like you even cared!" he shouts. "How many goddamn times have I asked you about planning the wedding and been put off?"

"And thank God I did, since you've been over there lying to me about Christina and hooking up with her behind my back."

"For fuck's sake," he growls. "You're totally overreacting."

I laugh, the sound sharp and unhappy. What would Harper do in my shoes? What would Olivia do? He has no idea how badly I could react under the circumstances. "Oh, you think?" I ask. "You've been lying to me, you've been completely cavalier about my feelings and you *cheated* on me, but I'm the one at fault?"

"I didn't say that," he argues. "I'm just saying—"

"Stop." My head will explode if I have to hear one more of his asinine justifications, his blame-shifting. "I can't do this anymore."

"Can't do what?" he asks.

"Us. I can't do it. Not separated like this. Which you're now telling me isn't going to end until August."

"You're breaking up with me?" he asks. He sounds like he's been hit.

I don't know what I'm saying. I can't possibly be ending this, can I? We're engaged. I've been with him most of my adult life.

"I don't know. But I'm definitely not doing this bullshit anymore. I'm not listening to you tell me every night how much fun you're having over there with *Christina* while I sit in our home alone. I don't know if it's going to work when you get back, but I know for a fact that it's not working now. I just can't believe..." I have to stop or I will burst into tears. I really can't believe she was there all along, and that he just told me in *passing* he'd be staying another two months.

"Erin, come on, honey. Don't do this right now. You're upset. It's not the time to be making big decisions. Look, I'll call tomorrow. I'll call before you leave for work, and we can Skype. I need to see your face."

I'm not doing that. The idea of seeing his face makes me want to weep. It will only make it harder to do what I know for a fact needs to be done.

"No, Rob. We're doing this now. I ask so little of you that it doesn't even occur to you to tell me until now that you're staying all summer. All the things that make me want to get up in the morning are things you've crapped on. It's my fault for letting you do it, but it's also your fault for not caring enough about my happiness to ever try to correct course."

His voice is rough when he finally speaks. "Jesus, Erin. Where did all this come from? We've been together nearly four years, and you're just telling me this *now*?"

"I don't think I even realized it myself until now. Until lately."

"I don't want this to end," he says.

My chest aches. I don't either, not entirely. I don't know *what* I want. Rob is like family. I've certainly spent more time with him than my own family, and he's been better to me than they have, at least until recently.

"We'll figure it out when you come home," I tell him.

"So you're saying what? That we'll start over then? What happens in the meantime?"

I close my eyes and let out a long breath. I'm tired of worrying. I'm tired of feeling like I can't trust him. I'm just tired.

"I'm not going to sit here every night wondering what you're doing and if Christina is with you. So do whatever you want."

"What the fuck, Erin?" he asks, on the cusp of shouting. "I

don't want to be with someone else. I love you. I love our life. That's what I want."

The right words, delivered far too late. "Then," I tell him as I hang up, "you probably should have acted like it sooner."

❧ 30 ❧

ERIN

I was so firm on the phone. But after the call ends, I desperately wish I could take every word of it back. This, with Rob, has been my home for nearly three years. *He's* been my home.

Telling him we could start over when he returns, that was my safety net. It was based on the assumption that what happens when he gets home will be my choice, but what if it's not? He will sleep with Christina—I basically told him to, didn't I? What if he chooses her and doesn't even want to try when he comes home? I wanted to punish him, but it seems very possible that I'll come to find I've only hurt myself.

I wake the next day feeling blown, as if I haven't slept. Even though I've stopped crying by the time I get to work, it doesn't feel that way.

I find an ominous Post-it from Timothy on my computer that reads *See Me Immediately* when I get in. I'm going to get ripped to shreds for taking one damn day off and I'm almost too upset to even care.

I enter his office, but he continues to look at something on his computer for a few seconds, pretending to work when we both know his entire job involves shuffling *my* work out to the university and acting like he was somehow instrumental in its creation.

Finally, he turns to me. "We need to talk about what happened on Friday. I needed that brochure mock-up for the chancellor's office and had to show up empty-handed," he says. "I'm writing you up for insubordination."

I've had it. The past twelve hours have finally taken their toll, and I've had it. Timothy lives in constant fear of discovery as a fraud. Let him dig his own grave with this.

"Good," I say flatly. "Write me up."

He blinks. "You must not understand what the word *insubordinate* means."

"I know what it means. I'm saying good because I welcome the opportunity to go to Human Resources and explain that you've written me up for taking my second day of sick leave in nearly four years."

I'm a little impressed with myself. My hands are shaking with anger, but I sound calm, bored almost—like Olivia might, but without the potential assault charge.

"Are you threatening me?" he asks.

"No, I'm just informing you of the logical course of action anyone would take under these circumstances."

He does his best to look scary, glaring at me and sitting bolt upright. But today I'm too upset about things that actually matter to care. He's just a little man, the kind who would bully children because he knows he can't scare anyone else, and I am not a child. In fact, I've been the *only* adult in this situation for years, and maybe it's time someone other than me realizes it.

I return to my desk, staring at my computer without seeing anything. My whole life is going to hell, and going there quickly.

"What's up with you?" asks Harper, regarding me with suspicion as she walks into my cubicle. "Oh my God. You've been crying? Let me guess: Tim used the word *stakeholders* one too many times, and you stabbed him to death?"

"You really think I'd cry if I stabbed Tim to death?" I ask with a shaky laugh. And then my eyes fill again. I wanted to keep it all to myself until I knew what I was doing, until I was certain I wasn't going to call Rob and take it all back. But I can't. There's no way I can make it through the day like this, especially not with Harper's nose for drama.

"I broke up with Rob last night," I whisper. My voice cracks. "Well, maybe not. We're going to take a break."

She wraps her arms around me and that does it—the tears begin to flow and it all comes out: how Rob extended his trip again without even telling me, that I've been realizing of late how much I've given up because of him. And that he's been hanging out with Christina there the entire time.

All along she's been nodding and sympathetic. When I tell her the part about Christina, though, her jaw drops. "Are you fucking kidding me? I can't believe he did that. Good fucking riddance."

"He didn't necessarily cheat," I argue. "She was just there and he—"

"Hanging out with that girl for six weeks without mentioning it to you?" she demands, cutting me off. "Going to Belgium with her? You seriously believe he didn't cheat?"

I swallow. "I'm not sure."

She looks as if she feels sorry for me, which I hate.

"It doesn't matter," she says. "He should have told you, and he shouldn't have been taking you for granted all this time. So good riddance."

It should reassure me that I've made the right decision, but it's always easy to sum up another person's life as black and white: a bad, inconsiderate boyfriend, who may have cheated. Things are rarely that clear-cut.

Maybe he did things he shouldn't have, but we were happy. Not mind-blowingly happy, but I'm not convinced anyone is. And I'm certainly not happy right now without him. So maybe I just gave up a relatively good life for nothing at all.

∿

I GET HOME, FEELING EXHAUSTED AND OVERWHELMED. HARPER'S roommate is in Europe so I can use her room until she gets back, but the prospect of leaving is hard. This has been my home for years. I chose every paint color, every piece of furniture in this house. There's such finality to moving out. I text Rob, asking him to give me a week to get my stuff out since I'm leaving for Squaw Valley on Thursday, and he calls immediately.

"Babe, don't move. It's your house too. Come on. At least stay until I get back. Please."

I don't know. It seems like a slippery slope, claiming independence and still living in the lap of luxury, just waiting to get seduced back into all the ways being with him made my life better.

"Rob, maybe I need to be on my own, completely on my own, so that if we try this again, we're making a clean start."

"We *are* doing this again. I know that for a fact. So don't leave."

I tell him I don't know. And then I realize after I get off the phone that he's already back to ignoring the things I want. So I text him to say I'm moving. And I ask him not to call me again until he's home for good.

BRENDAN
Three Years Earlier

Gabi is amazing. And it's not just her looks, although in a country full of beautiful women, people still stop on the street to stare at her. She's fun, easygoing, and fucking brilliant—heading to medical school at Stanford in the fall. She can keep up with me on a bike as easily as she can keep up a conversation.

I guess I've been a little homesick, too. Talking to her is just easier than it is with anyone else here. I can quote *Talladega Nights* without her looking at me like I'm insane and she shares my craving for a really good burger. She fills a void I didn't know I had, and I don't even mind that we haven't slept together yet—although when she looks up at me from under those lashes of hers, I sometimes wonder if I'm not going to explode waiting for it to happen.

She's full of questions about my past. Rob comes up—how could he not when he was a part of nearly every high school story? The drunk nights out, getting into fights, hung-over mornings eating burritos at King's Chef Diner—I'd almost forgotten there was a time when I didn't resent him the way I do now.

I'm more reluctant to answer her questions about my relationship history—if she's looking for reassurance, I doubt the truth is going to offer any. I've never dated anyone longer than a month.

"So you've never been in love?" she asks.

"I think I was, once," I admit.

"What was so special about this girl?"

I don't know what to tell her, because it was no one thing. It was Erin's looks, but it was also just *her*—her laugh and the way she tilts her head when she's listening intently, the way she sings when she's doing something mindless and how her eyes light up when she's excited.

"I don't know," I tell her. "It was just everything."

"You sound like you're not over her," Gabi says.

I swallow. "There was never anything to be over. We never went out once. And now she's with a friend of mine."

"Ouch," she says.

I blow out a breath. "It's fine. It would never have worked out anyway." This is something I tell myself all the time, and it's probably true. I just wish it *felt* true.

"Maybe you were meant to meet me here instead," she suggests.

I really hope she's right. Because I'm not over Erin, and I need to be. I had my chance and I'm not getting another one.

❧ 32 ❧

ERIN

By Thursday morning, when I meet Brendan at the airport for our flight to Reno, I'm recovered enough to at least pretend things are fine. And I'm really *not* that upset. Not too upset, certainly, to think about how good Brendan looks in everything. Right now he's wearing khaki shorts and a navy T-shirt —nothing fancy, and he still looks completely edible.

Brendan's heard from Rob by now, I'm sure. He seems to know almost everything even before I do. I'm just grateful he's behaving as if things are normal.

"I have to warn you," I tell him as we find our seats. "There's something about planes that puts me to sleep, so I'm probably going to snore or drool on you."

"How's poor Rob ever going to join the mile-high club if you're always asleep?"

My smile falters a little. Did Rob tell Brendan we're definitely getting back together? Did he imply we hadn't *really* broken up? Neither are true but I don't feel like introducing the topic.

"Have you *met* Rob? Can you actually imagine him doing that?"

He looks at me out of the corner of his eye. "But you would?"

I flush. I've always been more interested in mixing things up than Rob. Over time I just stopped suggesting anything different, knowing I'd get shot down. "No comment."

"I always imagined you'd have a little wild side."

"Spent a lot of time imagining me in bed, have you?" I tease.

His eyes linger on my mouth for one long moment, during which my heart seems to flop over, again and again.

"No comment," he says softly. "Go to sleep, Erin."

I close my eyes, certain we've just had the one conversation that could make sleep impossible. How many times have I fantasized about having sex with Brendan? Countless. How many times have I squeezed my eyes shut, even with Rob, and pictured Brendan's face? I guess it'd be better if he weren't my fiancé's best friend, but is it really so different than what anyone else does? Brendan was in my head long before I even knew Rob existed, and there's only so much control you can exert over your own brain. God knows I've tried.

WE LAND AND GET THE RENTAL CAR. IT'S NEARLY AN HOUR drive from the Reno airport to Tahoe, where we plan to take a quick hike before heading up to Squaw Valley. This means nearly an hour of watching Brendan's thighs flex when he brakes, his broad hand resting on the gear shift, the way he leans back in his seat like he rules the entire fucking world. The effect of watching Brendan drive could be described as mildly pornographic *without* having had the dirtiest dream possible about him on the flight here. So I'm either the luckiest girl alive right now, or the most tortured. Both, perhaps.

I sneak a glance at him—the clean lines of his profile, his clearly delineated biceps even when he's not flexing. I should be too upset for lust, but obviously I'm not. And the very fact that

I've spent weeks lusting after someone other than Rob, and that I'm doing so now, makes me think perhaps I don't have quite as much moral high ground with the Christina thing as I'd like to believe.

"So you've now gone over a month without getting laid," Brendan says. "That's got to suck."

"You probably can't imagine holding out for *a week*," I reply with a roll of my eyes. "But that's something I can take care of on my own when I need to."

He flinches. "Jesus," he groans. "Don't say things like that."

"Guys do it. Why shouldn't I?"

He frowns, glancing at me and away again. "It's not that you shouldn't do it. It's that you shouldn't sit there wearing shorts that end just below your ass and put that image in my head."

I laugh, assuming he's kidding, and then take in the tension in his jaw. My eyes flicker to his lap, where I discern an unmistakable bulge that wasn't there a minute ago. Why does that thrill me? I shouldn't care. I should be embarrassed. Instead I feel like I'm going to come out of my skin with want.

I turn my flushed face toward the window. "Geez, Brendan. I'm flattered. I figured that threesome with supermodels you probably had before we left would've taken the edge off."

"I'm not that bad," he mutters. "I think your image of me is based a lot more on some bullshit of Rob's than it is the truth."

I laugh, but it feels a little bitter. "It's not any bullshit of Rob's. You took home more girls during that summer we worked together than I've even *met* over the course of my life."

His frown deepens. "I was twenty-four, Erin. Twenty-four and stupid, with some money and my own apartment for the first time in my life. That doesn't mean it's who I am now."

He's so full of shit. I turn toward him, curling up in the seat. "No? How many girls have you had in that hammock?"

"Honestly? Not a single one," he says. "I didn't get the hammock to have sex in. I don't have girls over to my place."

My jaw hangs open. "Never?"

"It's best to keep sex separate from your life," he says, "so no one gets the idea that it means something."

And for Brendan, having it mean something would be the end of the world. Reason number ten thousand why it's for the best that nothing ever really happened between us. He'd have broken my heart more than he already did.

∼

WE ARRIVE AT THE RUBICON TRAIL FASTER THAN EXPECTED, thanks to Brendan's inability to obey the speed limit, and take off for our hike. I'd forgotten how much I enjoyed it...that when I first moved to Colorado, it was moments like this I was after: the silence, the movement, the way the air gets clean and clear as you ascend. The best parts of running are present here too—muscles working, heart beating hard, getting out of your own head long enough to realize nothing is as bad as it seems.

We reach the top all too quickly and sit on a boulder, taking in the view.

"I'd love to lead tours here," he says with a sigh, leaning back.

I feel a small shot of panic. Not even two months ago I didn't want him moving home. Now the idea of him moving away makes me feel slightly ill. "Instead of Colorado?" I ask.

He shakes his head. "No. But I'd like to expand to tours in other states. I'm sure Will and Rob would tell me it's crazy, but there it is."

If Will and Rob had their way, Brendan would have gone into some normal nine-to-five job indoors like they both have. But something like that would kill what I love about him. Correction: it would kill what I *like* about him.

"Nothing great was ever produced without a little risk," I reply. "I'm glad you never listened to them."

He looks at me for a long moment then looks away. "Me too,"

he says, climbing to his feet. "Come on. We need to make a pitstop on the way to the car."

He leads me down to the tall rocks overlooking the bay. The water is a blue so deep it hurts your teeth, the sun full in my face, the air bracingly clear. I breathe in deep. "It's so beautiful here."

"It is," he agrees, and, without warning or hesitation, he pulls off his shirt.

I stare. Unabashedly. Brendan has muscles for days. His chest deserves its own calendar and commemorative stamp.

He smirks, pulling off his shorts. His boxer briefs are filled out just enough to leave very little to the imagination and I'm so flustered I can't even summon the shame to look away.

"You ready, Doyle?" he asks, with such a dirty smile I can't help but take his words in an inappropriate direction. Can't help imagining his hand moving to the waistband, sliding the briefs off, saying *now it's your turn.*

He dives in before I've managed to craft a response, and I watch the lake until he surfaces, shaking the water from his face and doing a leisurely backstroke away from the rocks. The boxer briefs are clinging. I can't look away.

"Come in!" he calls. "It's pretty warm. There must be a spring underneath."

I don't feel like hiking back to the car in damp clothes, but I desperately need to cool a few things off.

"Turn around," I call down to him.

His smile fades. "You're not planning to strip, right?" he asks. "It's the middle of the day."

"You mean, strip like *you* just did?" I reply. "I know I'm irresistible, but I'm sure as hell not jumping in fully dressed. I'll freeze to death walking back."

He faces the other way, looking none too happy about it, and—after removing everything but my bra and panties—I jump, feeling mildly terrified and exhilarated at once.

I hit the water and gasp. It's so cold that I am momentarily paralyzed by it. So cold that it burns, that it steals my breath. I'm pretty sure it's only a desire to beat him senseless that propels me back to the surface.

"Motherfucker," I gasp as I emerge. His laughter echoes over the water. "You fucking liar."

He keeps laughing as I scramble onto the sun-warmed rocks, pulling myself out half-naked and too cold to care whether or not he sees. I use *his* clothes to dry off before I struggle into my own.

He's still laughing, the bastard.

"I'm sorry," he calls, beginning to climb out. "I bet you feel better, though, don't you?"

"Not as good as I'm about to feel," I reply, gathering his clothes and pitching them into the water.

I lay back on the rock and bask in the sun, laughing to myself as he jumps in after his stuff. This is a moment that never would have happened with Rob. In part, because Rob wouldn't have jumped in the first place, and he certainly wouldn't have lied about the temperature. But I wouldn't have thrown his clothes in, either. We never had that kind of relationship, and I sort of wish we had.

Moments later I feel Brendan's shadow looming over me, and before my eyes are open he's wringing out his soaked clothes on my face and chest.

"Now we're even," he says, pulling on his shorts, though not before I get another significant eyeful of what's underneath his now-soaked boxer briefs. I feel a hum of desire in my chest and flinch, willing it away.

He lies down beside me and I breathe deep, marveling at how content I feel. Yes, we had a good hike, and we've got good weather, but I have a feeling I could be doing anything with him, in any weather, and I'd feel the same way.

"This has been a perfect day," I tell him.

After a moment he replies. "You're like a different person here."

I squint at him. "How so?"

"When I first met you, you were game for anything. Happy," he says. "And then you got together with Rob and it's like that side of you went away."

"Oh, is *that* why you kept trying to get him to dump me?" I ask with clear sarcasm. "*My* well-being? I guess you're thrilled about the break-up. You've finally gotten your way."

He stiffens and slowly sits up. "*What* break-up?" His eyes are wide, his jaw locked tight.

I'm shocked that he doesn't know, but I guess that explains why he hasn't mentioned it this entire trip.

"I thought Rob told you," I reply.

He flinches, pinching the bridge of his nose. "Rob only tends to tell me what he thinks is worth bragging about."

"I don't know why you're acting upset—wasn't it your dearest wish that he find someone better?"

"I didn't think he'd find someone better, I just..." He shakes his head, as if he can't get his mind around this. "Why?"

So many reasons. Many involving you. "We haven't been getting along for a while. And then he drops this bomb about Christina—"

"*Christina?*" he asks. "Are you trying to tell me he's been hooking up with *Christina* over there?"

I swallow. It still hurts that Rob didn't tell me. And it bothers me even more that, even if he is telling me the truth, I'm not sure I trust him. "He says all they've done is kiss," I reply. "But for six weeks he never once mentioned her name until it came out by accident, so I find it hard to believe things are entirely innocent."

Brendan's teeth are clenched. "Of course they're not innocent."

He's the second person I've told, and they've both assumed Rob is cheating. Do I just know Rob better than they do, or am I incredibly naïve?

He puts an arm around me. "I'm so fucking sorry, Erin."

I *hate* that he's sorry. It's as if he's confirming that I have indeed lost something.

"I'm fine," I say, brushing at my eyes. "Honestly. And nothing is over, necessarily. We're just taking a break until he's home, and then we'll see."

"Why wouldn't you just end it?" he asks, jaw gaping. "You deserve so much better than that."

"We've been together a long time, Brendan. It's not a decision you make overnight. And he swore he didn't cheat, and I believe him." *Sort of.*

He pulls on his T-shirt abruptly. "The sun's gonna set soon. You ready to head out?"

I nod, sorry our afternoon is ending on such a low note. He seems more unhappy about my break-up than I am, which doesn't make a whole lot of sense.

We walk back to the car in silence. My clothes are still wet, and with the sun setting and under the shade of trees, the cold catches up with us fast. I'm shivering and miserable on any number of fronts. I wish I hadn't mentioned the break-up. It's cast a pall on everything.

It takes us an hour to reach the car, at which point I'm shaking with cold. I jump in place, trying to get warm. "Can you pop the trunk?" I ask him. "I need dry clothes or I'm going to die."

I turn to find him behind me, standing frozen in the middle of the parking lot, with his hands in his pockets. His eyes close and he curses under his breath. "I don't have the key."

"What do you *mean* you don't have the key? I saw you put it in the pocket of your shorts!"

"Yeah," he says. "The shorts you threw into Emerald Bay."

ONE HOUR AND SEVERAL TESTY CONVERSATIONS WITH A HERTZ employee later, it's concluded that we will have to wait until morning, when the Tahoe office opens, to get a replacement key. It's now dark, and I'm unbearably cold.

"I'm so sorry," I whisper to Brendan for the hundredth time.

He grins. "It's really okay. You're the only one of us suffering, Frosty."

This is true. I don't think I've ever been so cold in my life, and I live in a state where it hits thirty below in the winter.

Adding to my misery, there's some big convention going on in Tahoe, and after we Uber into town, it takes us over an hour to find a single available room, which has *one* bed.

"Nothing else?" Brendan asks, pleading in his voice.

The woman stares at her computer. "I'm sorry. This is all we've got at the moment."

I want a hot shower so badly I'd agree to sleep on their lobby floor at this point, and I can tell Brendan's about to turn it down.

"It's fine," I reply, teeth chattering. "I'm freezing, Brendan. Please."

Once again, he gets that look on his face, as if I've asked him to scale Everest, or clean a public restroom the morning after St. Patrick's Day.

It'd probably hurt my feelings except I'm too damn cold to feel anything, emotional or otherwise.

I TAKE THE WORLD'S LONGEST HOT SHOWER WHILE HE RUNS across the street to find us some food, and as my temperature returns to normal, I begin to recognize just how awkward tonight might prove. Brendan is huge, and I don't know what size that bed is, but it sure isn't a king. The whole thing would be easier if I hadn't gone two months without sex, but I have, and when I picture lying that close to Brendan all night, my heart goes triple time.

I emerge from the bathroom, wrapped in nothing but a towel because my clothes are still wet. He's sitting on the bed and for just a moment he looks surprised. His eyes go to the top of my towel before flickering away.

"I bought you a T-shirt across the street, so you'll have something dry to wear tonight." He hands me a T-shirt that says, *I Put the 'Ho' in Tahoe.* He is unable to keep a straight face. "It was all I could find."

I don't bother to point out that he has purchased himself a perfectly non-offensive T-shirt; I'm just excited to wear something dry. I eat while he showers, trying not to focus on the idea of him in there, naked. What would Harper do in my shoes? I know for a fact she wouldn't be sitting on this bed right now, eating a cheese-burger. I picture opening the bathroom door, climbing into the shower with him.

It's absolutely not what I should be thinking about at the moment.

I'm under the covers when he gets out, my stomach a storm of anticipation and excitement—two emotions that should not be there in the first place because nothing is going to happen.

He turns off the light, but for some reason it only heightens my awareness of him. The bed sinks a little under his weight as he climbs in beside me, and then his bare leg brushes mine.

He stiffens. "Please tell me you're wearing something," he says.

"Of course I am," I reply. "Did you really think I was going to climb in here naked with you?"

"Well I just came into contact with a lot of skin, so I had to ask. Whatever you're wearing has got to be minimal at best."

"I'm dressed."

"Okay." He sighs unhappily. "Well, good night."

"Good night," I reply.

I think about earlier today—the sight of him without his shirt. His wet boxer briefs clinging to his thighs...and other parts. And now here I am in this little bed with him so close that I hear his every breath and notice every movement. His leg brushes mine again and my whole body is strung so tight that I jolt in shock when it happens.

He exhales. "So what, exactly, are you wearing?"

"The stupid T-shirt you bought. Everything else was wet."

He groans. "So you're wearing *nothing* but the T-shirt?"

"Did you think I was going to sleep in wet clothes? Should I also keep one foot on the floor?"

He sighs. "I'm not blaming you. I'm just—"

"Just what?"

He hesitates. "Nothing."

I could pry further, but the truth is I can't worry about what's up with him. I'm having a hard enough time with the things that are up with me.

33

BRENDAN
Three Years Earlier

It takes me nearly three weeks to get Gabi into bed, which feels like four hundred weeks in Brendan time.

"I'm not the kind of girl who sleeps around," she warns me. "So once we do this, I'm not going to be with anyone else, and you aren't either."

Of course we're both naked at this point, so I'd probably agree to anything, but I think I'd agree clothed too, though it's the kind of statement that would have sent me running in the past. If anything good has come out of my experience with Erin, it's this: I know now that sometimes you've got to make an exception. Sometimes you have to stop worrying too much about how messy it might be when it ends, and just go with it.

I'm not in love with Gabi, but it's not a stretch to see it happening eventually. Either way, there's not much harm in agreeing to her terms. I haven't wanted to see anyone else since she got here, and she only has a few months left before med school anyway.

My misgivings are probably just fear of the unknown. I ignore the voice in my head that says they are something else entirely.

❦ 34 ❧

ERIN

Somehow Brendan and I both manage to fall asleep in the tiny bed, but when we wake the next morning, he's flat on his back, and I'm draped over him like he's a massive body pillow.

"Sorry," I whisper, disentangling myself.

"Do me a favor," he says, "and turn the other way for a minute."

I roll my eyes. "I've seen you in a pair of shorts before."

"Fine, smartass. I was trying to be a gentleman." And with that, he throws back the covers and reveals the kind of bulge that would catapult this moment straight into an NC-17 rating. "Happy now?"

"Good Lord," I say, covering my eyes. "Put that thing away, perv."

"I woke up with your tits pressing against my arm and your bare leg draped over my stomach, Erin. That doesn't mean I'm a pervert. It means I'm straight."

I pull the pillow over my face. "Ugh. I wish I could un-see that."

"Yeah, I bet," he says. "I just made it a thousand times harder for you to get back together with Rob, didn't I?"

"Sorry to burst your bubble, but I've got no complaints about Rob in that department."

Though Rob is far from...that.

"You sure?" he asks with a laugh. "I can pull it out if you want to do an honest comparison."

I throw the pillow at him. It seems a better option than telling him the truth, which is that I wouldn't mind a much closer look.

SOMEONE FROM THE RENTAL COMPANY MEETS US BEFORE LUNCH, and once we've changed out of yesterday's clothes, we climb in the car and head north. We drive with the windows down, cool air rushing in, and I feel oddly free. It's the kind of freedom I normally only experience under certain conditions: at the end of a race or as I collapse on my towel after a few hours of surfing. It's the experience of no longer giving a fuck, but in the best possible way—where I'm well spent and all the normal comforts of the world feel extraordinary. When I've pushed myself so hard that I'm beyond caring what anyone else thinks about me. That's how I felt yesterday with Brendan, and that's how I feel today, as we drive to Squaw Valley. I think it has to be him, or at least what he's reminded me about the person I used to be. I just hope I can somehow hang on to the parts of myself I'm reclaiming after this is done.

The house Olivia and Will have rented for everyone looks packed, even from the outside. The driveway and road in front are already full of cars. Olivia's crew might be just ten people, but ten people with several significant others, plus Dorothy and Peter and Will and Olivia and two children is...a crowd. Part of me wishes I had Brendan to myself a little longer.

"There they are!" Olivia shouts as we walk in. She detaches

herself from the group of people in the living room, with Caroline in her arms and Dorothy in her wake.

My heart gives a sudden thud at the sight of Caroline. When I saw her last, she was a newborn—squinty-eyed, with a pursed, pouting mouth, asleep seventy-five percent of the time and nursing the rest. Now she's an actual baby, with Brendan's eyes and Olivia's features, and she's so gorgeous it hurts. I pull her from Olivia, who sighs loudly.

"Oh my God," she groans. "Tell me you're not crying."

"She's so beautiful," I reply, my voice cracking.

"Erin cries every time she sees my kids," Olivia tells Brendan. "Keep an eye on her. I'm worried she might walk off with one of them."

Brendan reaches out and I hand Caroline over reluctantly. His face goes soft and wistful as he gazes at her for the first time— surprising for a guy who claims to be adamantly against having kids. And while I watch him, Olivia watches me.

"Let me show you your room," she says, her eyes alight, and I know exactly what I'm in for.

I follow her up the stairs. "We're just friends," I tell her once we're out of earshot.

The Cheshire-cat grin doesn't leave her face.

"We *are*."

"Right," she says, rolling her eyes. "The two of you are both single and sharing a hotel room instead of coming here. But you're *friends*."

"We didn't share the hotel room on purpose, and as I told you on the phone, Rob and I are just taking a break. I'm not planning to spend that time screwing his best friend."

"Something's changed with you two, though," she says, opening a door to the room I presume is mine. "He's different. Proprietary."

"He looks at me like a little sister," I reply, though I'm not so sure of that anymore. There have been plenty of moments over the last few weeks that you don't have with a sibling.

She cocks her head. "Tell me something: if I'd put you two in the same room all weekend, would anything happen?"

I'm saved from having to reply by Matthew, who comes barreling in and throws his little arms around my neck. Which is good, because when I think about last night and the way I was about to combust lying next to him, I don't like the answer.

~

WE ALL EAT DINNER TOGETHER, AND THEN PACK THE GEAR IN the van for tomorrow.

It's an early night for everyone, since wake-up is at four AM, and by the time I get downstairs from reading Matthew a bedtime story, the only person still around is Brendan.

"Come on," he says, raising a bottle of champagne and heading out to the deck.

"Isn't that for tomorrow night?" I ask.

"We're pre-celebrating. There's tons left for tomorrow." He takes one of the chairs outside, drinking straight from the bottle before handing it to me. "Come on, where did firecracker Erin go?"

So far doing things Brendan's way has worked out pretty well for me. I grab the champagne and take a swig off it, laughing when it dribbles down my front.

"My God," I laugh. "If Rob could see me now, drinking stolen champagne straight out of the bottle and spilling half of it."

"Yeah," Brendan says. "Because he's straight-laced."

"*I'm* straight-laced."

"I'm not convinced that's true." He looks over at me as he says it, and it feels as if he's reading every filthy thought I ever had. I hope not. They're all about him.

We finish the bottle of champagne and begin a second one. I'm getting tipsy, which I usually find unsettling, having watched my dad do it for so long. But tonight it's just lovely, all of it—the sky, the breeze, Brendan. It's perfect, aside from the fact that I can't stop taking in his profile, the sharp jut of his jaw in the moonlight, the softness of his mouth. And his legs... Normally it's his upper body that's my weakness, but right now only his legs are on display, and I'm forced to admit that they're every bit as perfect as the rest of him.

"I'm sorry I was so shitty to you," he says, apropos of nothing. "That night when you asked if we were becoming friends."

"You weren't shitty. You just didn't seem that interested in being my friend."

He laughs wearily. "It wasn't lack of interest, Erin. I didn't know if I *could* be. Isn't that obvious by now?" The heat in his gaze makes my heart feels like it's fluttering somewhere around the middle of my throat.

"No," I whisper.

"It should be," he says. "It's just always been easier to avoid the whole thing by being an asshole."

I could tell him right now that it's mutual, that for years I've felt like I can barely function when he's around. Except this is a conversation we should not be having at all. Nothing good can come of acknowledging it, so I stare off into the distance and remain quiet.

After a moment he rises. I half expect that he'll just walk inside, but instead he comes around behind my chair with the champagne in his hand. "Tip your head back."

"Why?"

He offers me a deliciously dirty grin. "I've got something I want to put in your mouth."

"I'm warning you, Langstrom. I use my teeth."

"Christ, you've got a dirty mind, woman." He laughs. "And make sure you swallow everything."

"Right. I'm the one with the dirty mind."

He lifts the champagne high overhead. "Mouth wide," he warns.

"No, Brendan, it's going to go everywhere," I complain. "I can't swallow it all."

"That's what she said," he answers.

And then we're both laughing, and he tips the champagne so it seems to explode from the bottle—over my face, my shirt, my shorts—and I laugh even harder. This moment, like so many from the last few weeks, reminds me of biking downhill faster than I should. It feels thrilling and wild and reckless, the danger and the excitement weighted equally. When I compare this moment to the rest of my history, it feels as if I've been tethered to the ground my entire life. Right now I finally feel free.

I climb to my feet, still giggling as I wipe my face with my shirt. "Your pouring skills are legendary."

He sets the champagne down and moves toward me, closer than he should. I can feel the warmth radiating from him. It makes me want to move closer too. His hand presses to my stomach, and I hold my breath.

"You need to change or you're gonna freeze out here. You want me to go get you clothes?"

I shake my head. As much as I don't want to be the voice of reason, and as much I want to remain out here with him, I have just enough common sense to know it's the last thing I should do.

"We should probably head in. We've got to be up in four hours," I tell him. "But I wish we had more time." I wish this was a night we could stretch into a week's worth of hours, or more.

His eyes are brighter right now than I've ever seen them. "I wish a lot of things were different, Erin."

My pulse races. The prospect of admitting even a tiny portion of the truth to him is terrifying. "I wish they were different too."

His hands frame my face, sliding through my hair, and my breath stills somewhere between my lungs and my throat, waiting for his mouth to descend. Waiting for this thing I've wanted for years and years.

His lips brush mine—once, twice, then harder and more thoroughly. It's everything I remembered, and yet it's better. So much better.

Kissing him is like that first moment you plunge under water—

when you are disoriented and thrilled all at once. Nothing about this makes sense and nothing else exists—only tangled limbs and warm skin and hearts that beat too fast. My mouth opens under his, and he groans, one hand sliding down around my hip, pulling me into him so that all of his heat is pressed against me, pulsing and ready.

"I've wanted this for so fucking long," he says, his mouth moving to my neck, his hands sliding to the hem of my shirt, grazing my skin.

There are a million reasons why this is a terrible idea, and I don't care about any of them. I love his calloused fingers. I love his insistent mouth. I love the fact that he's not gentle with me, that he doesn't treat me like something too fragile to touch but something he wants to destroy and put back together. There's so much of him, and I want all of it. I want that smooth skin and those arms and the trail of hair that dips below his belly button. His mouth and the smell of his neck and the feel of him pressing into my abdomen.

His fingers slide beneath the seam of my shorts. "Fuck," he groans. "I knew you'd be soaked. All day I thought about doing this, about sliding my fingers inside you and how you'd feel tight and ready, just like this."

I wrench his zipper down, slide my hand into his boxers to free him. His cock flies forward like something that's been caged, desperate for release, so thick I can barely get my hand around it. I don't want discussion or foreplay. I want him to do this before I can remember all the reasons he shouldn't.

He doesn't bother removing my shorts. He simply holds them to the side so I can feel him against me, both of us slick and ready. He slides over me once, twice, making me moan, and when I dig my nails into his skin, he finally lines himself up to push inside me. I hold my breath, waiting.

"You have no idea how many times I've thought about this," he says.

And then... a sound neither of us has made. It's the squeak of a screen door flying open.

Matthew. Standing there in his little jammies with the turtles all over them, his bear clutched in one hand, his thumb in his mouth, staring at the two of us like we're some kind of performance art he can't quite understand.

Brendan sets me on my feet, pressing close to me so one very prominent piece of his anatomy isn't flying free.

"What are you doing, Bwendan?" Matthew asks.

He looks so much like Olivia, but at this moment, oddly, he reminds me more of Will. There's something calm and self-possessed about him, as if he's older than both of us. As if he already knows the answer to the question and is waiting for us to discover it ourselves.

Brendan glances at me. A look that says *what the fuck am I supposed to say?* And I have no idea so I just stare back, my eyes wide.

"I'm, uh..." Brendan flinches, zipping up his shorts. "I'm kissing Erin."

"Because you love her?"

Brendan looks horrified. It'd be funny if it wasn't so awful. He runs a hand over his head and exhales heavily. "Sometimes people just kiss."

His words are the splash of ice water I needed. Because this isn't love. We aren't even dating, and I have a boyfriend, sort of. Who is Brendan's best friend.

Ah, yes. The thing I was trying *not* to remember.

"Mommy says that's what people do when they love each other," Matthew informs us.

Brendan turns toward him. "Yeah, uh, sometimes."

"So you love Erin."

Brendan flinches. "Uh...buddy, you should be in bed."

"I heard a noise. You said the f-word."

"Jesus Christ," Brendan murmurs. "He must have the hearing of a bat."

Glancing back at me with a look I can't decipher, Brendan grabs Matthew's hand and walks him inside. I give them a moment and then escape to the safety of my room, locking the door behind me, praying to God that flimsy safety measure is enough to keep me from making a terrible mistake.

❦ 35 ❦

ERIN

When my alarm goes off at four AM, I stumble through the room half-asleep and too tired to worry about the awkwardness of seeing Brendan after last night.

By the time I'm downstairs, however, I feel not just awkward but terrified. Being around Brendan and knowing he's an option is like walking into a buffet after twenty years of deprivation. I'm not sure I'm capable of restraint, and I have to be.

Yes, Rob and I aren't technically together. I suppose I could use this as an excuse to do whatever I want right now. But I can't— not with Brendan. I can't allow this thing to come between him and Rob, and while I trust Brendan, I don't trust *myself* with Brendan. Allowing myself any piece of him is like jumping into the deepest chasm. I can't begin to imagine how I'd ever climb back out. He only wants temporary, but I'd want everything, just like my mother did, and I'd go through my entire life waiting for it to happen.

There's no sign of him downstairs, but the crew is already up and raring to go, creating in me that same mix of excitement and queasiness I felt during my own racing days, only now on Olivia's behalf.

I walk over to Will. "Did she sleep?"

He sighs. "A little. Not enough."

"Is she going to be okay?"

His jaw is set, his face grim. "I wish I knew."

An endurance run of this length comes with special dangers—renal shutdown, heat stroke, low blood sodium. Western States comes with even more. Much of it takes place in the wilderness, inaccessible except on foot. There's wildlife and multiple chances to slip off a path and straight down the side of a mountain. There are rivers to ford, and weather you can't depend on—there's been snow some years, and in others the heat coming off the rocks has reached 114 degrees. For Will, who was fiercely protective of Olivia long before she became his wife, the anxiety must be excruciating, and for her sake he's got to pretend it isn't. Her anxiety would triple if she thought he was worried too.

We watch her walk down the stairs, clad only in running shorts and a singlet, though it can't be forty degrees outside. She's shivering, but I suspect it's more from nerves than cold.

She tries to cross the room, appearing to see only Will, just as he appears to see only her, but every member of the crew stops her to insist she's going to win—which is nothing she wants to hear right now because she's busy assuring herself she will lose. There's no one alive who can psych herself out the way Olivia can, and by the time she's halfway to us, she looks like she's going to pass out.

"They should know by now just to leave her alone," Will growls. "I've got to get her out of here. Can you manage these guys?"

I nod. We've done this before, Will and I, he the protector of Olivia's sometimes fragile psyche and me left to man the ship. He breaks through the crowd, draping a blanket over her and pulling her to his side.

"I don't have it today, Will," she whispers. "I feel weak."

"You have it." He pulls her closer. I think he'd drape his whole body over her like a cape if she'd allow it. "Let's go."

Olivia—who on a normal day takes orders from no one—leans against him and follows blindly. I've watched it before, but today it makes my eyes well over. In part because I'm so happy for them both, that they found each other. And in part because it reminds me what I've lost: Olivia is able to lean on Will because he's never let her down. I once thought I had the same with Rob, but he's done nothing *but* let me down these past few months. Maybe even for the past four years, though I haven't seen it until now.

I get the crew out the door, with Brendan still nowhere to be found. We head down to the mountain's base, where the race will start, and then begin the process of double-checking everything. Given that we're going to end up a hundred miles from where we began, leaving something necessary behind could present a real problem later in the day. And the whole time I'm taking inventory, I'm thinking about Brendan, though almost any topic *but* him would be preferable.

God. What was wrong with me last night? I was ready to do anything he wanted. Without a condom, for God's sake. And with *Brendan*, who never sleeps with anyone twice. Who, if Rob and I work things out, will probably be the best man at our wedding. It would have ruined everything.

And yet I think about that kiss, and I know I regret the interruption. I'll be thinking about that kiss on my deathbed and wishing, just once in my life, I'd allowed myself to have what I actually want.

It's ten minutes until the five AM start when Olivia appears, a grim, forced smile on her face. Everyone hugs her, which she bears with something approaching grace, and then she slings the Camelback over her shoulder and walks toward the start with Will still at her side, a cross between bodyguard and avenging angel.

"You think she's okay?" Brendan asks, coming up behind me.

My whole body stiffens, as if I need to shield myself from him, whereas he seems completely relaxed. Of course he does. Fucking a girl against the side of a house is probably all in a day's work for Brendan.

I tell him briskly that Olivia's always like this before races, and then I head in another direction. Maybe he's capable of putting it all behind him. I suspect it's going to take a little more effort on my part.

THE STARTING GUN FIRES, AND WE CLIMB INTO THE VAN AND head to the first checkpoint. I sit in the front of the van with Lee, a runner from Seattle who volunteered to come out and, like myself, will be running a portion of the race with Olivia. He's cute in a crunchy, endurance-runner kind of way—wiry and muscular, hair down to his shoulders, sweet. He might have appealed to me before Brendan. Now I barely realize he's male.

"You're running the Cal Loop, right?" he asks.

"Yeah," I say with a short laugh. "It's not gonna be pretty. I doubt I'll be able to keep up with her."

"She'll have run seventy miles by then," he reminds me, which is exactly what I keep telling myself, though it doesn't help.

We both ran cross country in college, and that's where the conversation turns next, though it doesn't help my anxiety any, given that I was the slowest girl on the team and Olivia was the fastest. He's still talking about it twenty-four miles later when we arrive at the first crew checkpoint, and I'm relieved to escape the car.

We begin carrying gear and setting up. Lee remains by my side as we set up, and though I'm a little tired of discussing all things related to running, I appreciate that he's helping me avoid someone else. Brendan's stripped down to his T-shirt, and just the curve of his biceps is enough to make me feel weak.

It seems as if we've barely gotten set up before Olivia blows in, looking like she just jogged across a parking lot instead of running a hard twenty-four miles through the mountains.

"You're in the lead, babe," says Will with a broad grin.

She smiles, collapsing in a chair. "Don't jinx me." But she's over her early-morning qualms. He pulls her shoes off to check for blisters and changes her socks. "Where are my babies?" she asks.

"On the way. Mom called, and everyone just woke up. You okay?" Will asks, raising a brow and nodding in the direction of her chest. "You're looking a little swollen there."

"I fed her this morning before we left," she says. "I'm fine."

"Oh my God," Brendan says with disgust. "I thought you were talking about Olivia's *feet*."

Olivia scowls at him. "With all the shit we've heard *you* talk about, you're giving us crap for discussing breast milk?"

"Yes. Jesus. The only thing worse is when Mom and Peter talk about needing 'alone time', like none of us knows what *that* means."

She grins at him. "Nursing is a part of life, Brendan. You'll see when you have kids of your own."

He runs a hand over his head. "Which is never happening, thank Christ," he replies.

Olivia looks like she doesn't believe him, but I don't have that luxury.

Remember this, Erin. Listen to the words coming out of his mouth.

He doesn't want a wife. He doesn't want kids. He doesn't even want a girl he's slept with more than once. I need to remember every one of those things when I catch myself thinking he could be more.

Once Olivia's feet are bandaged, she takes off and we begin packing down to drive to the next crew stop. Lee is helping me fold chairs, telling me about some bar they saw driving in, when suddenly Brendan appears in front of us both, looming over Lee, smiling at him the same way he did that football player—like he's two seconds from throwing a punch.

"Can I talk to you for a minute?" he asks me, though it sounds less like a question than a demand.

I nod, following him in silence toward the van. He opens the back, and I sit on the tail, avoiding his gaze.

"What's up?" I ask.

His eyes assess me as always. He looks as if he knows everything I've thought in the past twelve hours. I feel my cheeks heat as I remember how filthy some of those thoughts were.

"You tell me," he replies.

"I don't know what happened last night," I say.

"I could draw you a diagram."

I sigh, staring at my hands. "I mean I don't know why it happened and why it went so far. But we were drinking." A lame excuse. And one that doesn't exactly explain why it's all I'm thinking about now. "And we stopped before it went too far. So it doesn't count."

"Doesn't *count*? Erin, *we* didn't stop. Matthew stopped *us*."

I blow out a frustrated exhale. "What do you want me to say, Brendan?"

He steps closer. He is too close, again. "I want to know what you're thinking." His voice is low and husky, sending a shiver up my spine—one I need to kill, stat.

"I'm thinking it was just a tiny drunk mistake, and we pretend it never happened, and everyone's fine."

He nods, his jaw locked tight. "Neither of us mentions it to Rob, right?"

"Right." I confirm.

I look up at him and forget everything I've just said. His eyes have darkened and now dip to my mouth, as if he's just come across something he's starved for. It's probably how I'm looking at him too.

I hop down, and we close the back doors.

"Do me a favor," he says. "Stay away from Lee."

I roll my eyes. "He's harmless."

"Yeah, he is," Brendan agrees. "But I'm not."

He turns and walks off, and I remain behind watching him go. For someone who only wants no-strings, he sure is acting like the type of guy who wants a lot of them.

36

ERIN

Late in the afternoon I change into a singlet and shorts to run my ten miles with Olivia. Once she's done getting her blisters dealt with for the thousandth time, we take off.

The pace is punishing, for me, but Olivia is—for better or worse—not tired at all and wants to have a conversation.

"So according to my son," she begins, "you and Brendan are in love and probably having a baby."

Oh God. If he told Olivia, then he probably told Will, and Peter and Dorothy, and...*shit*. Matthew never stops talking. He probably told everyone.

"We're not together," I groan. "It was a misunderstanding."

"Yes," she says with a brow raised, "so many misunderstandings involve someone accidentally putting his tongue in your mouth."

"We just made a mistake," I reply. "Shit. Who did he tell?"

"Everyone who will listen. He wants to know how soon the baby is coming, and he wants you to name it Rubble—that's his favorite *Paw Patrol* character."

I groan. "It's not funny, Olivia. I almost cheated on Rob last night. It's not funny at all."

"You didn't *cheat* on Rob. You have no *agreement* with Rob. You can do anything you want. Just like he is."

As if I'm going to listen to Olivia. She's never liked Rob, and she adores Brendan. He could rob a bank and make meth in her basement and she'd stand off to the side cheering him on.

"Well just because I can do anything I want doesn't mean I'm hooking up with Rob's oldest friend," I tell her flatly. "We were a little drunk, and we kissed because we weren't thinking, and it was just this...blip. Matthew walked out, and that's where it ended."

"Do you like him?" she asks.

"Does it matter?" I reply. "This is Brendan we're talking about. I could have been anyone and he'd have gone for it."

Her arm flies out to hit my shoulder. "Give me a break, Erin. You've never been just anyone to him."

There's a part of me that wants to believe her. That wants to have her detail all the ways it's possible something could work between us. But allowing her to change my mind would be the stupidest thing I could do right now.

"Well, it doesn't matter either way. I'm probably getting back together with Rob, and Brendan has clearly stated he doesn't want a relationship with anyone, ever."

"So which is it?" she asks. "Is it that you *might be* getting back with Rob, or is it that Brendan doesn't want a relationship?"

The question jars me, and it's one I don't have an answer to. "Brendan and I don't want the same things. Conversation closed."

She sighs, disappointed. "Fine. Will, at least, will be relieved."

My head jerks toward her, surprised and a little hurt.

"I'm his children's godmother," I say. "He'd really have that big a problem with me dating his brother?"

"It isn't about you. It's about Brendan. He thinks Brendan runs through women, and he'd end up hurting you."

And that, I admit, is exactly what I think too.

❧ 37 ❧

BRENDAN
Three Years Earlier

I n June, the number of tours picks up dramatically, and for the first time in my seven months here, downtime becomes a rarity. Gabi makes the most of it, however. Italy is the ultimate adventure to her and she squeezes every second out of the experience...outside *and* at home. I've never met anyone who wants to have sex as often as she does. It's like she doesn't even need sleep.

We're on the third day of the Vineyards of Tuscany tour, sitting in the shade while our clients do a wine tasting. Gabi asked Seb to put us on the same schedule, which seemed excessive, given that we spend every free moment together already. I feel a little suffocated, to be honest, but when I think about Erin and Rob, I resolve to try harder.

Gabi texts her mom, and I check email, feeling a twinge of dread when I see Rob's name.

Rob has many good qualities. He's had my back in every stupid fight I've ever gotten into. But ever since he started dating Erin his emails have begun to irritate the fuck out of me. Today he mentions that he had to replace his Range Rover because it wasn't under warranty anymore. He sends pictures of the new house, the one Erin moved into. It's massive, of course. He says he wants to put in a basketball court, but he wonders if they'd use a tennis court more. He suggests that Gabi and I come visit. *You can stay in the pool house*, he says.

None of this surprises me. It's been Rob's M.O. since we were kids—asking about my grades before revealing he got straight As; patting me on the back for my college acceptances, and then casually mentioning he got into better schools. His SAT scores were slightly lower than mine, and seven years later he's still fucking bringing it up, mentioning he had a cold that day.

And I just don't get it—I've never tried to compete with the guy. I don't want a big-ass house. I didn't care about getting straight As or going to an Ivy. It's all Rob. Something in him seems continually dissatisfied with the fact that I just don't fucking care. That I don't want any of his shit, and I don't want to be him.

Maybe that's why he can't stop throwing Erin in my face. Because subconsciously, he knows he's finally got something I want.

38

ERIN

I've never been so relieved to finish a run as I am when Olivia and I arrive at the next checkpoint. She still seems fresh as a daisy, of course, while I'm barely able to stay upright. Brendan stands waiting, his arms crossed in front of him, as we come in.

"Your legs are shaking," he says.

I shrug. "It'll stop. I'm fine."

He ignores me, kicking one of the crew members out of a chair and making me sit.

"Well done!" says Lee, walking over, oblivious to Brendan's glare. "I told you you'd do great. We're about to start breaking down the tent, but I set up a solar shower for you in back if you're interested."

Forget about Brendan and his biceps. Lee is my new favorite person.

"That would be amazing," I reply, following Lee around the corner before Brendan can come up with a way to ruin it.

He shows me how to turn it on and then I climb in, sighing with pleasure as the water hits my skin. Few things in life are as underrated as a shower after a long run. I emerge feeling like a new person. Matthew asks if he can try it too, so I let him dance around under the spray for a few minutes before wrapping him in a towel and carrying him back to Dorothy, who has clean clothes ready. She looks so healthy it's almost impossible to believe she's the same woman I saw in a hospital bed a little over a week ago.

"I was sorry to hear about you and Rob," she says as I tug the shirt over Matthew's head. I'm about to awkwardly explain that we aren't necessarily over, but she continues. "Having said that, I've waited forever for you and Brendan to get together, so I can't say I'm truly sorry it happened."

Groan. Matthew really *did* tell everyone.

"Oh...uh...it's really not like that. We're just friends."

"Erin," she says, "the two of you have *never* been just friends. I knew he liked you the moment I first saw you together. Just be patient with him. I was so worried, after Gabi, that he'd never try again."

I can't imagine why all these women who know Brendan so well believe he's capable of a relationship. Or think he'd even want one in the first place. And I hate that I'm disappointing her, but I want to make sure she isn't misled. "Things aren't like that with us," I tell her. "Truly. And I'm sure Brendan will try again someday, but I get the feeling that's still a long way off for him."

She laughs. "I know that boy better than he knows himself, so let me tell you something, Erin: he's already trying. *You* might not know it, and *he* might not know it, but he is already trying."

There's nothing I can do but pretend to agree, even though I hate giving her false hope. I just have to make sure not to give myself any either.

JUST AFTER NINE PM, OLIVIA COMES THROUGH THE FINISH LINE in Auburn, taking first among the women. We celebrate with her in mid-field, but it's been a very long day on little sleep, and soon we are all piling into the vans to return to the house.

I find her after we've returned, sitting on the front porch nursing Caroline. She is barely keeping her eyes open, but she looks as dreamily content as her daughter does right now.

"Happy?" I ask.

"So happy," she replies, smiling at me. "Mostly happy it's over with."

I grin. "So you can stop working out and eat pounds of chocolate all day?" We both know she'll be training for something new by Monday morning.

"Exactly," she says. "Now, are you out here because you want girl talk, or are you out here because you're avoiding Brendan? I noticed you hauled ass out of Auburn in the first van with Lee. He was not pleased."

"I don't have a lot of willpower around him, Olivia, but I just can't... It will mess everything up."

And it will. It'll mess up our friendship and open me to a lifetime of wanting something unavailable. Then there's his friendship with Rob. And things with me and Rob too—how could I ever walk down the aisle toward him and his best man, knowing I'd slept with them *both*?

"If I can just manage to avoid him until I fly out tomorrow, I'll be safe. Thank God we're leaving separately."

"*Or,*" she says with an evil smile, "maybe you should just sleep with him and get it out of your system."

I watch her face to see if she's serious. It appears that she is. "You can't honestly think that's a good idea."

"You're so sure you want to marry Rob, yet you're obviously dying to be with Brendan. Put it to the test. Sleep with Brendan, and if it's out of your system, problem solved."

"What happens if it isn't?"

"If it isn't," she says, "then you had no business getting engaged to Rob in the first place."

I go upstairs determined to ignore her, and hit the landing just as Brendan's exiting the bathroom. The sight of him there leaves me grasping for a single rational thought. He's clad only in a towel, with miles of smooth, tan skin over a body that is nothing but muscle.

Our eyes lock, and my heart beats hard—like I've had ten espressos, like I've just run a sprint. It's beating so hard I'm unable to think. I only know—the way I would if I were being stalked—that I need to get away, as fast as possible.

I start toward the bathroom, willing myself not to even look at him. "I'm just going to—"

"Erin?" His voice is soft and certain, as is the hand that lands on my hip, pulling me toward him.

And then it isn't merely his hand on me, it's all of him, his mouth against mine, his chest bearing down, his hands reaching behind me, running below my hips, tucking me into him so there isn't a whisper of space between us. I taste the champagne from the celebration earlier on his lips, suck it from his tongue, and he groans, moving me backward toward his room, shutting the door behind us.

Certain forces in life are just too strong to fight. The lure of sleep when you've pulled an all-nighter, a wave breaking overhead. From the moment he begins kissing me, I know Brendan is one of those forces. There's no use even trying.

My hands are on his skin, pushing the towel away while his remove my shorts and rip my T-shirt over my head. His urgency thrills me.

So different from Rob. The thought makes me hesitate, makes me wonder if I'll regret this.

"Don't think," he says, his breath hot against my neck. "It'll be fine."

It's weak, accepting words you know can't possibly be true in order to get what you want. But I am weak, which is not news, and I'm especially weak where Brendan is concerned, which isn't a surprise either.

He pushes me backward toward the bed. The moon is bright

through the open window. Bright enough to watch him crawling over me, to see that look on his face—hungry and feral and tender all at once.

His fingers slide up the inside of my thigh, light as a whisper. His sudden lack of haste is agonizing, and when his hand finally reaches its destination, fingers pushing inside me, I make a sound I've never heard myself make. He groans in response.

"Hurry," I plead. He reaches over me to the nightstand, and I hear the sound of a condom wrapper tearing. It's been ages since I've heard that noise, and I find it oddly thrilling. I feel him lined up, and knowing what is coming makes the ache unbearable. I pull him down, closer, finding his mouth, my nails pressing into his back, and in a single swift thrust, he's inside me.

"Jesus, Erin," he groans. "You feel amazing."

He pulls back just enough to push back in hard—hard enough that the headboard slams against the wall, hard enough to make me gasp. And before I've even recovered, he does it again, his mouth seeking mine, his arms planted on either side of my head.

There are no words. No way to tell him—if I were capable of speech at the moment—what this is like, how different this is from anything I've ever had. That I've waited for this and dreamed about this for years, and it's better than anything I could have created in my head.

"Oh my God," I breathe. "Keep going."

He flinches and pulls out entirely, trailing kisses down my stomach. "Why are you stopping?" I cry. "I'm close."

"Because if I hear you gasp like that one more time while I'm inside you, I'm gonna blow." His mouth moves between my legs, and I gasp again. I don't seem able to *stop* gasping as his tongue sweeps over me. This is something Rob never does, and I'd forgotten how amazing it is.

And it's especially amazing with Brendan. He isn't tentative or careful. He devours me like he's desperate to do it, groaning against my skin with each noise I make. My hands fist the sheets as every muscle draws tight, and I explode in one spectacular, blinding moment, so shocked I cry out before I can stop myself.

Even after my body finally settles back onto the bed, though, he doesn't stop.

"Brendan, I don't... I'm not going to come again."

He raises his head, grinning up at me with the cockiest smile I've ever seen. "That sounds like a challenge."

And not two minutes later, it's a challenge he wins.

The moment I'm done, he's sliding over me, lining himself up. "I can't wait anymore," he says, his eyes shut as he thrusts.

The headboard slams again and again. He holds out, but I can tell he's struggling as he drags his lower lip between his teeth. I'm sure that I'm done, but as I watch him like that, grabbing the headboard with one hand, pushing hard, I discover I'm not.

"Oh my *God*," I whisper. I sound shocked, almost frightened. "*Again?*"

And the moment it hits me, he loses the fight, coming with a low, agonized groan, his mouth buried against my neck.

A few moments later, in the complete silence that follows, I realize Brendan and I were just *unbelievably* loud.

"The entire house just heard that, didn't they?" I ask with a sigh.

"They're all asleep. No one is listening."

I reach up, just for effect, and slam the headboard to the wall once, demonstrating the loud noise we just made at least thirty times.

"Okay, yeah, everyone heard that," he says. "But you know what? It was so fucking worth it."

I push a hand through my hair, stunned and overwhelmed and inexplicably happy. I know it will all come crashing down around me tomorrow, but for now what's done is done and I just want to enjoy it. "I thought multiple orgasms were a myth."

"I think maybe we should see if it was just a freak occurrence." He is already hardening again, pressing into my thigh.

"I can't. I can't possibly come again."

He rolls me onto my stomach and grabs my hips to drag me to my knees. "When are you going to learn not to challenge me, Erin?"

〜

I HAVE NO IDEA WHEN WE WENT TO SLEEP. I HAVE NO IDEA HOW many times I came...at a certain point I grew too tired to keep an accurate record. All I know is that when my eyes blink open, the room is flooded with sunshine, and the bedroom door is flying open, with Matthew launching himself toward us. Brendan manages to yank the sheets up, but not fast enough.

Matthew, frowning, asks me where my pajamas are. I cast a panicked glance at Brendan, who looks tempted to laugh.

"They must have fallen off while I was asleep."

Brendan laughs under his breath. "Smooth."

I ignore him. If Matthew decides to get any more observant, we're going to be explaining tied-off condoms too, since I don't ever recall Brendan getting up to flush them.

"Let's go downstairs, Matthew," I say.

"Erin," says Brendan with mock seriousness, "you can't go downstairs. Your pajamas fell off, remember?"

"It seems like a better idea," I reply between my teeth, looking at the floor and nightstand behind him, "than staying in *here*, don't you think?"

Understanding comes into his face, and he swings the covers away. "I'll take him."

In spite of the situation and the presence of a small child, I take one last moment to let the glory of Brendan sink in. The future may be a mystery to me, but I guarantee it'll never involve anyone quite as pretty as him walking out of my bed, bare-ass naked.

"Your 'jamas fell off too, Bwendan?" Matthew asks.

"No, my pajamas didn't fall off," Brendan replies, grabbing shorts from his backpack. "Real men don't wear pajamas."

Matthew follows him from the room, nodding as if he's just learned something valuable.

Once they're gone, I stumble into the shower. My whole body is sore, and there are certain parts rubbed so raw that even soap hurts. I emerge feeling almost beaten, dying to climb back in bed and sink into the sort of deep sleep Brendan and I only got a small taste of. But I can't, of course, because I'm leaving in a few hours, and also because if the girl who just ran a hundred miles can rally, I can too.

Wearily, I descend the stairs. Most of the crew is here, and there's a look on their faces as I enter the kitchen that lets me know, in no uncertain terms, that we were every bit as loud as I thought last night. I catch Brendan's eye and watch as he tries to maintain a straight face while simultaneously laughing so hard his shoulders shake. Olivia isn't even trying to hide it.

"I hate both of you," I mutter as I walk past them to the coffee.

The discussion, fortunately, has turned to a blow-by-blow of the race. Will comes down and unceremoniously hands Caroline over the table to Olivia.

"Hungry," he grunts. I'm unsure if he means himself or the baby until I watch Olivia pull her shirt over Caroline's head and start to nurse.

Brendan flinches. "It's so awkward when you do that."

She rolls her eyes. "Not nearly as awkward as you trying to push the headboard through the wall last night. I mean, I ran a hundred miles yesterday, and even *I* couldn't sleep through that."

He groans. "Olivia, my mother is sitting right here at the table."

"I slept here too, Brendan," says Dorothy. "It's not like I'm just figuring it out now."

"I'm going back to bed," I grumble, turning on my heel to leave the room.

"Don't worry, Erin!" Olivia shouts. "We'll keep Brendan away as long as we can!"

39

ERIN

B rendan was sprawled out on his bed, asleep, when I woke up again on Sunday to catch the airport shuttle. That was the first moment I thought *one more time wouldn't hurt*. I've thought it about a thousand times since. Sleeping with someone you're not supposed to sleep with is an awful lot like breaking a diet. Once it's happened, it's pretty easy to justify breaking it again. It's tempting, in fact, to scrap any attempt at discipline at all.

I can't act on it, of course, because Rob trusts us. We need to stop while it remains an accident—granted, an accident that occurred *seven* times. Except even now that I'm home, Brendan looms so large in my head it's as if there's no room to want other things. Rather than dampening my desire, sleeping with him has opened up some bottomless well inside me, one bubbling over with dangerous urges and possibilities.

Timothy drones on endlessly about the importance of branding during the Monday meeting, and I only hear the way Brendan's voice grows raspy just before he comes.

I spend lunch thinking about the cocky way he sits, leaning

back in his chair with legs spread wide—as if he's just about to demand you get on your knees and finish him off. I've fantasized about doing it more times than I can count. Now it's just another missed opportunity, one more thing I should have done Saturday when I had the chance.

I'm still thinking about Brendan when Timothy stops by my cubicle. It's hard not to scowl openly at him. Going from fantasies about Brendan to the reality of Timothy is a difficult transition indeed.

In his hand is the only completed piece for the new branding campaign, a postcard featuring the cringe-worthy tagline Timothy insisted upon: *ECU: A Place to Know, A Place to Grow*, which sounds like the title of a Dr. Seuss book. He throws it on my desk like it's an accusation in and of itself.

"I was surprised you weren't here on Friday," he says, lips pursed.

I sigh heavily. I knew this was coming. "I told you I was going to Tahoe. You signed my leave slip."

"I thought you'd just be gone Thursday."

Who takes a long weekend by going away Thursday and coming back Friday? I pull the document out of my drawer. "The form clearly stated I'd be gone both days."

He doesn't take it from me. "Well, this project is important, and you deciding to take off and miss a meeting does not signal commitment to your job."

You have got to be shitting me. I know people who didn't finish high school, yet make more than I do, and I routinely work fifty to sixty hours a week. I don't know if my Brendan-focused lust has left me unable to give a fuck about anything else in my life, or if it's just four years of outrage welling up inside me, but I've officially had it with Timothy's shit.

"When I left here Wednesday afternoon, there was no meeting planned. And, I *reiterate*, you signed the leave slip."

His frown deepens. "Your job review is coming up," he warns.

"I'm going to need to see an attitude adjustment, or you're not going to like what you hear."

I act as if he hasn't spoken and return to my computer screen. I'm glad I paid Sean's tuition, but God, I wish at some point in the past four years I'd gone down a different path. I'm hard pressed to imagine a job that could make me less happy than this one.

～

I SPEND MONDAY NIGHT PACKING. IF I'D HOPED IT WOULD GIVE me something other than Brendan to think about, though, I was sadly mistaken.

Tuesday is more of the same. Me: throbbing and needy and miserable with want, barely capable of pretending to do my job much less actually doing it. But I'm determined to put Saturday night behind me.

And then I get home and find a FedEx addressed to Brendan on the front step.

"Seriously?" I ask aloud, softly banging my forehead on the door. I've been fighting the desire to contact him since the moment I left on Sunday, and now fate is practically forcing my hand.

No. I'm not using this as an excuse to see him. The safest course is just to deliver it with no phone call or face-to-face contact. Before I can change my mind, I turn around and get in my car, driving as fast as possible to his place, as if the clock is running on my self restraint.

I park on the street and climb the stairs, thinking of the last time I was here. I don't regret sleeping with Brendan, but I hate that I messed up our friendship. I loved spending time with him, and I can't imagine how we will ever go back to the way things were. I've barely slid the envelope under the door when it flies open and Brendan stands in the frame, looking from the envelope to me with narrowed eyes. "You were just going to slide this under my door without knocking?"

My heart hammers in my chest. I'm already finding myself hungry for the sight of him, wanting to stay, wanting more. "I didn't know if you were home or—"

He raises a brow. "Yes, that's why people knock."

I sigh. "And how awkward would it have been if you'd had a girl here?"

"I already told you, I don't have girls here."

He opens the door wider, gesturing me in. I really should not cross the threshold. What I should do—what a decent person would do—is make an excuse and hightail it back down those stairs. Yet here I am, walking into his place. *Stupid, disobedient feet.*

He doesn't ask if I want a drink; he just opens a beer and hands it to me. I imagine, with the anxiety I'm feeling right now, I look like I need one.

I lean against the kitchen counter, staring at the beer bottle as if the label I'm peeling off is a bomb in need of defusing. I try not to look at him, but even in my peripheral vision I see his legs—lean and muscular at once, smooth. The hair on them is light, sparse, and barely visible. Why does he have to be so perfect? Even his damn *leg hair* is perfect.

"How was the rest of the trip?" I ask. "Lose any more car keys?"

"Leave that poor label alone," he says, and I'm forced to meet his gaze.

His pale blue eyes are hazy right now, like the grayest morning in autumn. He isn't smiling. I take a big pull off the beer, the way a man would, out of sheer nerves. I'm sure it's not an attractive sight, but there's something that's gone avid in his gaze. You'd think I just tied a cherry stem with my tongue or slowly sucked on a popsicle with the way he's watching me. And in the space of that moment I remember him on Saturday night. Above me, flinching as he tried not to come. A muscle spasms low in my abdomen.

"What are you thinking?" he asks.

Oh God. I'm so caught. I can tell just by the way he asks, by the look on his face, that he knows.

"Nothing," I squeak.

I need to get out of here. *Now.* I set the beer down on the counter so quickly it wobbles. My hand shoots out to steady it, and his wraps around mine as he steps forward, eliminating the space between us.

Only our hands are touching but I feel the press of his skin everywhere—a spark at the base of my spine, firing through my bloodstream.

"I should go," I whisper. His nod is barely there, more just a tip of the chin. He releases my hand.

I head across the room and he follows in silence. I am hyper-aware of his smallest sounds—his feet against the hardwood, his breath.

But when I reach for the knob, his hand covers mine once more. "Wait," he whispers.

I turn to face him. "I—"

His hand curves around the back of my neck, and then his mouth is on mine. There is no time for me to object, though who knows if I actually would have. The spike of adrenaline that began when we both grabbed that beer bottle is now coursing through my veins, taking over. He kisses me until my breath comes in small wisps and my knees shake.

"My room, now," he says, breaking away as he starts to pull me past the couch. I allow myself to be led for a moment, but already I'm thinking of all the things we didn't get to on Saturday night, all the missed opportunities I've been ruing. If we're really doing this, I want to leave with fewer regrets than I had when I arrived.

"No," I say, pulling against his hand. I push him toward the nearest chair. "Sit."

He raises a brow but does what I ask, perhaps as surprised as I to discover that I'm taking charge.

I push his shorts to the floor and straddle him, sliding my hand between us, still outside the tight boxer briefs that leave almost nothing to the imagination. My fingers can't quite wrap around him, but even through the fabric I swear I can feel him pulse. "Erin," he growls, and moves as if he's going to lift both of us.

I press my mouth to his ear. "You need to learn some patience."

"Fuck that," he hisses.

I laugh under my breath. We've barely begun but already triumph dances up my spine. It's not some kind of supreme confidence in my own abilities. It's simply that I'm so determined to walk away from this with what I want—the memory of him begging and desperate against my tongue.

I slide to the floor, pulling his boxers with me. Using hands and tongue, I play—giving him a little of what he wants, but not enough, memorizing his sharp inhales and his hands tightening in my hair. It's not until he begs, his breath labored as he thrusts upward, that I take him in my mouth.

"Oh Jesus," he whispers, air hissing between his teeth. His fingers press to my scalp and already I feel him swelling, wanting release and fighting it at the same time. "Erin...fuck."

His breath comes faster and I grip tighter, timing the slide of my hand and the pull of my mouth with those feverish inhales and exhales.

"I'm gonna come," he gasps too late, not that I'd planned on going anywhere. The pained noise he makes as he finishes is the hottest thing I've ever heard in my life.

"Jesus Christ," he says, his chest rising and falling rapidly. He looks down at me. "Where the fuck did you learn *that?*"

I laugh. "You really want me to answer?"

He shakes his head and then joins me on the floor, pushing me to my back. "No, but at some point I'm probably going to ask you to do it again."

≈ 40 ≈

BRENDAN
Three Years Earlier

At the end of June, Gabi arrives at my apartment with her suitcases, crying. She tells me her roommate kicked her out and asks if she can stay with me for a while.

My stomach sinks. Things are good with us just as they are, and I'd rather not mess with a winning formula. I already see Gabi nearly every day, and I spend every night with her when we're on a tour. I'm not sure I'm ready to hand over my remaining moments of freedom, but what am I supposed to say? She's got less than two months left, and she really has no place else to go. I tell her it's okay, but even as I say it, I feel as if there's slightly less air in the room than there was before she arrived.

∾

AT FIRST, HAVING GABI AS A ROOMMATE WORKS OUT PRETTY well for me. I seriously can't believe there's a female alive who wants to get laid more often than I do, but I've got no complaints. It's all going okay—until suddenly it isn't.

"Your friend Rob," she ventures one afternoon, looking up from my iPad. "He's the one dating that girl you liked?" I wish, now that I know Gabi better, that I'd never told her about Erin. She's jealous about the most innocent of things, and my feelings for Erin were never innocent, not for a moment.

"Yeah."

"So her name is Erin?" she asks.

My jaw drops. "Are you reading my email?"

"It was just open when I picked it up," she says with a shrug.

She's lying. I haven't heard from Rob in weeks. I want to give her the benefit of the doubt but I just can't. "Please get out of my email."

"Do you have a picture of her?" she asks. Her voice is neutral, but I catch a glimpse of something in there, something needy and fearful. And if she's jealous now, seeing a picture of Erin sure as shit won't help.

"No," I reply, even though I do.

"What's her last name?" asks Gabi.

"What are you doing?" I sigh. "I never even dated the girl. Why does this matter?"

"It doesn't. I was just curious."

The conversation ends, but it also remains. It is wedged between us all night, Gabi's unhappiness almost palpable. I'd like to end it, reassure her that it's over for me. I just don't think I can do it convincingly.

41

ERIN

In spite of the lack of sleep, I arrive at work feeling absolutely wired. I want to stand on my desk and announce my discovery to the world. "I finally get it now! I understand why sex is such a big deal to you people!"

I was able to rationalize how amazing it was with him on Saturday: there'd been so much build up between me and Brendan, and I'd gone without it for so very, very long. But none of those factors were in play this time, so how is it even possible that it *improved?*

I left in the middle of the night, even though I wanted to stay. I'm guessing Brendan would be a hundred percent in favor of morning sex, something Rob never had time for and rarely seemed to want. It's just one more thing I gave up to fit in the space Rob carved out for me, but now it's back on the table—along with everything else I gave up—and it leaves me feeling like I've been set free in a candy store.

Is it like this for Brendan? Probably not. And yet it was so amazing that surely even *he* wants to repeat it again.

It's only as the afternoon winds down and the office begins to empty that reality sets in. Of course Brendan wants to repeat it. I'm sure he'll repeat it tonight, just with some other girl.

By the time I get home, my joy has ebbed away completely. What did I think was going to happen? Did I really think one good blow job and a little intercourse was going to make him *infatuated* with me? If so, I couldn't have been more wrong. It didn't even make him want to do it again.

The next morning I get in a good, long run before Pilates. Operation Forget Brendan has begun, and working out is really the only strategy I've got so far. I return so exhausted I'm certain I don't have the energy for either lust or obsession, but by the time I'm standing under the showerhead, he's already taking over my brain. I imagine him behind me, wet and soap-slick, sliding into me with ease. I add shower sex to the never-ending list of things we didn't get to do.

My phone is silent all day. I pretend I'm not watching it, reminding myself that it doesn't matter if he contacts me because nothing I want can happen again anyway. What we did was wrong, and it has to stop.

It's just as I've truly begun to give up on him that he finally texts.

Brendan: Want to help me paint tonight?

There is no reference to Saturday night, Tuesday night, or a desire to repeat either. Maybe he legitimately wants help. Maybe suggesting a friendly activity is his way of reinstating our friendship, making things normal again, and how can I say no to that?

I'll live if he just wants to be friends. But I can no longer pretend that I don't want more. That I don't want it so much it feels like I might explode even as I sit here staring at a memo someone has sent out about labeling food in the break room.

Operation Forget Brendan, I've got to say, is sort of a bust.

∽

I CHANGE CLOTHES AFTER WORK AND HEAD TO HIM, CLAD IN running shorts, T-shirt, and ponytail. No matter how I feel, I don't want to *look* like a girl who's spent the last thirty-six hours obsessing over the things he can do with his tongue.

I bring over some of the cupcakes I made the night before, because that's the kind of thing Friend-Erin-Who-Doesn't-Necessarily-Want-To-Sleep-With-You would do, but when I walk into his apartment the ruse gets a little harder to keep up. He looks the way he always does: frayed khaki shorts, gray T-shirt, muscular thighs, hard jaw, and clear blue eyes. The problem is that's enough. It's too much, actually. The sight of him alone is hormonal overload.

I inhale and thrust the cupcakes toward him. "I brought snacks."

Fuck. My voice sounds all breathy, like I just ran ten flights of stairs.

He hears it and holds my eye for a second, calm as ever. I wish I were calm the way he is. Right now I'm a chaotic mess of worry and lust, and he's as still, as cool and impenetrable, as a steel beam.

He takes the box from me, his fingers brushing mine, staying there a moment too long. Acting normal is almost impossible. I stare at his unshaved jaw and remember how it felt against my lips, the delicious scrape of it against my skin.

"What's going on, Erin?" he asks, setting the box on the counter behind him. His voice is low, smooth, *leading.*

"Nothing," I reply.

"You bite your lip when you're nervous," he says. He pulls me against him. Slowly his lips trail down my neck, tugging at the soft skin just beneath my jaw, and for a single, delicious moment I let myself have it—his size and his smell of soap and coffee, the feel of his smooth skin under my hands, the prickle of shaved hair at the back of his neck, how ridiculously muscular he is. If I *wanted* to push him away, it would be like pushing a brick wall.

His hands are sliding inside my T-shirt when I come to my

senses. "We can't do this," I say. But even I hear the pleading note in my voice saying *Brendan, convince me, convince me.*

His hands spread over my rib cage. "If you want me to stop," he whispers, his breath next to my ear, "say so now. Because otherwise I've got about fifteen things I plan to do to you."

I know there is a logical and well-reasoned argument against this somewhere inside me, but mostly I want to know what fifteen things he has in mind, and I want him to have already gotten them underway.

"Condom," I demand.

"Not yet," he says. He slides my shorts past my hips and lifts me, depositing my bare ass on his counter. "And by the way," he adds, pulling me to the very edge and pushing my legs apart, "I'm in charge tonight."

IT'S LATE WHEN I FINALLY CLIMB FROM THE BED. HE WATCHES AS I start hunting for my clothes. "Why did you try to stop me when you came over tonight?" he asks.

"You know why." For the first time I feel guilty. Sleeping with Brendan once was an anomaly. But three times is something else entirely. It's intentional.

He sits up. "You're seriously worried about being loyal to Rob after what he did?"

"Not exactly. But it's messy. How will you and Rob get past this? And if Rob and I get back together, we'd never be able to hang out, the three of us. You'd be his best man—" I trail off, swallowing hard. Just envisioning it makes me sick.

"Erin, I'm not going to be his best man, and you and me and Rob are never going to be hanging out. I'm not going to tell him about it, obviously, but I'm also not going to spend the rest of my life lying."

I sit at the end of his bed, clutching my shirt and bra to my chest. "I don't get what you're saying."

"I made a choice when I slept with you. I can't continue pretending to be his friend after that."

My stomach drops. What I've done is bad enough, but for me to be the cause of their friendship's demise is worse. "Brendan, he's been your best friend for years. You can't do that."

He shakes his head. "I like Rob, or at least I did until he cheated on you, but we haven't lived in the same place for over a decade, and we've both changed. You saw how it was when I got back—we have nothing in common anymore. He's obsessed with making money. Status matters more to him than anything else. And any respect I still had for him was lost when I heard what he did with Christina."

"I don't know that *anything* happened with her," I argue.

His mouth flattens. "You want to believe he's innocent so badly you won't even look at the facts."

He's wrong. At this point I *hope* Rob cheated on me, because if he didn't, it makes what I've done with Brendan ten times worse.

"Come here," he says softly. He cups my chin and kisses me. He kisses me until I forget what we were discussing entirely.

I even forget that I'd planned to leave.

HOURS LATER I STUMBLE INTO MY OWN BED. THIS TIME I SLEEP late, missing my get-over-Brendan run and my get-over-Brendan Pilates. They didn't seem to be doing me much good anyway.

I wake feeling banged up and rejuvenated at the same time, as if I just went on the best hike of my life and capped it off with ten cups of coffee, or ran a marathon and came in first. Somewhere in the back of my mind I feel the insistent buzz of guilt, but I ignore it. Instead I put on my highest heels, my favorite dress and practically skip into the office.

Nothing can touch me. Not traffic, not Timothy's snide comment about my arrival time, even though I wasn't late. I didn't know orgasms could make me invincible, but it appears they have.

I sit at my desk and reread all the texts Brendan's sent me. None of them are even vaguely romantic, but my heart still does this ridiculous fluttery thing, the way it did when I was in sixth grade and Bradley Peterson passed me a note asking if I liked him. But of course, my ridiculous fluttering heart would probably send Brendan running. He likes me precisely because he believes my heart is too busy fluttering for Rob to flutter for him too.

I'm still reading them when Harper pops into my cubicle and comes to a dead stop.

"Hey," I say, dropping the phone as if it's burned me. "How was your trip?"

She doesn't even answer. Just stands there staring at me, tapping her lip. "Something's different," she says, eyes narrowing. "What did you do?"

"Nothing," I chirp, running my fingers through my hair, feigning innocence. I'm quite sure I look completely normal, although I'm so relaxed I feel entirely liquid right now.

"Bullshit," she says. Her eyes widen and a smile flashes across her face. "You little slut!" she cries gleefully. "You got laid!"

I blink. "What?"

"Oh my God, we both know you can't lie for shit, Erin. Don't even try. Who was it? You didn't get back together with Rob..." she says, mumbling to herself. "No, no, you'd have texted me if... Oh. My. God. Brendan. You slept with Brendan? Oh, don't open your lying mouth to me again. You totally slept with Brendan."

I slump in my chair, exhausted by the mental gymnastics she performed entirely on her own. "You need a psychic hotline or something."

"Wow," she mouths, sitting on my desk. "Tell me everything. Was it amazing?"

I smile. "It was okay."

"Like I said before, you're a terrible liar. There's not a chance sex with him was merely *okay*. So what now? Are you a thing? Have you talked about it?"

Yet another female with far more faith in Brendan than he

deserves. As if Brendan would ever talk about a relationship, aside from discussing his desire to avoid one.

"No, of course not," I say. "There's nothing to discuss. He doesn't want a girlfriend, and I *have* a boyfriend."

"*Had*," she emphasizes. "Had. You're a free agent now, my friend."

I shrug. "Rob's coming back, Harper. It's not like we could keep this going even if we wanted to, and Brendan isn't the sort to want to."

"Whatever. Until Rob gets here, I want you to tag him as much as humanly possible."

I laugh and blush at the same time. "I'm pretty sure we already did that. My vagina is broken."

"Well, go let him break it some more. Or if you're done with him, send him my way."

I feel an odd little flare of jealousy, which is beyond ridiculous. I don't even know if I'll see him again.

"He's all yours," I tell her.

Just not yet.

42

ERIN

Over the weekend, Mr. Tibbles and I move to Harper's place. The finality of leaving Rob's house—with the possibility that I might not return—hits me harder than I expected. I lock my engagement ring up in Rob's safe, wondering if I'll ever see it again, and then walk around the house one last time. For the three years I lived here, I assumed it was my future. I'd even chosen a room for the nursery. So it's not just my home I'm losing; it's all the potential lives that might have been led here. They'd have been good lives. Maybe not transcendent. Maybe not sex-til-two AM, floating-into-work-ebullient-each-morning kind of lives, but also not anything to complain about.

And for most of my years, I've believed living a life I couldn't complain about was enough. If Rob and I don't get back together, I have to wonder if the day will come that a life I can't complain about sounds like enough, if I'll curse myself for wanting more than I had. But right now, I'm so busy craving Brendan—his smooth skin, his smell, the way he laughs, the sight of his name—that it's hard to imagine.

On Sunday I go to Littleton to take my brother to lunch. For once it's not painful to see Sean. He's put on a little weight, and he's excited about the future—about his last semester of school, which begins in a week, and about working to become a counselor after he graduates. It was worth every penny I've spent if it helped get him where he is at the moment.

I tentatively mention that I've been spending time with Brendan. It's juvenile, but I just like saying his name, as if it will somehow make what is happening feel more real. Which hurts a little, because I know that it's not.

Sean frowns. "You mean as friends, right? Isn't Rob due back soon?" he asks.

"Oh," I reply, staring at my flatware, carefully aligning each piece as if I'm Martha Stewart. "No. Actually, he's staying until August, I think."

"August?" His tone demands eye contact, which I reluctantly provide.

I wish I'd never brought any of this up. The less my family knows about my life the better. "We sort of broke up. I mean, we may get back together when he's home, but I sort of doubt it, to be honest."

All the excitement I saw in his face only moments before is gone. His eyes are dark. "It was about the money, wasn't it?" he asks. "He didn't want you to pay my tuition. I could tell when I spoke to him."

I wave my hand. "No, of course not. Honestly, Sean, money is pretty much the only thing we don't have a problem with."

"But you're going to need that money back if Rob isn't supporting you," he insists.

"I can always earn more," I tell him.

My mood is unrelentingly sunny, no matter what Sean says. It's Brendan, I'm sure. He makes me feel invincible. He makes me believe anything is possible.

Even though I haven't heard from once, all weekend long.

IT's NOT UNTIL TUESDAY, WHEN I'VE BEGUN TO DESPAIR, THAT Brendan texts. It almost feels intentional, the way he's waited until I'm about to give up before he makes contact. And the truth is that I'm mad. Was he off with other girls all weekend? Am I only good enough to fuck on work nights?

Brendan: I woke up feeling like my walls could use some more work.

Me: The walls? Are we still calling it that?

Brendan: Fine. My dick. My dick could use some more work. I was trying to be subtle.

I know I should refuse. Anything that can cause me this much grief, this early on, is clearly something to be avoided. But apparently my brother and father aren't the only members of my family with an addictive personality. Every time I get a little of Brendan, I need even more. No matter how bad it is for me.

WE DON'T END UP PAINTING, OF COURSE.

And when I'm startled awake by a ringing phone in the middle of the night, I nearly fall out of the bed trying to grab it, certain it's my father...only to find it's not my phone at all. It's Brendan's. He's on his feet and moving into the other room before I've fully put it together.

For a moment I'm merely puzzled.

And then I'm pissed.

The only calls a single guy receives in the middle of the night are booty calls, and of course he gets booty calls—he has a whole host of girls he can and *does* sleep with. Which prompts the question yet again: Why am I even here? I've never settled for being one of many to *any* guy, and I'm sure as shit not doing this with a guy who takes the call while I'm in his bed.

Beneath my rage, though, my chest feels like it's been split in half, and if I were alone I would dissolve into tears. No matter how strong I feel, Brendan has the power to make all my threads unravel. He always has.

I begin searching the bed for my underwear. I'm nearly dressed by the time he gets back to the room.

He stops just inside the door and stares at me. "Where are you going?"

"Home," I reply, my voice flat. I refuse to let him hear my anger, or my grief. He owes me nothing, and I owe him nothing.

I move toward the door, but he sidesteps me to block it. "Why?"

I summon all of my inner fortitude to sound calm, when really I'd like to slap him and scream. "Look, I know how you roll, but I don't need to be a part of it. I can do better than a guy who gets booty calls and *answers* them while I'm still in his bed."

"It wasn't a booty call."

I shake my head. "Please, Brendan. Who else calls this late?"

He stares me down. "Do you trust me?"

Maybe it was Gabi on the phone, but the truth is I'd be upset by that too, so I don't want to contemplate his question. What I want most of all is to end this now, immediately, before it does me real damage, though I suspect it's already too late.

I fold my arms over my chest. "It doesn't matter," I say. "I need to go."

"Look me in the eye and answer the question, Erin. Do. You. Trust. Me?"

I meet his gaze reluctantly, and almost immediately feel something seep through my blood. I don't want to believe him, but I do anyway.

"Yes," I whisper.

"Then when I tell you it wasn't a booty call, do you know I'm telling the truth?"

Whether or not it was a booty call is irrelevant. He's going to break my heart, and I should not be here. I want to weep for the moment when it will officially happen, as if I can dilute the pain ahead of time.

I nod and he moves closer to me, pressing his mouth to my ear as his fingers go to the button of my jeans. "Then get back in bed," he says, "because I'm not done with you yet."

43

BRENDAN

Three Years Earlier

The schedule gets so busy that Gabi and I can't always lead tours together. I'm okay with that. I'm finding she has these little habits that grate on my nerves if I'm around her for twenty-four hours straight. She employs the words *amazeballs* and *awesomesauce*, for instance, more than the correct number of times, which is zero.

Even the sex, which was so amazing at first, isn't that great. The more we sleep together, the more she seems to want it. I guess that should be flattering, but at times it almost feels like she's trying to prove something to me or to herself, though I have no idea what that would be.

Or what she possibly could need to prove: other than Erin, I've never seen a girl get as much unsolicited male attention. The guys at the tour company make no bones about their desire to sleep with her. It doesn't bother me, but occasionally I wonder if it should. It bothered me when guys even *looked* at Erin, much less commented. It makes me wonder if I've made a mistake, letting this thing with Gabi go as far as it has. Especially because it's starting to seem like we have different expectations of where it's headed.

"You know," she says over coffee, "there are lots of places to do bike tours near Stanford—Big Sur, the redwoods, Napa."

"I thought medical school was pretty demanding," I reply. "Are you going to have time to work?"

She laughs. "Not me, silly. *You*. Wouldn't that be great, leading tours along the coast?"

Yeah, except I'm already someplace great, and I'm nowhere near being ready to move for Gabi. I wish I could be in this thing with both feet, instead of constantly missing what this is not, but there's a hole inside me I'm increasingly sure Gabi can't fill.

"I was planning to go to Bali next," I tell her.

"Will you at least consider it?" she pleads.

I tell her I will. I want to be someone who considers these things. I tell myself I want the things Rob has at home. Except I'm pretty sure I just want one specific thing Rob has.

🦋 44 🦋

ERIN

I learn from Olivia that Brendan and Will aren't speaking. Will is pissed that Brendan didn't tell him about Dorothy's cancer, but mostly he's pissed that Brendan is hooking up with me. Olivia wants details, but I really have none to give, since I don't even know what's going on with us myself. I know that I hear from him every day. His texts are always funny and frequently dirty, but what they never are is *sweet*. I wait for them to evolve, for him to say *I wish you'd stayed over*, or *I'm sorry I didn't get to see you last night*, but those words never come.

I know that I'm with him more nights than I'm not. I know that we've fallen into a sort of haphazard domesticity—he'll make us dinner, I'll bake. I start staying the night and he doesn't seem to mind. But we are not dating. We don't go out, we don't hold hands. And I don't know where he is on the nights we're not together.

That's what troubles me most.

Brendan's unexplained absences have become a blank screen on which I project worst-case scenarios: cheerleaders with D cups, sex-crazed models. Or nights spent with Gabi—the girl I suspect he hasn't left behind.

~

HE GOES TO BOULDER TO VISIT HIS MOM WHEN SHE STARTS radiation. I don't see him for three days, but I have no idea whether he's with her the entire time. I'm not even sure I'll hear from him again. I'm forced to wonder—not that I ever really stop wondering—when we will end, and if he'll warn me before it happens.

I go to his place when he gets home. He's standing at the stove when I arrive, but takes one look at me and turns the burner off.

"Get undressed," he says, his voice a low growl.

Mere seconds later we are both rid of our clothes, bare skin meeting bare skin. He manages to grunt the word "bed," but we only make it as far as the couch.

When it's through, his gaze follows mine across the room, which we've littered with clothing.

I laugh. "Your apartment looks like a crime scene."

"I did plan to try to talk to you for at least a few minutes first," he admits. "It's those fucking heels of yours. Seeing you naked is mandatory when you come here in those things."

"What's shocking is that you still want to," I admit. "I can't believe you're not bored yet."

"Why would I be bored?"

I shrug, feigning ambivalence. "It's sort of what you're known for, isn't it? Never the same girl twice?"

He studies my face. "Does that bother you?"

"I just want to make sure it ends well." I grind my teeth together on the last word to keep it from sounding tremulous, because that's suddenly how I feel when I say it aloud—not ambivalent, the way I'm supposed to be about our dirty little secret, but invested. You cannot be invested in something as brief as this, particularly something you've always known will end, but I am.

"You worry too much," he says. "We're in the bubble right now. That's why this works."

"The bubble?"

"Like a pocket of air in a submerged car. It's a little space to breathe that you know won't last. This works because I know you're getting back together with Rob," he says. "If you weren't, I'd have to worry that...you know, you might get attached."

It's not so different than what I thought, but it bothers me anyway. It bothers me to hear him say, so definitively, that it won't last. I'm hurt, and angry, and I don't have the right to be either one.

He seems to realize he's said the wrong thing. "But if you weren't getting back together with him, you wouldn't want this," he adds. "You'd be off looking for someone just like him."

"Why do you say that?"

He rolls on his back, staring at the ceiling. "You want stability, Erin. You want the boring guy like Rob who's going to work unrelentingly until he can retire at sixty-five, and who's never going to have more than one or two drinks when he goes out."

"Being a hard worker and responsible drinker doesn't mean someone is *boring*."

Brendan rolls his eyes. "Fine. Not boring—controlled. You want someone who's always controlled, and reliable, and steady. And that guy will never be me."

I no longer believe that *controlled* is what I need, but I still want someone I can count on. If I were a smarter girl, I'd ask myself why, given that fact, I am here at all.

"Why are you so against relationships?" I ask. "They aren't all bad."

"The problem with a relationship," he says, "is that it's a sort of promise to the other person—not that you're staying together but that you at least think you might. And it fucks people up when you realize you were wrong. I'm not ever making that promise to anyone again."

He must be thinking of Gabi. I'd always assumed that he was the one who was hurt when it ended. Now I'm not so sure.

"Brendan, it's not a promise," I argue. "It's an attempt. Until you marry someone, you're only promising to try. No one can blame you when it doesn't work out."

"You just never know how someone will react," he says. His eyes close for a moment and then he turns toward me, brushing a hand over my stomach. "This is really not what I want to be discussing right now."

He's trying to change the subject and just this once, I refuse to let him. "How could someone react?" I ask. "You're great and everything, but you can't possibly think that I'm going to turn into some psycho who stalks you after this is done?"

"No," he says softly, removing his hand, closing in on himself again. "It's just me. I seem to bring it out in people. And when that happens, you bear some responsibility for it, for what you've turned someone else into."

"No, you don't," I argue. "I became someone else with Rob—to keep the peace and to make him happy. But he didn't *make* me change, and he also isn't responsible for how unhappy I became when I did. The only person whose feelings you're responsible for are your own."

He sighs and glances at me before he jumps to his feet. "I wish I could believe that, but I just don't," he says, walking out of the room.

❦ 45 ❦

ERIN

I decide I can live with the uncertainty, because Brendan makes me happy. I float into the office each morning, and the minute I can escape, I'm heading to Brendan's, my clothes shed within seconds of climbing his stairs.

We don't talk about the future. We are, like he said, in the bubble. It's temporary, but until that bubble pops, I've decided to enjoy it as if these are my very last days on Earth.

If only there was such an easy fix for my boss as well.

"I came by your desk yesterday afternoon and you weren't here," Timothy says, leaning into my cubicle on Wednesday, staring me down the way a parent might a misbehaving child. "Is there a reason you're suddenly leaving early?"

I don't know what his problem is, but I'm done jumping when he says jump for a shitty salary and no chance of promotion.

"I'm not leaving early," I reply, my teeth grinding. "Our hours here are eight to four-thirty."

"That's the *minimum* requirement, Erin. And as one of the senior employees here, I thought you understood that more was expected of you."

Senior in what way? I long to ask. I don't have a better office or better pay or better leave. If the only benefit to being a senior employee is longer hours and higher expectations, I have a few suggestions for what he can do with the honor.

"Anyway," he continues, "the chancellor wants to see mock-ups of the entire branding campaign tomorrow at three, including the new stuff he asked for."

I very nearly laugh. What he's asking is impossible. He wants copy for a ten-page promotional brochure, a four-page magazine article, and four recruitment pieces—and then he wants a designer to have them all laid out—in a day.

"That's impossible," I argue. "We don't even have copy yet."

"I didn't come here for a status report, Erin. I came here to tell you my expectations. And all of those items had better be on my desk by two-thirty."

I watch his retreating back and imagine quitting. I imagine showing up tomorrow at the requested hour, empty-handed aside from my resignation letter, and saying, "Here's your campaign, asshole." It's the kind of thing that works for other people—I guarantee Harper could do it and somehow wind up floating out of here on wings of glory, moving a week later into a far better job. But I'm not Harper. My arc has never gone the way of a Lifetime movie with its inevitable triumph. Which means I will not be seeing Brendan as planned, nor experiencing everything else he detailed in the filthy text he sent this morning. That fact alone makes me hate this job more fervently than anything else that's happened here over the past four years.

I call Brendan and explain that I can't come over because I will instead be crafting twenty pages of starry-eyed prose about the glories of ECU.

"You sure about that?" he asks. "I'm making fajitas."

I groan in dismay. "I wish I could, but I won't even have time to eat."

"Just come over," he says, sighing. "Bring your laptop. You can work while I cook."

I wonder if he has any idea that he sounds like a boyfriend right now. A *good* boyfriend. I don't point it out. He'd find the revelation horrifying.

"We can't be having sex the whole time," I warn.

"Erin," he says, sounding exasperated, "I'm capable of controlling myself when I have to."

I snort. "I guess I haven't witnessed that yet."

"What do you think I was doing," he counters, "for the two months before we slept together?"

I ARRIVE AT HIS PLACE EXPECTING HIM TO UNDRESS ME immediately, but he doesn't.

"Dinner's almost ready," he says, grabbing a plate.

He's wearing my favorite T-shirt, the one that brings out the gold in his skin and makes his eyes look Photoshopped. I instantly regret the prior claims I made about sex, and us not having it.

"I didn't really mean we couldn't have *any* sex," I volunteer, and he just laughs.

I walk toward him, and he turns to me sternly, wielding the tongs like a weapon. "Don't even think about getting laid until you're done with your work."

"I think you're underestimating how long this is going to take," I reply, a hint of pleading in my voice.

"That's okay," he says, returning to the grill. "Just get your work done. We don't need to have sex."

I suspect he's doing it just to torture me, because *we don't need to have sex* is not a phrase I ever imagined coming from his mouth. I bet the words burned his throat a little as they came out.

After dinner, we settle in on opposite sides of his couch: me with a laptop, him with a book, legs entwined. He seems disappointingly unaware of my presence, whereas I am aware of little other than his. Every time he shifts, every time his foot brushes my leg, I grow very aware of the fact that he is there, and that we have not had sex in nearly eighteen hours. Just the way he *sits* makes me think of things I should not.

"A quickie might take the edge off," I venture.

"Get back to work," he says, without even glancing up.

Minutes later, I've only typed about two sentences, and I am hyper-focused on the fact that his foot has just brushed mine. Such a small, simple motion. It could happen with anyone and be meaningless, except that it's not anyone, it's Brendan, who has the filthiest mind and mouth of anyone I've ever been with. So that little brush of his foot has an entire library of memories accompanying it.

"I'm having a hard time focusing," I whine. "Maybe we should..."

He cocks a brow. "Not a chance, blondie. You asked for self-control. You're getting self-control."

Great. Trust Brendan to turn it into a personal challenge.

"You want to try it in the hammock?" I suggest. "I promise I won't get mad if we fall out."

He laughs but doesn't even glance at me.

I even tell him I'm wearing the red thong—he once described a particularly graphic fantasy about me in the red thong and heels—but even that doesn't work.

"I give up," I say with a sigh as I pull off my cardigan. He glances over, and I catch the look in his eyes before he returns to his book.

Seconds later I catch him looking again, surreptitiously, just for a moment. *That's* when I realize how to win this battle.

I am no longer worried about my project. I can get up at five AM to finish it. Or maybe Timothy can fucking provide a week's notice next time. I set the laptop on the couch, still open, and stand. I start taking off my jeans.

"Seriously?" he groans.

"What?" I ask. "I'm not comfortable. They're cutting into my waist."

"Right," he mutters.

I return to the couch and pick up my laptop, laying down so my back is flat, my knees up, feet slightly apart. It makes me think of going to see a gynecologist. But I'm pretty sure it won't make Brendan think of that.

And then I feel his foot skimming the outside of my thong. Skim and retreat. Skim and retreat. I push forward a bit the last time he pulls away, chasing. The next time his foot returns, I release a small huff of air, a slightly desperate noise, and he groans, diving toward me. Before I've even shut my laptop he's pushed the fabric to the side and put his magical tongue to work.

"You like that, tease?" he demands.

Yes. Too much. I'm already close and he *just* began. After waiting so long, I feel like I've earned this. I want it to last, and I know for a fact that it won't. He adds two fingers and my whole body jolts, my head hanging off the arm of the couch helplessly as I come. I haven't even finished before his pants are down, a condom is on, and he's pushing inside me, knocking the air from my chest.

"I'm going to fuck you so hard you won't be able to stand when I'm done," he grunts.

And say what you will about Brendan, but he always keeps his promises.

❧ 46 ❧

ERIN

The next afternoon, with thirty minutes to spare, Harper brings me the mock-ups of the ad campaign.

"You should walk in there and forcibly shove these up his ass," she says.

"That would kind of defeat the purpose of staying up all night."

She sighs. "Yeah, well, you shouldn't have done that either. You look terrible."

I *feel* terrible. If I had a body scan right now, it would show that I am ninety percent coffee, and yet I still can't keep my eyes open. I take the mock-ups and knock on Timothy's door. "I've got your stuff for that meeting."

He takes a cursory glance at the pieces and hands them back to me. "The meeting was cancelled, so you'll have a little time to get these cleaned up. Looks like they need it too."

He returns to whatever he was doing before. The stuff I just spent twenty-four hours on is forgotten. This is where Olivia might turn violent, but I've never thrown a punch in my life. I've never even pulled someone's hair.

I fold my arms across my chest. "I stayed up all night working on this."

"You wouldn't have had to stay up all night if you'd gotten it done sooner," he says, still not even bothering to glance up at me.

My voice trembles. "I didn't know you *needed* it done until yesterday afternoon."

"Well, now you have extra time to go over these and refine your work," he says.

I cross my arms over my chest. I hate him. I really fucking hate him. I do not make less than Olivia's nanny to stay up all night and put up with this shit.

"My work is about as refined as it's going to get, Timothy," I reply. "If you need more refinement, consider giving me a damn raise. In the meantime, I'm going home, and I'm going to bed."

He calls after me, his voice stern and full of reprimand, and I just keep walking, straight to the chancellor's office, because he needs to put a face with the work he demands at the last minute all the time.

I'm exhausted, running on nothing but rage at this point. I must *look* like I'm running on rage too; when I step into his secretary's office, she appears slightly alarmed.

"Can I help you?" she asks.

I tell her who I am. I add that I'm a former student, and that I know the chancellor from my days on the cross country team, which is a bit of a stretch. I only met him a few times, and I guarantee he doesn't remember me.

A few minutes later, I'm ushered into his office. It's clear by the look on his face that he has no idea who I am. I introduce myself, mentioning that we met a few times at events in honor of Olivia, who's probably the only ECU graduate to go on to even marginal fame. That softens him up a little. Olivia, in the years since she left, has put our athletics department on the map. He asks what he can help me with.

"I have the marketing campaign you asked for," I tell him,

trying my best not to sound as pissed as I feel. "It's a little rough, since we didn't learn until yesterday that you needed it."

It only occurs to me as I slide the pieces forward that I've just bypassed our workplace hierarchy. I'm going to be written up for this, at the very least. Probably worse. Right now I'm too tired to care much, however.

The chancellor looks confused. "Marketing campaign?" he says. "I didn't ask for this."

I stare at him in confusion for a moment, and then my body goes cold. I think of all the last-minute requests Timothy's made—requests that mostly occurred when he wanted to punish me for something. I wonder if *any* of those requests came from the chancellor.

I can't believe I'm just figuring this out now. And I can't believe I just risked my job for no reason at all.

"I'm sorry," I tell him. "Timothy gave us this project late yesterday and said they were needed today. I thought it must have been something important, given the turnaround time."

"I didn't ask for any of these," he says. He looks at the pieces again. "How on Earth did you get it all done so fast?"

My rage is gone, and the exhaustion hits me so suddenly I think I could curl up in this chair and sleep.

"We stayed up all night—me and one artist," I say, rising with dejection pressing down on my shoulders. "I'm sorry I interrupted you."

I did all this work for nothing and may very well have gotten myself fired the first time I tried to do something about it.

"Does this happen a lot?" he asks. "Last-minute projects like that?"

I hesitate. The diplomatic response would be to assure him it doesn't. But fuck Timothy. "It happens every week."

He nods slowly. "And do you see much of Olivia these days?"

I tell him I do, and he asks me to say hello for him. I get the feeling my connection to Olivia matters far more than the work I did. I just pray it matters enough that he chooses to keep our conversation to himself.

~

WHEN I TELL BRENDAN THE STORY LATER THAT NIGHT, HE looks even more pissed about it than I am. "Please explain to me why the fuck you're still there."

The question doesn't surprise me. Brendan comes home each night raving about the tour he gave that day, spilling over with plans for bigger and more extensive adventures. His income is almost an afterthought because he has a job he'd do for free. "Normal people require this thing called money, Brendan. I have bills."

"But you act like that place is the only job in the entire world," he argues. "There are lots of jobs, and there are lots of jobs you might enjoy, or where you have a chance of getting promoted and don't have to deal with a tool like your boss."

"But I like ECU. In terms of marketing jobs, it's a good cause. What if my next job is marketing cigarettes to children? Or cocaine?"

He cocks a brow. "I haven't seen a whole lot of cocaine advertising directed at kids."

"And I might not make the greatest salary, but it could also be a lot worse. If my dad gets fired again, my parents will need help. And Sean always needs something. That's not changing anytime soon."

He slaps his palm to his face. "Are you fucking serious right now? You're talking about two grown-ass men who can handle their own shit."

"I've just made a lot of huge changes at once," I tell him. "People do that when their lives suck, but mine didn't suck. It just needed improvement. And I'm worried that if I keep changing everything, I'm going to look back and regret what I've done."

He stiffens. "Are you talking about work?" he asks, not looking at me. "Or are you talking about Rob?"

"I don't even know anymore. I don't know what I'm doing." Three months ago I had job security and a fiancé and a very nice home. I had twenty grand in savings. Now I have none of those things. Sometimes people burn a bridge because they must. But you're not supposed to burn them all at once.

BRENDAN
Three Years Earlier

I go to work on Monday, but my tour's been cancelled. Seb, the owner, asks me to go with him to shop for bikes instead. I agree without a second thought. Shopping for bikes is like porn for me. Once it's suggested, it's almost impossible to resist.

The first text from Gabi asking where I am arrives around noon, and it isn't *until* it arrives that I realize I've been waiting for it, bracing myself almost, the way you do before you reach for a light switch when you know it's going to shock you.

It's puzzling even to me, recognizing that I dreaded this text and that I somehow knew it would make me grind my teeth, that I would loosen this tired sigh before I send her a simple reply, telling her I'm looking at bikes.

She's been doing this more and more, ever since the discussion about Erin, keeping tabs on me the moment I'm out of sight.

My irritation with her over something so mild also makes me feel like an asshole. She's my girlfriend. Of course she wants to know where I am. Why the fuck should that bother me?

But just seconds later comes the next text, asking when I'll be home, and I'm annoyed anew. *Because* I'm annoyed, I tell her I'm not sure, knowing even as I write the words that I'm making the problem worse. Gabrielle is not the type to handle any kind of ambiguity well—she approaches life as if it is science, and she wants a precise *why* and *when* and *what* for every question. This is probably why laid-back dudes who lead bike tours don't usually wind up with medical students.

When the follow-up text comes from her—*why don't you know?* —I do the ultimate dick move and just turn off my phone. I want to enjoy this. I love looking at bikes, and she's ruining it by aggravating me. So I'm not going to let her. I'm going to enjoy this, and I'll deal with her afterward.

It's late afternoon by the time I'm done. I head home, checking my phone. There are thirty texts, all of them from her.

She's pissed when I get to the apartment, but I'm pissed too.

"Texting someone thirty times might work with your little pre-med boyfriends," I tell her, "but it's not going to work with me."

Her face falls, which is when I realize I *wanted* to fight with her. I wanted her to stay pissed off. I guess the truth is I want a little air, a break from this thing. I miss not having to be on my best behavior all the time.

She starts to cry, and my irritation vaporizes, replaced by guilt. I'm responsible for this. She's younger than me, and she's also just...young. She has so much less life experience than most twenty-two-year-olds. In this moment, as I watch her weeping, her hair clinging to her face, I know I've made some kind of grave error.

"Gabi," I plead, "don't cry. I'm sorry."

"Are you cheating on me?"

My jaw drops. How she could come to this conclusion when we spend every fucking minute together is beyond me. "What? No! I was seriously looking at bikes. That's it."

"I'm sorry," she says, pressing her face into her hands, crying harder. "I'm not good at being with someone. And now that I've slept with you, I feel like there's nothing to keep you coming back."

I wrap an arm around her, wanting to say anything to make her feel better. "Gabi, that's crazy. Of course there is. I like you. Did you think this was all about me sleeping with you a few times and moving on?"

"I don't know. It's what you've done before, right? I love you, Brendan. I love you so much."

She waits there, wide-eyed and broken, wanting me to say it back. And—because I know the truth will hurt her, because I've fucked this whole thing up so badly, and she's leaving in a little over a month—I do.

❧ 48 ❧

ERIN

"Stop looking so nervous," Harper says, poking her head into my cubicle.

I laugh. "Is it that obvious?"

I've spent the day feeling sick, waiting to be called into Timothy's office. It hasn't happened, but it's made me realize just how often I've waited here, exactly like I am now, to be punished for something, and typically something that isn't my fault.

She pushes more files off my desk and takes a seat.

"You know, you could just hand me the files instead of throwing them on the floor," I suggest.

"It's more fun my way," she says. "So what did you do last night? I barely see you anymore."

I blush and she laughs. "Yes, I know you had many, many orgasms. I meant what did you do before that?"

She wants to know if he took me out, and it bothers me a little. I enjoy our nights in, but I sometimes wonder if we're staying in for reasons he'd rather not discuss.

I shrug. "We cooked dinner? I don't know. It was pretty much the same as always."

Harper's frown tells me she's displeased with my answer. "Well," she sighs, "on the bright side if there's a zombie apocalypse, the two of you will be the only ones to survive."

I tell him what she said when I get to his place that night.

"Of course we'll survive an apocalypse," he says with a cocky grin. "I'm a badass."

I laugh. "I think she meant because we never go out in public."

He's quiet for a moment, long enough that I'm sure I'm about to get the speech: *Erin, we are in the bubble; we aren't dating.*

"My friend Beck has a bar in Elliott Falls," he finally says. "A bunch of friends from school are getting together up there this weekend. You want to go?"

"You want me to go *with* you?" I tease. "In public? You mean actually go out, or would I be wearing an invisibility cloak or something?"

"It's so hot when you reference Harry Potter. Yes, with me, in public. Visible. Unless you're worried about Rob finding out. But he doesn't know any of the people coming."

I tell him I'm not worried, but my smile dims. I hate being reminded that Brendan and I have an expiration date.

"So he's *finally* taking you out," Harper says as I get ready on Friday.

"It's not really a date. It's just a party."

"Which you are attending with a guy. A guy who invited you and with whom you are fornicating. It is, therefore, a date. And since I've conclusively established that you and Brendan are dating..."

"We're not dating."

"Just because he doesn't realize it's a relationship doesn't mean it isn't one," she counters. "So I'm wondering what you plan to do when Rob comes home?"

The question rests like a barbell on my shoulders, pushing so hard I actually want to rub them in response. "You mean what's going to happen with me and Rob?"

"You and Rob. You and Brendan. Brendan and Rob. Wow, it just occurred to me that would make for one unbelievable threesome."

"We won't be having a threesome, I can promise you. And in response to your question, I don't know. I guess no one will be with anyone." Rob can never find out about this, so it has to end with Brendan at some point. And I can't imagine wanting to get back together with Rob now, but if I did, I'd have to tell him about Brendan, and I can't, so...it's probably off the table no matter what.

"Enjoy it while it lasts then," says Harper. She insists that I wear her clothes instead of my own—skinny jeans that are way tighter than I'd normally be seen in and an off-the-shoulder blouse.

I'd never admit it to Harper, and I can barely admit it to myself, but I'm excited for tonight and it *does* feel like a date. He's introducing me to his friends—that has to mean something, right?

Brendan arrives to pick me up and his eyes widen when I open the door.

"Wow," he says, looking me over, head to foot. He yanks me toward him, free hand sliding over my ass, mouth finding mine for a soft, slow kiss—one that lets me know where he'd like it to lead.

I forget, for a moment, that we are not at his place. When his mouth moves to my neck, I groan so loudly that Harper, two rooms away, laughs.

"Erin," he says, pulling away only slightly, "unless you're going to let me fuck you right here in the foyer, we'd better get in the car."

I grab my purse. "I guess you'll just have to wait," I tell him over my shoulder as I walk out the door.

"I have a feeling," he says, his mouth close to my ear, "that this may be a very short night out."

WHEN BRENDAN TOLD ME HIS FRIEND HAD A BAR, I EXPECTED something small. A glorified shack with six bar stools and a juke-box. Instead, the place is sprawling and impressive, with a huge deck—and already so crowded at nine PM that we struggle to find a parking space. I don't know why it matters, but I'm thrilled—I know it's not really a date, necessarily, but suddenly it sort of feels like one.

"Wow. This is not what I was expecting."

"Yeah," he says with a half-hearted smile. "It's something."

I'm not sure what happened to the Brendan I drove here with, but the one beside me now seems to have lost his interest in this night out entirely over the course of five seconds.

I slide my fingers through his as we walk toward the bar. "You okay?"

He nods, pulling his hand away as he reaches for the door. Inside, a group of people wave to us from the deck. I follow as he heads in their direction, wondering what he's told them about me, remembering the summer we worked together and how infuriating I found the endless parade of girls he brought out at night. Is that how his friends will see me? Or has he let them know that we are different?

I have my answer pretty quickly.

"This is Erin," he tells the group. "My sister-in-law's best friend."

No, I'm not a part of the parade. I'm *less*. He's just explained my presence here in a way that makes it sound like he was forced to bring me. He didn't even introduce me as *his* friend. He finds me a seat at a table with only one available chair, and then he walks away—no kiss, no hand to my shoulder, no promise that he'll return. I smile awkwardly at this group of people who all know each other while my stomach sinks to the floor.

I didn't realize how much I wanted this to be a date until now, when I discover Brendan doesn't consider it one. And what makes it all worse is that it's clear he wants no one here to think it is either.

"So you're friends with Olivia?" one girl at the table asks. "Are you visiting from Seattle?"

"No," I reply. "I live here. How do you all know Brendan?"

"College. He was with a different girl every night," she says with a rueful laugh, twisting the wedding ring on her finger. She glances over at him, currently talking to a very pretty girl in the corner. "It doesn't look like he's changed much."

They start exchanging stories I'd rather not hear. Brendan with twins. Brendan getting stalked by girls on campus. Brendan caught climbing out of a girl's dorm window. I listen in silence with a forced smile on my face.

Even after the conversation moves on to other things, my brain does not. As soon as I can extricate myself, I go the bathroom, where I'm forced to listen to two girls at the sink plot ways to get their married boss in bed. It reminds me of the conversation I overheard at a work dinner of Rob's, long before last year's disastrous holiday party: Christina saying that the second she got the chance, she was going down on Rob "like it's the end of the world." Only *Christina* would think giving someone a blow job was a good way to spend her last few moments alive.

I was so mad at the time, and I'm still mad. She's gotten her wish by now, I'm sure. Probably multiple times. I can't tell if what I'm feeling is jealousy, or just pure rage that she got what she wanted.

Why? Why is my entire history littered with men I couldn't trust, men who didn't want me quite as much as they claimed? And Brendan is worse than all of them: happy enough to fuck me as long as he never has to acknowledge it to his friends. I was stupid to think I meant anything to him, and I was stupid to believe this might be a date, but that doesn't mean I have to continue being stupid.

I walk out of the bathroom, heading for the front door. A hand closes around my elbow to stop me and I want, so badly, for it to be Brendan.

Even though I know it won't be him, I feel that familiar,

sinking disappointment when I see a stranger standing there. It was a ridiculous thing to hope for anyway. What possible explanation could Brendan offer for tonight that I'd find acceptable?

"Hey," the guy says. "I think I know you from somewhere."

He's tall, though not as tall as Brendan, and cute, but not as cute as Brendan. He's got the same kind of confidence, though—a guy who's used to getting what and who he wants. He starts trying to figure out how he knows me, without success.

"I think I just have one of those faces that looks familiar to everyone," I tell him.

"Maybe it's because you look like that actress. The British one. Sienna somebody. Do you know who I'm talking about? She—"

Suddenly a massive shape inserts itself between us. Brendan, glaring down at me with the wrath of a hurricane.

"I've been looking for you," he says.

The guy I've been talking to wraps his arm casually around my back, hanging a hand off my hip.

"Remove your hand," Brendan says, his voice a low growl, "or I'll fucking help you remove it."

The guy removes his hand, not that it matters. Brendan's already pulling me away, his fingers twining with mine, too tight and restrictive to ever be considered sweet. He pulls me around the corner of the bar and presses me to the wall.

"I thought you were all ready to get back together with Rob?" he spits out. "But based on the way you were flirting with that guy, it sure didn't seem like it."

"Since when do you care? You invited me to this thing and then ditched me."

"I care," he says angrily. "I saw a guy Rob knows walking in when we pulled up. I just thought it was best if it didn't seem like we were here together."

No matter what his logic, I'm not ready to forgive him. Did he really have no idea that I'd be hurt by the way he introduced me to everyone? Or when he stood across the deck flirting with someone else? "You could have just told me that," I reply. "And you took it way too far."

He flinches, running a hand over his head. "I know. I just..." he trails off, his teeth grinding. I don't want to forgive him, but I can feel myself softening.

"You just what?"

He shakes his head. "Nothing," he says. "But I want to take you home now." His voice is low, skimming my skin.

It's a weird, primal thing, the way just the sound of his voice and the look on his face can create this shift inside me, making my skin feel stretched too tight over my bones, lips tingling, everything so sensitive, seeming infinitely fragile. I go from feeling nothing to feeling everything in a second.

"Maybe I don't want to go home with you. You seemed pretty interested in the girl out on the deck. Maybe she'll be game."

His lashes lower, his mouth hovering so close that I swear I can feel it before it touches mine.

"She's my friend's wife. I don't want to take anyone else home, and you don't want me to."

"I'm still pissed," I say. But the words are slightly breathless, unconvincing.

"I know," he says, "but I can probably do a thing or two that will make you forgive me."

As we drive back down the mountain in utter silence, I try to figure out what happened tonight. I glance over at him, making out the silhouette of his jaw in the moonlight—blade sharp, his mouth grim. He's every bit as unhappy as I am.

"What's the matter?" I ask.

It takes him a second to reply, and he sounds reluctant when he does. "I'm sorry about before. I shouldn't have pulled you away from that guy. You probably *should* be meeting people. Seeing what's out there."

My heart begins a long, dizzying spiral downward. I don't want to meet guys. I don't want to meet anyone who isn't Brendan or be with anyone who isn't Brendan. And I don't want him to want me to.

"Why?"

"Rob's going to push hard to get back together. You should know what your options are, before he comes home."

I could tell him I don't want options. That I can't imagine getting back together with Rob now. Except that would puncture the bubble, wouldn't it? The fact that we should not be doing this, that we both believe this must end, is also what makes it possible.

We get to his apartment, and there are no slow kisses, no leisurely removal of clothes. It is quick and silent—as if it is urgent, or as if he wishes it weren't happening at all.

BRENDAN'S CELL RINGS LATE THAT NIGHT. ANOTHER CALL HE rushes to the other room to take. I remain in bed, but even from where I lie, I can tell the woman on the other end is yelling at him. I wonder if it's Gabi, or maybe someone else, just as besotted as me, who can't seem to move on.

Either option is painful, because whoever this girl is, he's still taking her calls. Which most likely means she still matters to him, and if tonight was any evidence, she probably matters more than me.

❦ 49 ❧

BRENDAN
Three Years Earlier

"D o you love me?" Gabi asks every morning.
There are no words for how uncomfortable this
question makes me. Because I said it once, I can't
exactly stop saying it now. So she asks every morning, looking up
at me with that mixture of expectation and unrest in her face, and
I tell her I do. She asks every afternoon. She asks when we go to
bed. She asks and asks, and I have to wonder if the reason she
keeps asking is because she knows, like I do, that what I say isn't
true.

Her need for constant reassurance begins to wear on me. It's
not enough that we're in the same place. She has to be right beside
me with her fingers wound through mine. She's jealous of Erin.
She's also jealous of the book in my hand, the television show I'm
watching, phone calls to my mother. She's jealous of anything that
directs my attention away from her. I've begun counting the days
until she leaves.

∼

ON A RARE AFTERNOON WITHOUT HER AROUND, I GO ONLINE and look at pictures from the wedding. It's an exercise in masochism, but I can't seem to stop. I remember watching Erin walk down the aisle. It was the moment I finally knew I could commit. God, I wish things had happened differently. I wish she'd been willing to hear me out. Mostly, I wish I'd been worthy of her in the first place.

When Gabi gets home from her tour, I don't really feel like having sex. That makes her cry, of course. *Everything* seems to make her cry these days.

She asks if I'm cheating. Is jerking off to thoughts of your best friend's girlfriend cheating? I doubt it. I tell her I'm not.

She isn't reassured because she knows I *never* turn her down. It even surprises me a little, the fact that I don't want to. I guess maybe I'm kind of bored with our whole thing.

Or maybe it's that I know it would be better with someone else.

❧ 50 ❧

ERIN

I call Sean for the first time in nearly two weeks, and the moment he answers, I know something is wrong. He doesn't sound happy to hear from me, and as we talk he volunteers no information. With Sean, these are very bad signs.

"You sound distracted," I say. "Are you in the middle of something?"

"Uh, no. Just studying."

Something feels off about the conversation. I couldn't begin to pinpoint what it is, but I know when Sean is lying, and he's definitely lying right now.

I ask how classes are going, and in the lag between my question and his answer, my stomach slides to my feet. Sean only needs a few credits to graduate, but I've already paid tuition for the counseling program he'll start in September, so we're on a fairly rigid timeline. I wonder if he's already flushed my life savings down the toilet somehow.

"Oh," he finally says. "Yeah. They're good."

"What are you taking again?" I ask, though I know exactly

what he's taking. I filled out his registration form myself when he missed the summer deadline.

"Hey, I've got to run," he says. "Can I call you back?"

There's nothing I can do but agree, knowing he won't call back. Knowing something's gone wrong, and he's going to avoid me until he's fixed it. Or made things worse trying.

LATE THAT NIGHT, WHEN THE PHONE RINGS, I KNOW BETTER than to hope it's Sean. He wouldn't call this late, and it's been weeks since I've heard from my father. I knew the reprieve wouldn't last.

I grab it on the second ring and take it to the other room, but no sooner have I sat on the couch and begun whispering to my father than Brendan takes the seat beside me.

I don't want him here for this. The two times we've driven to Denver, my father was comatose. This—my father sobbing—is worse in some ways.

I wave him off. "Go back to sleep," I whisper.

He shakes his head. "Your dad?" he mouths, and I nod.

He gets his phone, directs Uber to the address my father gives me, and the two of us sit there, me with my head on Brendan's chest, watching the car's progress on his phone while I listen to my father cry on the other one.

"Your dad needs help," he says after we finally hang up.

My eyes close. "I tried that, the summer after my junior year. My mom threw me out." I kept up appearances the whole time, though. It felt like someone in the family had to prove to the world we weren't a lost cause, but it just made me feel like a fraud.

"I don't know why you've never given up on them," he says. "They don't deserve you. They don't deserve your loyalty."

"I can't just walk away," I reply. "This is a problem I helped create."

"How can you say that?" he asks. "You're not holding a bottle to your father's mouth every night. You're not buying Sean coke."

I've been through enough family therapy to understand the role I've played. The role I continue to play. I just can't seem to stop. "I've spent my entire life covering for my dad and rescuing him, doing the same thing for Sean. I've kept them from getting better, from learning the lessons they should have learned. My brother and my father are sick, but my mom and I...we're sick too."

He's quiet, and I hold my breath, wondering if I've said too much. "That's why you hid it all from Rob," he says after a moment. There's astonishment in his voice. "Not because your family is such a disaster but because you think you're just as bad. You think he'd like you less if he knew."

"He would. Anyone would."

"I don't," he says, pulling me closer. "I think maybe I like you better for it."

We sit like that for a while, and I feel something changing inside me. A secret you keep to yourself festers and grows until it begins to seem monstrous in your eyes. But now, in one fell swoop, it isn't something quite so poisonous, something I can barely stand to acknowledge. It isn't pretty, and it isn't admirable, but it isn't quite as ugly as it seemed when I kept it to myself.

Eventually he leads me back to bed, and pulls me closer than he ever has, his fingers tracing some secret pattern over my skin as I fall asleep.

🦋 51 🦋

ERIN

I should have known going to the chancellor would catch up with me.

It's just after lunch when Timothy returns from a meeting with him, slamming the office door so hard it rattles the drawers of the file cabinet.

"Erin," he says. "My office. Now."

When I walk in, he is crumpling up one of the new campaign brochures, and then he swivels in his seat and throws it at me. I watch in shock as it bounces off my arm and hits the floor.

"The chancellor's notes are on there," he sneers. "Did you really think you'd get away with going above me?"

I stare from him to the paper on the floor.

"Pick it up. Fix it. And don't let me see your face until it's done."

I'm so shocked that I feel blank—not worried, not scared, not even angry. But I know I'm completely over this situation. "No," I reply quietly. "You don't get to treat me like this. You don't get to treat anyone like this." I return to my cubicle, determined to do what I should have done long ago.

216

I grab my purse and walk across campus to Human Resources, and as I go my shock finally gives way to rage. I'm ready to report him for this and a hundred other things he's done. The late nights, the disrespect, the threats. As I think about it, the list grows in my head...and then fades when I reach their office and find it closed. A note on the door informs me they're away for a team-building retreat and will return after the weekend.

I'm left with a whole lot of anger and no outlet for it. Fifteen minutes later I find myself in Brendan's apartment, ranting, and it's not until my whole story has spun out that it occurs to me that showing up here unannounced is a girlfriendish thing to do, the kind of thing I'd expect him to hate. Fortunately, he's so pissed off on my behalf that he doesn't seem to notice. "I have an easier way to deal with this than going to HR," he says, his hand curling into a fist.

"You and Olivia. She suggested I build a car bomb the last time he bothered me."

"I promise I won't use a weapon," he says.

"Brendan, this isn't the Wild West. Physical violence solves nothing."

"You know who says that? People who know they can't win a fight. I don't have that problem."

I smile. He is ridiculous but also sweet. I shouldn't, but I like his outdated chivalry. "I am *forbidding* you to beat him up, Brendan." I bite my lip. "Sorry I just showed up without calling. I wasn't thinking. Do you have another tour?"

He shakes his head, running a thumb over his lip. "You want to do something?" he asks.

"Are we going to the movies again?" I ask.

The theater last week was actually his suggestion. I should have known when he insisted I wear a skirt that he'd planned a Brendan-like twist on the experience.

"No movie today," he says, "but definitely wear the skirt."

He takes me to a vineyard a friend of his just bought. The bar and tasting room haven't opened yet, but a small shop on the ground floor is selling wine and cheese. Brendan buys a bottle of pinot noir and way more food than we could possibly eat—four kinds of cheese, crackers, prosciutto, Marcona almonds—and leads me across the grounds to a spot near the lake.

It's a perfect day for a picnic: a light breeze, sunny but not hot. I spread the blanket, and he lays out the food. Does he realize how romantic this is? It may be the most romantic, date-type thing I've ever done in my life. All we need is a violinist and maybe some swans and we're straight out of a Nicholas Sparks novel.

He opens the bottle of pinot and pours some into plastic cups for both of us.

"You bought a lot of cheese. We're never eating all this."

"Don't try to act like you're a delicate little sparrow," he says. "I saw you pound a large movie popcorn last week, remember?"

I flush, remembering what else occurred in that theater.

He hands me a glass of wine. "You're blushing, Erin."

"No, I'm not."

He catches my eye, his mouth turning up almost imperceptibly. "What are you thinking about?"

"Syria," I reply primly. "Did you know we've now got a large percentage of our military deployed to Syria?"

I completely made this up, but I don't see Brendan reading *The Wall Street Journal* too often, so I'm probably safe.

"Do you always blush when you're talking about Syria?" he asks. "Where, by the way, we do not have a large military presence. Just admit that you'll never enter a theater again without thinking about last week."

"Will you?"

That light in his eyes turns feral. God, it's ridiculous how little it takes to make me want him. He takes the wine from my hand. "Yeah, but there are one or two more things I wish we'd done there, though."

He pushes me onto my back, wrapping a hand under one knee to pull my legs apart. "What are you doing?" I ask, but my voice has already gone breathy and slightly desperate. He pushes my skirt up around my waist. "Someone could see us."

"They can't. I've checked every angle from the main building." He slides my panties off and pockets them. "And sex out here is on my bucket list."

"You're sure no one can see us?" I ask.

"Positive."

I smile. "Then get on your back. I have a bucket list too."

52

ERIN

On Monday, I stop by Human Resources on my way in to work. They've apparently done enough team building that they can do their jobs today, but I hate the counselor from the moment I enter her office. She speaks to me in an overly soft voice, but there's something patronizing there too, as if she's humoring me, before I've even said a word.

I tell her about the incident, about Timothy's habit of putting assignments on my desk late in the day and demanding they be done by morning. When I conclude, she asks me why I didn't report this sooner.

"I came by on Friday," I reply. "But the note on the door said you were at a retreat."

"You could have emailed, though, or left a message." Her voice is still gentle, but there's an undeniable message of *you fucked up* underlying it.

"Or I could come back first thing Monday morning, which is what I'm doing," I reply.

"The problem, Erin, is that when an employee comes in to file a complaint after she's already been written up, it looks somewhat suspicious."

"Written up?" I ask. "I haven't been written up."

"Timothy submitted a complaint Friday afternoon. He said you refused to complete your work and walked out of the office without requesting leave or informing anyone. He also said you've shown a pattern of 'volatile' behavior over the last few months."

"He crumpled up a brochure and threw it at me, then told me to pick it up and fix it," I tell her. "Was I just supposed to *obey?*"

"His version is somewhat different," she says. "You're welcome to file a complaint, of course. Just be aware that your credibility is suspect, under the circumstances."

When she hands me a brochure *I* wrote about the Employee Assistance Program, it takes every ounce of restraint I possess not to ball it up and hurl it at her, since that kind of behavior is apparently not a big deal around here.

I fume all day long. Timothy says nothing, but seems to be watching every move I make, eager for me to slip up. I wonder how exactly he thinks he'll benefit if I'm gone? No one else here is going to take over my workload, and they'll never find someone who'll work the hours I do for the little they pay.

The only person I want to discuss this with is Brendan, but he's in Boulder while Dorothy gets her final round of radiation. I know that he won't call, but I keep my phone close by just in case. When it rings that night, I dive toward it, only to discover Rob's name instead of Brendan's. Until now he's respected my request that he not call, and I'm not sure why I answer. It's mostly guilt, I suspect.

"Hey babe," he says softly. "I know it's late there. I just...miss you. How are things?"

I think I'm falling in love with your best friend—your best friend who claims he's no longer friends with you, by the way. The most important things in my life all revolve around Brendan, which means there's little I can say.

I focus on work instead. I tell him about the argument with

Timothy and the complaint to HR. I really only tell him so I have something to say that isn't related to Brendan, but he actually gives me pretty good advice in response. I'd forgotten his strengths during this time apart—forgot that he's smart, and focused, and no one is better in a crisis. If there's ever an apocalypse, Rob will be the one person who acquires food and shelter without breaking a sweat.

As we get off the phone, he tells me he wishes we hadn't broken up, that he misses me. Though I choose not to say the same, talking to him has reminded me of something I absolutely *do* miss, something I don't have right now: I miss being with someone I know for a fact is mine. I miss that a lot.

ON FRIDAY I'M ON MY WAY TO MEET BRENDAN AT HIS FRIEND Beck's bar, already late thanks to Harper's insistence that I allow her to add a few highlights to my hair, when Rob calls again. I answer only because it's three AM in Amsterdam, and nobody calls that late without a reason.

"Hey, what's up?" I ask. Already I sound eager to get off the phone.

"I just wanted to hear your voice," he replies.

I sigh, rubbing a hand over my eyes. It's funny how his sudden desire to hear my voice coincides with my sudden desire to *not* hear his. "I was just on my way out."

"With a guy?" he asks.

There's a part of me that would like to say *yes, with a guy, because this is what you did. This is what happens when you take things for granted*. But that only opens questions about *who* that guy might be.

"I think this isn't a good line of discussion, for either of us," I reply. "I don't want to know what you've done and I don't owe you details about what I've done."

"I miss you, Erin," he says. "I miss you so damn much. I wish I'd never let you go. I wish I'd never left in the first place."

Guilt hits me hard, and unexpectedly. He made mistakes, but I do care about him. I don't want him to be unhappy, so I hate what I have to say next.

"I think it was probably for the best."

The silence on his end of the phone makes me feel even worse. I've heard words like that before, the kind that land like a punch to the gut. I hate that I'm the one responsible.

"You sound like you don't want to start over," he finally says.

"I changed a lot when I was with you," I tell him, "in ways that weren't great for me. I'm not saying it was your fault, or even that we weren't happy together, but...I'm happier now."

There. I said it. I wish I felt proud of myself for my honesty, but really I just feel sick.

"I had no idea I was making you unhappy before. You have to at least give me a chance."

"Rob..." I begin, but I don't know what to say after that. "I just don't see it working out."

"It will," he says. "You'll see. I can change. And when I come home I'm going to prove it to you."

Except I don't want him to change. I don't want him to prove anything. I want him to walk away.

I'M NEARLY AN HOUR LATE BY THE TIME I FIND BRENDAN, sitting at a table with friends. We haven't been out with other people since the disastrous party a few weeks back, so I approach warily, but he stands and pulls out the chair beside him. I guess this means he's going to acknowledge my presence tonight, but it's a little sad that I've got the bar set so low. For all Rob's faults, he always seemed proud to have me beside him.

Brendan introduces me to everyone again. At least this time it's not as his *sister-in-law's* friend.

"So what happened?" he asks, pouring me a beer. "You were supposed to be here an hour ago."

"Sorry," I sigh. "Harper was messing with my hair and then Rob called."

The softness leaves his face. "I thought you told him not to call."

It sounds like an accusation, which is ridiculous—*he's* the one who doesn't want a relationship. How can it possibly matter if I've spoken to Rob? "I did."

He sets the pitcher down heavily. "So is this first time you've heard from him?"

Another accusation. I sit straight in my chair, muscles tensed. "No."

"What did he want?" he asks, his voice tight.

I shrug. "Just to talk about stuff. What's going to happen when he comes home, that kind of thing."

He sets the glass down, too hard, and his chair scrapes the floor as he pushes away from the table. "I'm gonna get another round," he announces. He doesn't even glance at me as he goes, just leaves me there with a bunch of people I barely know, all of them pretending not to notice the sudden tension between us.

His friends continue their conversation but I struggle to follow it. I'm too busy trying to figure out what the hell just happened.

Is he pissed off? It feels like I can't win with Brendan sometimes. He wouldn't even be spending time with me right now if he knew I'd called it off with Rob for good. These are *his* rules. He can't get mad at me for following them.

I glance toward the bar. He's not alone—there's a ridiculously beautiful girl hanging all over him. Literally. She's got one hand on his shoulder and the other on his arm, leaning against him. And he might not be encouraging it, but he sure as hell doesn't appear to be *discouraging* it.

My blood begins to pulse behind my ears. The roar is so loud, I can barely hear anything, although the sound of Brendan returning to his seat is as explosive as a detonating bomb.

"You guys remember Paulina?" he asks, introducing the girl from the bar.

The night is warm, but suddenly I'm shivering, the fair hair on my arms standing on end.

I knew one day Brendan would be done with me and return to girls exactly like Paulina, the same kind of girls he always left with back when I was in school. I just didn't realize it would feel like this, that it would cut this way and rob me of breath and leave me half blind. And I didn't realize it was going to happen *now*, in front of me. Him bringing that girl here hurts more than anything Rob did in all of our years together.

Brendan and his friends are moving around, trying to make room for Paulina at the table. A part of me doesn't want to give up my ground, wants to stay here and fight for him, charm him, lure him back. But I will not lower myself to fighting for a man, especially one who's treating me the way Brendan is right now, and my anger is on the cusp of turning to tears—just the kind of crazy, emotional response I'm sure Brendan dreads from any female.

"Take my chair," I tell her, rising, the words as small and cold as chips of ice. "I can't stay."

Every head at the table jerks toward me. Later on, I'll be embarrassed that I'm making a scene, that I didn't at least feign an emergency of some kind to explain the way I sat down at the table and left not ten minutes later. But right now I just need to get out of here before I burst into tears.

I walk out of the bar, my hands shaking as I pull up Uber on my phone. I can't believe I expected to leave with Brendan, assuming things would go well. They've never once gone well when we're in public.

I hear the bar door swing open, and a moment later Brendan stands in front of me. The phone is wrenched from my hand.

"Give it back," I demand.

"No," Brendan says, cutting down some narrow path that leads to the side of the bar, and moving so fast I have to run to catch up to him. Between the darkness and my three-inch heels, it's harder than it sounds.

"Give me back my fucking phone!" I shout.

He rounds on me. "What's your rush, Erin? Eager to have another romantic chat with Rob?" I've adjusted to the darkness just enough to see the rage in his eyes.

"What do you care?" I reply. "You *obviously* weren't going home alone. And since I'm clearly not enough for you, just go back inside and get her."

"I don't want her. I didn't even invite her to the table. She just followed me there."

Part of me wants to believe him, but another part of me insists it's time to face facts. What happened tonight is going to happen eventually—when Brendan tires of me, or when Rob comes home —and when it does, I'll be destroyed. That's why you don't give yourself to someone with whom there's an expiration date; because you're probably not getting all of yourself back when it ends.

"Give me back my phone. I don't need this shit."

"I think you do," he replies, and I find myself pressed against the wall. His mouth lands on mine at nearly the same moment, his fingers digging into my back, pulling me so tight against him I can barely get a full breath. It's not Brendan's usual kiss—there's something rough and desperate about it, the rasp of his unshaved jaw scraping my skin, the hard press of his mouth and the thrust of his tongue. I've never been so excited in my life, and I've also never been so heartbroken. Every bad thing I've felt over the past hour is something I know I'm going to feel again.

I hear the sound of his zipper, and then his fingers slide between my legs, pushing my thong to the side.

"Already wet," he says smugly. "That didn't take long."

He lifts me against the wall and pushes inside me so hard that I feel winded from it. He pins me there, effortlessly, capturing my small moans with his mouth. The relentless slap of his skin against mine is the only sound I hear.

"Oh, God," he groans. "This...*fuck*."

He doesn't complete the thought, and he doesn't need to. Sex with Brendan is always amazing, but this is different. Everything is slicker and hotter and more immediate. It's only just started, and I'm already close.

His hands tighten under my ass as he thrusts harder, once, twice, my breathing nearly as harsh as his. He buries his mouth in my neck. "Christ," he groans. "I'm not gonna last."

I dig my fingers into the bunched muscles beneath his shirt, tighten myself around him. "Don't squeeze like that," he pleads.

Except I can't help it. Because I can't last either.

"Oh, God," I moan, my head going backward, eyes squeezed shut. It's so good that I hear nothing, don't care that we're in public, am only vaguely aware of the low growl in his chest as he comes.

He's still holding me up against the wall, his head pressed to my shoulder.

"Holy hell," he breathes. "That was...I have no words."

I don't either, but everything I feel is too jumbled to make sense of right now. Sex with him is amazing and somehow just got better, but it's always tinged with the knowledge that it's not going to last. He makes me happier than anyone ever has, but he makes me sadder too.

He lifts me just enough to pull out, and when he does, something wet starts dripping down my inner thigh.

"Shit," I gasp, staring at my legs. "You didn't wear a condom. That's why it was different."

He looks as astonished as I do. "Fuck," he says, rubbing his eyes. "We can get a morning-after pill or something, right?"

"I'm not worried about *pregnancy*," I reply. "I'm on the pill. I'm worried about the fact that you've slept with more girls than most men even *meet* over the course of their lives and I don't feel like dying of AIDS just yet."

"The only other girl I haven't used a condom with since *high school* was Gabi."

I ignore him, sliding away and fixing my dress. "I'd like my phone back."

"You're still mad?" he asks.

I fold my arms across my chest. "You hurt me when you brought that girl to the table. Maybe this isn't a real relationship, but if you bring me somewhere, you don't let someone else hang all over you. How would you have reacted if I'd done that to you?"

His mouth opens, then closes again. "I just—" he begins, and then stops himself with a sigh. "You're right. I'm sorry." He closes the distance between us, so close that I can feel the whisper of his breath over my skin. "I'm so, so sorry." He presses his mouth to the corner of my lips, to my cheekbones, my eyelids. "Let's go home, okay?" he asks.

I tell myself I'm forgiving him because he called it *home*, as if his place is ours, and because he's so full of regret. But the truth is I was probably going to forgive him no matter what.

❧ 53 ❧

BRENDAN
Three Years Earlier

I come home from a tour, and Gabi is crying. My shit is spread all over the floor—personal shit she had no business going through. Sitting beside her on the bed are pictures of Erin. Erin grinning ear-to-ear after a crazy bike ride. Erin in her brides-maid's dress with her head thrown back, laughing. Erin turning back toward the camera with that knowing look of hers.

"Is this her?" Gabi cries.

I grit my teeth. "You had no right to go through my stuff."

"I was cleaning the closet," she says. "It fell."

I don't believe her, but I also feel like I've driven her to this—she's insecure because I've made her insecure, because I told her I'm not going with her to California, and when she talks about leaving for Stanford, my words of regret sound as forced as they are. Because when I sleep with her, I am thinking of someone else, and even in our best moments, I know I'd be happier with someone else.

Only an asshole would ask her to move out at this point, when she has just a little over a week left in Italy and nowhere else to go.

But God knows I wish that I could. I hate that she went through my stuff. I hate coming home to her at all, if I'm being honest. Sometime over the past week or so it's like a light switched off inside her. Everything about her just seems dark now—she's either angry or sad, every minute of the day.

She demands to know why I kept all of the photos of Erin. I tell her I didn't remember they were there, that Erin and I are barely even friends. At least the last part is true. Erin and I aren't friends. She's hated me ever since the night of the wedding, and while I could never hate her, I hated being around her during those weeks before I left Colorado. I hate who I became around her and Rob, how bitter I felt, how petty and resentful. So Erin and I aren't friends now, and we never will be. If it were up to me, I'd never lay eyes on her again.

❧ 54 ❧

ERIN

T hings feel different with Brendan after our argument. All weekend he is gentler with me, as if it's possible he's changed his mind about what this could be. I still want the kind of future I once envisioned with Rob: stability and children and Little League games. A small piece of me has begun to hope, though, that I could have some version of that future with Brendan instead.

We spend Saturday night inside. He convinces me to make him coconut bars and while I bake he sits on the kitchen counter with a map, discussing the first week-long bike tour he's planning for next spring. I catch myself wishing I could go. I catch myself thinking he might actually *want* me to. Dangerous, impossible thoughts.

Later, we're lying in bed. The song we danced to at Will and Olivia's wedding comes on and he pulls me to my feet to dance, though I'm clad in nothing but a T-shirt. What might have happened if the deejay's announcement hadn't interrupted us that night? When I got back to the reception only to discover he'd left with the wedding coordinator, my heart broke so thoroughly I thought it would never be put back together.

"We've danced to this before," I tell him.

He smiles. "At the wedding. Believe me, I remember. I wanted to kiss you so badly I'm still not sure how I held back until I got you around the corner."

My head falls to his chest, remembering it all. *Why didn't you wait, Brendan? How could have seemed so certain I was what you wanted only to change your mind minutes later?*

"Sometimes I wish that night had gone a different way," he admits. "But it all worked out for the best. I just would have hurt you."

I long to tell him he *did* hurt me, but this isn't the time for brutal honesty. "If I got hurt, that would have been on me, not you. How someone reacts to what you've done isn't your responsibility. It's not even your business."

"No," he says. "It's a pattern with me. Gabi's not the only girl I ever hurt. There were girls in high school, in college. One of them left school because of me. I just bring it out in people."

He sounds so lost and broken as he says it that my heart squeezes into a tight knot. Even if it can't be with me, I want Brendan to find someone. I want him to allow himself to really be loved and to give it back to someone. I guess, like Dorothy and Olivia, I finally believe he's capable of it, despite ample evidence he's not.

"You're giving yourself way too much credit, Brendan. You didn't bring the crazy out in those girls, you just chose poorly. Normal people don't drop out of school over a break-up. Can you see Olivia reacting like that? Or me? Just allow yourself to consider the possibility."

He pulls me closer. "I'm trying. I really am."

It's the first time in all the weeks we've been doing this that it feels like he's offered me a sliver of hope.

∼

THE WEATHER IS PERFECT ON SUNDAY, SO WE TAKE HIS KAYAK out to the Eleven Mile Reservoir. It's peaceful, being here with him. I find myself laughing more, smiling more, relishing the feel of the sun on my face, the breeze on my skin.

When we get back to his apartment, he pulls me to the hammock and we curl up together, a light blanket over us while the breeze from the French doors streams in.

His mouth ghosts over my cheek, his nose brushing across my skin, as if he's trying to memorize me using all of his senses at once. "I like you best just like this," he says, his tongue flickering out to taste my neck before he lowers his mouth and pulls at the skin, drawing a small, needy sigh from my throat. "Just you, sunburned and sandy." He pulls the blanket aside and slips my T-shirt over my head. The hammock swings and he puts a foot on the floor to steady us. "With miles and miles of skin to taste." His hand skates up the inside of my thigh, brushing lightly until it is exactly where he wants it, and then he draws a nipple into his mouth, pulling on it just enough to keep me on a tightrope between pain and pleasure. "So I can listen to you gasp." And then his fingers slide inside me, and I arch toward him, helplessly, gasping just the way he predicted.

His fingers continue to move, brushing over me in a pattern designed to tease but not satisfy. "More," I whisper.

He rolls over so he's above me. "Is that what you need, Erin?" he breathes as he pushes inside me, his eyes squeezing shut for a moment as if it's just too much to keep them open.

"Yes," I sigh. "That."

The light glimmers and dances around us, and I hear only the sound of our breath and his quiet words. I wish we could stay here, just like this, for hours and days and weeks.

I love him.

The words arrive like something I've known all along. Just like when, as a child, I'd bury my feet in the sand. I knew exactly what was there, if I was only willing to look. But I didn't want to see it.

I don't want to feel this way. Rob hurt me, but Brendan—he could destroy me entirely, irreparably. And it seems almost inevitable that he will.

❧ 55 ❧

ERIN

The sun is just beginning to rise when I pull up to Harper's house on Monday. I climb out of the car, grabbing my bag with the weekend's clothes shoved inside haphazardly, and start toward the house...to find Rob sitting on the steps.

I stare at him, wide-eyed, holding an overnight bag. Undoubtedly looking exactly like I feel: as if I've been caught red-handed.

It went without saying that if we broke up there'd be other people. I never doubted for a minute that he'd take Christina up on her generous offers, if he hadn't already. But seeing me stroll in at the crack of dawn is the equivalent of having it said aloud.

"I guess I don't have to ask if there's someone else," he says. There's nothing accusatory in his voice. He's just upset, which is so much worse. I've never seen his face as long as it is right now, and he doesn't even know the worst part.

"I...didn't know you were here," I reply lamely. "I thought you had six more weeks there."

"I did but I wanted to see you," he says. "I came here straight from the airport."

That shouldn't make me feel guilty—I didn't ask him to do it, and I didn't know he was here—but I feel guilty anyway. Especially when I consider what I was doing during those hours he spent waiting.

He stands, looking thinner and less sure of himself than he did before he left, and I'm struck by an intense wave of familiarity, homesickness. There are parts of our life that I miss, and seeing him reminds me of all of them at once. I could have been *happier* when we were together, but I also wasn't completely unhappy.

He wraps me in his arms. This is familiar too, all of it. His smell and his size and the way we line up together, and suddenly I grieve everything that's gone. With Brendan, I exist in a sick cycle of hope and panic—one day cautiously optimistic, and the next certain the end is coming. That was never the case with Rob, and it strikes me that there's a lot to be said for knowing where you stand with someone.

He pulls back after a moment. "I don't want any details. I never, ever want any details. I just need to know if it's serious."

Serious.

Could I possibly claim that it's serious, when the end is imminent? When Brendan won't even acknowledge me in public? Could I possibly claim that it's *not* serious when it feels like Brendan is holding my heart tight in his careless fist?

"No. It's not," I reply.

The sun falls across the yard in a sudden stripe of muted gold. I tell him I've got to get work.

"Can I see you later?" he asks.

"How long are you in town?"

He swallows. "I was hoping to talk to you about that. Do you think we could meet for lunch?"

It feels too soon. It feels like I need a month before I hear what he might have to say. But that's just cowardice, so I reluctantly agree.

He stares at me for a long second. "You're so beautiful, Erin. I know I've said it a hundred times, but I'm seeing you now, and I can't believe I ever let you go without a fight."

He leaves, and I find myself fervently hoping he hasn't decided to fight for me now, either.

∾

I SIT AT MY DESK ALL MORNING, SICK WITH NERVES, STRUGGLING to focus on my job.

As much as I want to call Brendan, I don't. I want to talk to Rob first, as if there's anything he could say that would keep Brendan from ending things with me.

Rob is already waiting when I get to the restaurant. His face, as I approach the table, is wistful and hopeful at once. We chitchat at first, like business associates. He asks after my family, and I give him the high points. I ask after his, and he does the same, although I doubt he has to do quite as much selective sharing.

"It's so good to see you," he says.

He reaches across the table, his fingers twining with mine. I'd have expected to want my hand back, but I don't. We've done this for so long, it's almost muscle memory at this point.

"I didn't even want to go the house," he says, "knowing you weren't there. Except you never even liked that house, did you?"

I shrug. "Maybe. But relationships are about compromise."

"Yeah," he agrees. "Except you did all the compromising. And because you gave everything up so easily, I thought none of it mattered to you. But it did. You stopped even asking me for the things you wanted."

If he were Brendan, I could explain that this is how I was raised: you ask for nothing, you fight for nothing, you keep everyone happy—whatever the cost. But Rob doesn't know about my ugly past, which is probably why he understands so little about me. Everything I am was created in that environment, and to reveal any of it would be to reveal all of it.

The girl he knows is basically just someone I substituted for the real me.

"I think maybe we just never had enough overlap, Rob. We just didn't want enough of the same things."

"I disagree," he says. "Because what I want most—more than my job or anything else—is you. I never put you first, Erin, but that's going to end now. I swear it."

Suddenly this conversation feels like a train without brakes. There are the words that could stop it, were I able to utter them. *I'm sleeping with Brendan.* I just can't say it.

"Rob, you're still based in Amsterdam. I—"

"I'm home for good," he says, cutting me off. "I told them I either came home or I was quitting. I'll have to fly back once a month, but that's it."

"Why?" I ask weakly. What I want is to say *Why in God's name did you do that? And please don't have done it for me.*

"Every success I ever had was a success for *us*, was something I saw benefitting us as a couple, benefitting our kids. Without you, it's just money, and it's meaningless."

There was a time when I would have loved to hear those words, but now I feel nothing. He isn't perfect, but he will make someone very happy. That someone, however, isn't me.

"Please don't decide right now," he says. "I know I fucked up, and I just want a chance."

He asks if we can go to dinner later in the week, just as friends. I nod, ruing the hours it means being away from Brendan.

And then I remember: there is no more time with Brendan. Every single plan, every single hour we might have had, died the moment Rob's plane landed.

I DRIVE BACK TO THE OFFICE, MY STOMACH SICK WITH DREAD. I know what I want Brendan to say when I call—that he loves me, that he doesn't want it to end, that we can find a way to make it work—and I also know he is not going to say it.

I wait until Timothy leaves the office and Harper steps away from her desk before I dial his number. When Brendan answers, I suck in the rasp of his "hey" like I can taste it. I hear the sound of glasses in the background, the murmurs of a crowd.

"Are you out?" I ask.

"I'm at Beck's place."

It's only three PM. I've never known Brendan to be out drinking in the middle of the day, at least not since he came home. I don't know why, but it feels like a bad sign.

"Rob's home," I tell him, my stomach tipping, lurching—that same roller coaster I've been on since he first kissed me weeks ago, only so much worse. "He was waiting on Harper's steps this morning."

"I heard," he says, still distracted. I hear the unmistakable clink of pool balls crashing.

I didn't expect that he'd already know. I also didn't expect that he'd sound like he doesn't give a fuck.

"Don't worry," he says. "I didn't tell him about us. Hang on. It's my turn to break."

I've slept with him pretty much every day for six weeks. I have spent every free moment with him. But this conversation isn't even important enough for him to pause his fucking game? I feel that infinitely small wisp of hope gasp and die in my chest.

He comes back to the phone. "Are you going to tell him about us?" he asks. "I don't want to be blindsided."

My hand presses to my chest, to the ache that seems to throb under my hand. I wanted him to offer something, at least express a little regret at the ending, but instead he sounds like some cavalier dick who had other plans tonight anyway. "Is that all you have to say?" I ask.

"What else am I supposed to say?" he replies. "It was fun while it lasted. I hope it all works out for you guys, if that's what you want."

Already I'm crying so hard that my shoulders are shaking and tears are dripping down my face. I will not give him the pleasure of knowing he's responsible for them, so I just hang up the phone.

56

BRENDAN
Three Years Earlier

Gabi has only a few days left in Italy when we take off to lead a three-day tour of Tuscany. And from the moment the trip begins, I know I'm fucked. Our typical clientele consists of middle-aged couples and active seniors. *This* trip mostly consists of women my age...really attractive women my age. And that's something Gabi won't handle well. We're still in the process of introductions and Gabi's already watching me, her smile long gone. I haven't uttered a word to these women, and I'm already in trouble.

We get our gear sorted and take off for our first stop of the tour. And even though Gabi made it pretty clear that I'm taken during the introductions, one of them—Tatiana—doesn't seem to care. The girl is a dead ringer for Selena Gomez and seems to view my relationship as a fun challenge, not an obstacle.

No matter how much I try to avoid her, she does not avoid me. She talks to me, rides near me, sits close at lunch. And in response, Gabi clings more, and her mood worsens. She's so rude to our clients that Seb and I spend most of the next day apologizing for her.

By the final leg of the trip, I feel so suffocated I just want to bike home on my own and leave them all behind. We reach Florence at last, but there's still the farewell dinner to get through. This is usually a celebration, but tonight it feels instead like a test of diplomacy, one I am failing miserably. On the one side of me is Tatiana, "accidentally" pressing her tits against my arm all night and talking about how much she loves anal, and on the other is Gabi, sulking and unrelentingly bitchy to everyone at the table.

When dinner concludes, the group heads to a bar down the street, while I return to my apartment with a pissed-off girl who will undoubtedly spend the next five hours crying, yelling at me, or both.

The door isn't even shut before she starts.

"You want to sleep with her, don't you?" she demands.

I rub my temples. "Don't do this, okay? It's been a long day. I'm going to bed."

"Just admit it!" she screams. "If I wasn't here, you'd sleep with her."

The answer seems so obvious—as if she's asked if I want to continue breathing oxygen—that I don't say anything at all.

This is apparently not the correct course of action.

Her face sags, waiting for a denial that does not arrive. "Go sleep with her then."

"You don't mean that," I reply.

"You would, wouldn't you?" she cries. "You'd totally sleep with her right now if you could!" She grabs my backpack and hurls it at me. "Get the fuck out."

"Gabi—"

"Get out!" she screams. "Get out get out get out get out! I never want to see you again!" She throws a book and barely misses.

I'm about to point out that it's my apartment we're in when she picks up a knife. I decide that discussion can wait.

I wander down the street, uncertain at first where to go. She'll be gone in two days. I can crash at Seb's place until then. As I head to the bar, hoping to catch him, I realize something: I'm free. Gabi said she never wanted to see me again. Which means, for the first time in months, I can do whatever the fuck I want.

I go to the bar. Seb's already left with one of the girls but Tatiana is still there. I tell her Gabi kicked me out and she informs me—tongue piercing flashing in the light—that she has a hotel room to herself.

I realize just how stifled I've been only now. The sense of freedom is overwhelming. I can go home with anyone I want, I can spend an entire night without listening to someone cry, without having to offer assurances I don't mean. Tatiana climbs into my lap and I swear, as she does it, that I am never going to be trapped again.

And as soon as I swear it, someone at the table gasps, and I look over to find Gabi standing there, weeping like I just broke her heart.

⚜ 57 ⚜

ERIN

I leave work early, feeling too sick to go on.

I cry all afternoon. I cry all night. Harper doesn't come home, which is for the best, except it makes me wonder if Brendan won't be going home tonight either. I want to vomit when I consider it.

How could it mean so little to him?

And how did I ever convince myself it was otherwise?

I think back to the way he looked at me in the hammock yesterday. The night we danced in his apartment. Everything I thought I saw in his face...could not have been real. And the way he acted on the phone today made it all so much worse. Losing him would have been hard enough, but now it feels like he's taken all of my memories and crushed them underfoot too.

I miss making dinner with him, having sex with him, sleeping beside him. I suspect there won't be a moment of my day—even the moments I didn't normally spend with him—that won't leave me missing something about Brendan. And I have no one I can tell —not Olivia, who'd immediately call Brendan and rip him a new one. Not Harper, who doesn't come home. Not even Sean, simply because he doesn't answer or return my call.

When I was with Brendan, I was consumed. He was like a drug, and with him I existed in this hazy space of believing the world was good and everything would work out without a shred of proof. It felt like I needed nothing other than him. And now the drug is gone, as I always knew it would be. I have to look at my life again—at the fact that I'm homeless and on my final warning at work—and admit that maybe I didn't need anything other than him, but I also didn't *have* anything other than him.

And I never really had him either.

HARPER DOES HER BEST TO CHEER ME UP WHEN SHE FINALLY comes home. She says all the things women say in these situations: *you're better off without him, he's going to come to his senses.* It doesn't help, though, because neither statement is true.

"You need to fix yourself up and get laid," she insists. "Brendan isn't the only hot guy in the world."

Except he's the only one I want. I can't imagine I'll ever feel otherwise, and I can't imagine how he was able to feel otherwise the minute I left.

I get through the next days fueled by daydreams about Brendan coming to his senses. I picture grand gestures: him waiting on Harper's steps so he can tell me he was wrong, or standing outside my window, playing the song we danced to at the wedding loud enough for the whole neighborhood to hear. Except the guy who can't even make a small gesture is unlikely to make a grand one anytime soon.

I leave him a message about picking up my stuff—my running shoes, my favorite jeans—and he waits a full two days to return the call. It's almost as if he's had to *force* himself to do it. I picture him sighing wearily as he lifts the phone, deciding he needs to get it over with.

"Hey," he says. "Got your message."

He sounds bored, as if we barely know each other. And just like that all my pain turns into rage. He has no right to act like we were nothing—either that or he had no right to act like it all meant something when it didn't. I'm so angry that it's an effort to speak normally. My words emerge clipped and precise, as if I'm calling someone about getting my furnace looked at.

"Yes. I need my running shoes. Is there a time when I can come by and get them?"

He yawns. "I'm on my way out, but I can set them outside the door if you're in a rush."

For the first time in days, I'm glad I have plans tonight. "I can't. I'm getting ready to go out to dinner."

"Oh yeah," he drawls. "The big dinner with Rob." He doesn't sound jealous. He barely even sounds *interested*. "So that's it then, huh? 'Mission Make Rob Pull His Head Out of His Ass' worked like a charm."

I'm not getting back together with Rob—I'm certain of it—but fuck Brendan and his ambivalence. "Yes, Brendan, I owe it all to you."

"Hey," he says with a laugh. "You deserve a little credit too. You laid there so well."

It felt like so much when we were together, and now he's making it sound ugly and cheap—as if I could have been a blow-up doll for all my contribution to the endeavor.

"Fuck you."

He laughs. "I was just joking," he says, and then his voice grows earnest. "I'm sorry. It was just a stupid joke, babe. I'm really happy for you."

I don't want you to be happy for me, Brendan. Your happiness breaks my heart.

58

ERIN

Rob shows up with the most gorgeous bouquet I've ever seen.

"You didn't need to do that," I say. And I wish he hadn't. My biggest fear for the evening is that he'll ask about Brendan. But my second biggest fear is that he'll push hard to get back together.

"I wanted to," he replies. "I wish I'd done it more."

I assume we'll be going someplace expensive, with a menu that consists only of things that are rare and unusual. Instead he takes me to the kind of place I prefer. Ribs and margaritas, outdoor tables, and live music.

"I know you don't want to eat here," I say. "You don't have to do this."

"Erin," he chides, "you wanted stuff like this enough that you broke up with me over it. So if it matters that much to you, you've got to fight for it a little."

Except that's not how I'm programmed. I'm never going to fight for something so minimal as where we eat and if we sit outside when we do it. And how is making him change to suit me any better than the way he made me change to suit him?

After we're seated, he reaches across the table for my hand. "I know you're not ready yet. I know I fucked up. But I just want a chance. I want the chance to prove to you that I've changed."

I stare at the tablecloth, so guilty that my voice rasps when I speak. "You didn't fuck up."

"Yeah, I did. I should have talked to you about the trip, I should have made sure you were okay with me staying. I should have come back for Olivia's race. I definitely should have told you about Christina. I'm so, so sorry I didn't."

Anything that happened with Christina is now so minor compared to my own failings that I can barely stand to glance up at him. "It's okay. But look, about this other guy—"

He squeezes my hand. "I'm begging you, Erin. Do not tell me. You didn't get home 'til sunrise the other day, so it's pretty obvious that things I don't ever want to think about happened. Can we just put it all behind us? Agree that I did stupid shit, and you did stupid shit, and now it's over?"

I wonder if he'd feel that way if he knew exactly what stupid shit I did, and with whom. "Rob, I don't see this working—"

"Stop," he says, squeezing my hand. "I know you're not ready. Let's just enjoy dinner. And when it's done, I won't ask you to give me another chance. I'll just ask you not to rule it out."

Over dinner he is funny and charming and I'm reminded of all the ways he swept me off my feet in the first place. He was so besotted back then, so convinced I was perfect. It was something I needed at the time, after a long summer of being rejected by Brendan. I don't need it now, but it's nice to be with someone who actually wants me for once.

It's only on the way home—just as I've begun to hope Brendan isn't going to come up—that Rob asks if I've heard from him. I swallow hard. I hate lying—which is ridiculous when you consider just how many lies I've already told him—and I also wonder why he's asking. If he knows something.

"No, not lately," I say, avoiding his gaze. "Why?"

"It seems like he's avoiding me," Rob replies. "Never can meet up, doesn't answer the phone, barely replies to texts. He's probably just busy with this new girl he's dating, but you know—I let the guy stay in my pool house rent free. You'd think he'd manage to pick up the phone."

This new girl he's dating.

My stomach goes into freefall.

"Brendan doesn't *date* anyone," I whisper.

"Apparently he's made an exception," Rob says. "I guess I should just be happy for the guy. It's cool he's finally met someone, even if his timing is terrible."

It's only been a few *days*. He couldn't have moved on that fast. But it would certainly explain his crushing ambivalence.

How could he have moved on? How could anything they have be better than what we had? What does she have that I don't?

Rob drops me off and I go inside, but I don't cry. Instead my tears sit caged inside me, and I long for something that will set them free. They're like a blister that needs to be popped, and God, I want to. I want something to make it all go away.

I've felt like this before—back in high school, when Sean disappeared and my father's drinking got worse, while my mother cried and begged me to somehow fix it. I was sixteen. Of course I couldn't fix it. I fell asleep back then apathetic about whether I woke in the morning.

I thought this kind of sadness and desperation was behind me. I thought I was better. As it turns out, I was simply numb. Brendan is the only thing with the power to bring this version of me to the surface. I tried to make myself hate him after the wedding. I tried to make him hate me too. I should have kept doing it.

Being numb, not caring, everyone says that's a bad thing.

But to me, right now, it sounds like bliss.

THE NEXT DAY WHEN I GET HOME FROM WORK, THERE'S A bouquet waiting on Harper's front porch, with my name on the card. For one insane moment I allow myself to hope it's from Brendan. I half-laugh and half-sob at my own stupidity when I find Rob's name instead.

Another bouquet is delivered to work the next day, and again to Harper's the day after that.

"How long are you planning to keep this up?" I finally ask him.

"Until you give me another chance," he replies.

He texts me frequently. He asks how I am, when he can see me. He is the anti-Brendan: he wants to give me everything. It matters to him that I exist. That shouldn't sway me, and it's not a reason to date him again, but there's something comforting about it.

He returns to Amsterdam for a week, but the flowers keep coming.

"My house looks like a florist's shop," says Harper. "And believe me, I'm not complaining. But how long are you going to let this go on?"

I rub my eyes. What Rob is doing is sweet, but it just makes me feel guilty. It makes me feel bad that I'm keeping the truth from him, and that I still don't want to give him another chance. "I already told him to stop."

"I don't mean the flowers. I mean *you*. You've been the most miserable human alive now for going on two weeks. Something's got to change. If Brendan is out of the picture, why aren't you going out with Rob?"

I laugh unhappily. "Because I slept with his best friend, for starters."

"So what?" she asks. "Rob told you he didn't care, and you know he slept with Christina. He's obviously in it for the long haul. Either way, it's time to move on."

Moving on. I want that too.

I was relieved when I first met Rob at Will and Olivia's engagement party. I was tired of wanting Brendan, tired of fighting it. I wanted it to end. I want it to end now. It has to, because while all of those high points with Brendan were amazing, I can no longer live with the lows.

❧ 59 ❧

BRENDAN
Three Years Earlier

Somehow I get Gabi outside of the bar. She's crying, but it's the sheer devastation on her face that kills me. She expected better of me, and I allowed her to expect better of me when I should have told her the truth up front, which is that I am exactly the guy I knew I was: incapable of commitment, careless with others. I allowed her to think we meant something because I hoped if I agreed, if I stuck it out long enough, maybe it *would* mean something. I should have known better.

She goes boneless when we get outside, sliding down the bar's exterior wall into a heap on the sidewalk. "I thought you loved me," she weeps. "You *said* you loved me."

We've only got two days left, and I know I should say something to smooth things over, but I just don't have it in me. I'm tired, and I've put up with more tears and drama in two months than most people do over their entire lives. I'm done.

"Gabi, you're leaving. I just think it's run its course."

"I'm not leaving," she says. "I deferred for a year. For you."

My stomach drops. How long ago did she do it? Was it weeks

ago, when I was busy counting the days until her departure? She will now start medical school a year late, entirely because I allowed her to believe things that weren't true.

I exhale heavily. "You shouldn't have done that."

"I thought you'd be happy," she cries, burying her face in her hands.

People walking by stare at us, then glare at me. They don't even know us, don't even speak our language, yet they know I'm the one who fucked up. And they're right.

I crouch next to her. "Come on, honey," I beg. "Let's just go back to the apartment, okay?"

"Are you breaking up with me?" she demands.

God, I don't want to do this here. I don't want to hurt her anywhere. But it's just all gone too fucking far. "You need to go to medical school," I tell her. "I don't want to be the reason you're staying."

"You're worth it to me. I don't even care. I'll skip it entirely, and we'll just stay in Italy if that's what you want."

I'm tempted to lie. I'm tempted to say whatever I have to in order to get us back to the apartment, where it won't be so fucking awkward to sort things out. But I can't lie anymore. *If only I hadn't lied in the first place.*

"I'm sorry," I whisper. "I'm so fucking sorry. But this isn't what I want."

❧ 60 ☙

ERIN

I'm having a hard time getting through the day. And just when I think the horrible branding campaign is behind me, full of trite phrases and insincere accolades, I discover it's not.

"We need a different group of kids for the cover," Timothy says, flinging a brochure about the Mitchell Scholars Program on my desk.

I run my tongue over my teeth, searching somewhere inside me for a calmness I don't feel. "These are the kids who actually won the award."

"They don't project the image we want. And we need more diversity."

"How much more diversity could you possibly want? We've got ten award winners, of whom *five* are minorities."

"Well, the minorities you chose are not a good representation of the school."

He has really picked the wrong week to piss me off. I don't have it in me to even feign civility at the moment.

"I have no idea what you're trying to tell me," I snap. "And I didn't choose them. These kids all *won* Mitchell Scholarships. How are they possibly not a good representation for the school?"

"Well, to be perfectly frank, none of them look that smart. And the African-American boy is too...urban."

Patience, Erin. You are not Olivia. You are not Harper. You don't get to lose your shit with impunity. "How exactly can someone be *too* urban?"

"The jeans, the T-shirt. Just all of it." He rolls his eyes as if this is obvious, when nearly every kid featured is wearing some version of that. He hands me a brochure for affordable housing, which features someone light-skinned, wearing a button down and a bow-tie. "I want something more like this."

Patience, Erin. Patience... No, fuck it. "The kid in this picture is one of the ten best students in the school, and he's dressed exactly like the other kids. So basically what I hear you saying is that anyone other than Carlton from *The Fresh Prince of Bel Air* looks like a criminal to you."

His nostrils flare. "As you are well aware, you're already skating on thin ice. And I'm not asking for your opinion. I want a new cover."

I slide the brochure back to him. "I'm not doing it."

"If you don't do it," he says, "you have no job."

I stand and grab my purse. "Then I guess that I have no job."

I stride out of the office feeling enraged, full of indignation. It takes me only two seconds after the door's shut behind me to wonder what the fuck I've done.

I GET BACK TO HARPER'S AND SPEND MOST OF THE AFTERNOON staring at my hands, shocked that my life has gone so wrong. Three months ago I had savings, a home, a fiancé and a job. Now I have none of those things.

Harper assures me everything will be fine. "When my room-mate gets back, we'll figure something out. And you don't want a boyfriend. And you don't want *that* job. You never did. Just wait," she says. "This is the start of something amazing. Your life is going to be so much better."

I guess I have to agree with her there, because I'm not sure it's possible for things to get worse.

She plies me with something she calls "cheer me up" shots until I collapse in bed, still sad but too drunk to remain upright. When I wake the next day there's a message from Timothy saying that as long as I'm in by noon, we can move past this, though "some disciplinary action will, obviously, be necessary."

I can't say there isn't part of me that glances at the clock, that doesn't imagine rushing off to put on work clothes and pretending none of this has happened. I don't want to promote nicotine patches or energy drinks. I want to care about the product, and I liked promoting my alma mater. Except my job at ECU now feels like the end of a long run; I reach the end certain I could keep going if necessary, but once I've stopped, once I've thrown myself down in the grass and kicked off my shoes, the idea suddenly feels impossible. If my life depended on it, I don't think I could get up and go back to work for that man. In fact, I have no idea how or why I stayed as long as I did.

Rob calls in the afternoon. I tell him about my job and it's a relief when he backs my decision to leave. "You were always under-appreciated there," he says. "Let me take you to dinner. Just as friends. We can talk it out."

I begin to say no, and then stop myself. Whatever we might lack in excitement, Rob can be a good sounding board. Plus, being around him reminds me of a time when I wasn't miserable, and that soothes me. If it was possible to not hurt once upon a time, it's possible it can happen again, and I'm desperate to begin piecing myself back together.

~

WHEN HE PICKS ME UP THAT NIGHT, HE'S FULL OF IDEAS FOR MY job search. He pushes me to consider a different kind of marketing, which is something he harped on while we were together too. I resented it a little at the time, but now I kind of see his point.

"Working for a non-profit is never going to make you money," he says. "Why not do what you're good at and make a decent living at the same time? You could make three times as much in marketing for the right for the right company. You could work for us. We're always looking for good people."

I picture it: writing cheerful missives to the people Rob's company will lay off, full of euphemisms about "new opportunities for growth" that will make me cringe with each keystroke. It leads my thoughts to Brendan, though my thoughts never seem to veer far from him.

What would he be saying in Rob's shoes? He'd be telling me not to settle. He'd swear somehow it would all work out. And a part of me wants that, wants to feel optimistic and hopeful about the future, excited by its possibilities. Except that sort of unrealistic thinking is just like Brendan himself: fun while it lasts, but gets me nowhere in the long run.

"I really appreciate you listening to me talk about this," I tell Rob when he drops me off. "Not that you'll ever get fired, but if you do, I hope I'm half as helpful."

"I'm not planning to get fired, but I do have a way you can return the favor, if you're inclined to," he says. "I need to make an appearance at this opening on Saturday. Cocktail attire. You know I hate going to those things alone."

I hate going to those things too, but my primary objection is that it's hard to imagine how dressing up and going to an opening won't feel like a date.

He grins. "You're so transparent. It's not a date, okay? I swear it. Just come with me, and then I'll drive you home and shake your hand at the door. Hell, if it makes you feel better, I won't even walk you to the door."

I sigh. "I don't know, Rob."

"I won't even fully stop the car—you can jump."

I laugh. "You're impossible to say no to. You know that?"

"That's what I'm hoping," he says, nodding toward the ring on my finger—not my engagement ring but an emerald he bought on our first anniversary. "Because maybe that ring isn't the only thing from our past worth keeping."

I frown, staring at the ring. Every conversation with him feels like it's full of landmines. I don't think I want to be with him, but I also don't want him under the impression that everything about us together made me miserable. "I like lots of things from our past."

"I could have done a lot better, though. The longer I'm back, the more I'm realizing it," he says, pulling my hands into his. "If you give me another chance, I'm going to devote my entire life to making you happy."

I walk inside, feeling much better than I did before I saw him. And if being with him makes me feel better, and Brendan only causes pain, isn't it obvious who I should want? What Rob and I had wasn't perfect, but at least it was real. At least it didn't hurt.

61

ERIN

I wear a dress of Harper's—slinky and silver—for the opening. I even put on makeup and curl my hair. It's not that I care about looking good for this, but Brendan moved on, so I can at least pretend I have too.

"You look unbelievable," Rob says when I open the door. "I'm going to be the most envied guy there."

I warm a little inside. I was merely a small blip in Brendan's existence, so brief and inconsequential I don't even mark a point in his timeline. So inconsequential he couldn't even walk away from his pool game to tell me so. But that's not the case with Rob. He's proud to be seen with me, and he wants everything I can give.

Once we're in the car he turns not toward town, like I expected, but up into the mountains. I glance at him. "Where are we going?" I ask. "There's nothing out here."

"It's a vineyard. I'm a minority partner, and tonight's the official opening."

I release my air in small, controlled puffs. It can't be the same vineyard Brendan took me to. It can't. But what are the odds that two different vineyards are opening up nearby at the same time?

"Blue Mountain?" I ask.

"You've heard of it?"

"I think Brendan is friends with the owner," I reply, my stomach knotting up. *Oh dear God, please don't let this mean Brendan will be there too. I can suffer anything but that.*

Rob's smile fades. "I dropped by his place yesterday—I only saw it from the hall but I can't believe he moved out of the pool house for *that*. It had holes in the wall, for Christ's sake."

I don't remember any holes in the walls, but I'm too busy thinking of the running shoes I haven't picked up, and all the other things I left behind. "Why were you in the hall?" I ask, my breath caught in the middle of my throat.

"The girl he's dating was there," Rob replies. "I've never seen him so whipped over someone."

I feel like I've been hit. Again. When is this thing with Brendan going to stop providing fresh sources of pain? He told me he didn't let girls sleep over. God, I was stupid. I was so fucking stupid to believe him, to believe I was special somehow. I wonder if he's delivering his speech about being in the bubble to this girl too. Or maybe *they* aren't in the bubble. Maybe she has what I did not, whatever magical properties are necessary to make Brendan want more.

We arrive at the vineyard, and I'm deeply relieved not to find Brendan there. It feels like the first break I've gotten in weeks. Rob starts introducing me to the other investors, and to Chris, the owner—who I never met with Brendan, thank God—and we fall into our familiar patterns. Bland social smiles, my hip brushing his thigh, his hand at the small of my back. This kind of event still isn't my thing, but I don't hate his role in it. I don't hate the way he wants to show me off—the small, possessive things he does that Brendan never did.

"Are you doing okay?" he asks, his breath grazing my ear.

I nod. "Yes. You?"

"I've never been happier than I am right now," he says, his hand wrapping around my hip. He leans down, pressing a kiss to the top of my head. "I'm gonna get us a sample of the shiraz. You'll be okay for a second?"

I nod and as he departs, a woman leans toward me.

"The two of you are adorable," she says. "Newlyweds?"

"Oh, uh...no. It's not... No." I want to claim we're not dating, but how can I when we're here together and he's kissing the top of my head when he goes off to get wine?

"Well, you should be," she says with a fond smile. "You'd have beautiful children."

There's a low, unhappy laugh behind me. A laugh I could identify anywhere in the world, under any circumstances.

"She's right," Brendan drawls. "You definitely belong together."

I turn slowly, bracing myself. His face is the only thing I've wanted to see for the past three weeks. I want to weep for how badly I've missed the sight of him: that sharp jaw and those slightly flushed cheekbones, eyes the palest possible blue against his tan. I've stared at that photo of him in a suit at Olivia's wedding a thousand times, but tonight he puts it to shame. He is so beautiful that he breaks my heart all over again.

"Hey, man, I didn't know you'd be here," Rob says, coming up behind me. "You know Chris?"

Brendan's eyes fall to Rob's hand as it wraps around my waist, and I get a glimpse of that sneer of his. It's a look I know well— I've seen it far too many times over the past few years.

"Yeah," Brendan replies. "You?"

"Only recently. I invested in this place a while back."

I see a hint of tightness in Brendan's jaw, a small twitch, and then he forces it to relax. A girl comes up to the three of us, handing Brendan a glass of red. She is beautiful, curvier than me, and I hate her on sight. I hate her ample cleavage, her leather dress, her perfect hair. I loathe everything about her.

"Crystal," he says, looking only from her to Rob, as if I'm not there, "this is my friend Rob and his fiancée." I don't even get a name now, apparently. Maybe he's already forgotten.

Crystal immediately starts gushing over my ring with the

precise level of enthusiasm you'd expect from a sixteen-year-old. "I love it!" she squeals. "Diamond engagement rings are so over."

Rob and I exchange an awkward glance.

"It's just a ring," I reply. "We're not engaged."

"Oh." She looks up at Brendan with a cute little expression of complete confusion—an expression I bet she has a lot. "You just said they were engaged."

"We *were* engaged, and now we're just figuring things out," says Rob.

"Well, that ring is fufleek either way," she tells me.

"*Fufleek?*" I ask, thinking I've misheard her. I'd assume she was just pulling from another language entirely except...come on, this girl doesn't speak a second language.

"Yeah, you know. Fleek as hell. Fucking fleek."

"Ah, of course," I say, casting a shaming glance at Brendan. "Yes, that's what I wanted. A ring that's fucking fleek. We went into Tiffany, and that's what I said. 'Take us right to your fucking fleek section'."

"Right on, girl," Crystal replies. "Have you thought about music?"

I blink, confused. "Music?"

"For your wedding."

What does this girl not understand about what Rob just told her? "I...no, not really. Like Rob said, we're not engaged."

"Because this is a good song for a wedding," she says, pointing at the small trio playing music in the corner. "I don't know what it's called, though. Classical music should have words, you know?"

"It's called 'Fur Elise'," says Rob. "It's Beethoven."

She looks appalled. "What the fuck? You mean like a fir tree or fur you wear?"

"It was actually titled 'For Elise', but someone misread Beethoven's handwriting," Rob explains. "He wrote it for one of his pupils."

"Good," she says with a sigh of relief. "Because I'm sorry, but I couldn't get behind a song about fur. I love all animals, even the mean ones like foxes."

Holy shit. This girl is so fucking dumb I almost feel bad for hating her as much as I do. Almost. "You're wearing a leather dress," I point out.

She looks down at her dress and back to me, her face completely blank. "Yeah? What's wrong with that? There's no *fur* on it."

My mouth twitches, the merest hint of the bitter smile I want to shoot at Brendan. It doesn't escape his attention.

"Have you guys been down by the lake yet?" he asks, holding my eye. "It's the perfect place for a picnic."

Our picnic. I can't believe he's bringing it up.

"Picnics are overrated," I counter. "I've never been to one that was worth my time."

"You'd love it," Brendan says, turning to Rob with a smirk. "Pack a big lunch. I bet she'd swallow everything."

All the air leaves my chest. Suddenly, I'm unable to stand another minute of having to watch him with that stupid girl.

I excuse myself and hurry to the bathroom. Inside, I shut the door behind me and press my face to the cool tiles, flushed by both anger and distress. I reapply my lipstick, willing my breath to slow, my hands to steady. And when I finally step back outside, Brendan is waiting.

I'm not sure if I want to laugh or cry at how little anything has changed. The last time we spoke outside a bathroom it was an identical situation, wasn't it? He'd brought someone hot and dumb then too, and I was blindingly jealous, just like I am now.

"Nice choice," I sneer. "But maybe next time you should look for some quality other than bra size."

"And maybe you should look for some quality other than the size of his wallet."

"Fuck you, Brendan," I say, as my hands curl into fists. "You know that's never been the reason I was with Rob."

"Oh right. It's probably everything else," he smirks, leaning against the wall. "It must get you so hot the way he immediately recognizes songs by Beethoven and can tell us all the story behind them."

I roll my eyes. "At least he realizes that leather comes from animals. I should have known you'd wind up with the one girl in the state who doesn't understand that."

"I haven't *wound up* with anyone," he snaps. "Unlike you, I don't move right from fucking someone like I'm never going to get it again to being all over someone else. I mean, how long did it take before you got back together with him?" he demands. "An hour? A day?"

"Does it matter? As I recall, you claimed all I did was *lie there*."

His eyes narrow. "You probably don't even have to do that anymore, do you? The only thing that guy gets hard for is the closing of the stock market."

"Yes, it's so terrible the way he makes tons of money and wants to be a good provider," I reply. "Women *hate* that."

He raises a brow. "Yeah, well if you loved it so much, why were you getting naked for me twenty seconds after he left?"

I respond with my most saccharine smile. "Maybe I just wanted to see if it could be better with someone else. By the way, it wasn't."

He closes the space between us until he is pressed up against me. His muscles are coiled and under the starch of his shirt, I smell *him*—skin and soap and heat. His pupils are so large that the blue is a mere shadow, his mouth slightly ajar, his body tense.

"You're so full of shit," he hisses, his mouth a breath away from mine. "Let's go in the bathroom right now. I'll prove it."

I won't do that to Rob. But I wouldn't do it anyway. Brendan has wounded me endlessly and unforgivably over the past three weeks. He's turned me back into the girl I was in high school and after Olivia's wedding, the one so overwhelmed by grief she could barely get through the day.

I shove him hard and push away. "Move on, Brendan. I have."

I march out to the patio, planning to ask Rob to take me

home, but Crystal won't let me get a word in edgewise. She's too busy trying to explain how being a Broncos cheerleader is really "the exact same" as being a prima ballerina. It's not until Brendan returns that she finally stops babbling.

"Where were you?" she whines.

"I ran into this girl I know," he says, glancing at me. "I'd forgotten what a liar she is. I'm not sure she tells the truth about anything."

I want to be angry, but my throat tightens instead. Because he's right. I'm not even sure which lies he's accusing me of: the one I'm telling Rob by omission, or the ones I've been telling for a long time—about my family, what I want from life. I do nothing but pretend. It's all I know how to do.

The realization exhausts me. I'm so tired of the effort it takes to lie, to be this person Rob thinks I am, to pretend I'm not heartbroken.

"I'm not feeling great," I whisper to Rob. "Would you mind taking me home?" At least this lie feels true.

"Of course," he says. He hastily says goodbye to Brendan and Crystal and then ushers me out to the car.

"What was going on back there?" he asks when we get outside. "With you and Brendan."

"He was just mad that I was being a bitch to Crystal," I reply.

He pauses. "Why *were* you?" It feels like he's asking so much more.

"Because she's an idiot."

He could counter that it's unfair to blame her for being an idiot, or that there's no reason to ridicule her for it to her face, but he says nothing.

We reach Harper's house, and he walks me to the door. He watches my face. He wants to kiss me, is wondering if I'll let him.

I do. And just like everything else with him, it is nice and familiar and eases something inside me.

"I fly out pretty early in the morning," he says slowly, holding my gaze as if these words are important. "But I'm home on Saturday. You know that I want you back, and I think you're ready to give me a chance, but before I go, I want to make something clear: I don't care what you did or who you were with while I was gone. I just need to know it's over."

There's something in the way he says it, in the way he's looking at me. It's almost as if he knows I was with Brendan.

❧ 62 ❧

BRENDAN
Three Years Earlier

Gabi cries all night long. All I can do is apologize, again and again. She's a nice girl, and I've fucked up so badly. I don't know why I allowed it to happen, or how to fix it.

The next morning I go to work, but she won't get out of bed. I lead the morning tour, and just as we're coming in, my landlady calls. She's yelling and speaking so fast I can't understand her, so I hand the phone to Seb.

"Did you leave a sink on something?" he asks me. "She says there's water coming through her ceiling."

I will always remember this moment. The innocent half-second when I ponder what might have happened, followed by the moment the Earth shifts. The moment where I realize the consequences of my behavior might be so much worse than hurt feelings, than grief.

It's the moment when it occurs to me my mistakes might be fatal ones.

63

ERIN

I cannot sleep, so instead I tally my losses: Sean isn't taking my phone calls. I've got no job, and when Harper's roommate returns in a little over a week I'll have nowhere to live and no money with which to acquire something. I've sent a few resumes out, but I've heard nothing back.

And all of that is minimal compared to the agony of picturing Brendan with that stupid, stupid girl. I know I'm not perfect. I can easily imagine that there are better girls out there than me. Girls who are prettier and smarter and less fucked-up. But she's not one of them.

Just the image of him with his arm around her waist makes me want to vomit. He never once stood like that with me in public. It's not even about wanting him back, because that was always a lost cause, always impossible. I just want him to stop breaking my heart. I remember when he told me we were in the bubble. *Like a pocket of air in a submerged car*, he said. What he didn't say, and what I should have realized, is that when the bubble is popped you don't shoot to the surface. You drown.

When my mother calls at two in the morning, I'm still awake. I see her name on the phone and for once I let it ring. Why does it have to be me? Why can't *she* go find him? Or maybe she could just let him spend a night in jail, allow him to actually see how serious a problem it is.

She calls a second time and a third, and my hand twitches, but I don't pick up the phone. Maybe I'm feeling sorry for myself, but I've had enough. For once in my damn life, I am not going to allow them to add their problems to mine.

I must fall asleep after that, because it seems as if moments later the phone is ringing again, but the clock says it's just after four. Which means she didn't go find him, and he's still missing, and I'm a terrible daughter for letting it happen. I know all of this before I ever pick up the phone.

My mother is crying so hard she's almost incoherent. She tells me my father was in an accident. And then she tells me something I already know.

"This is entirely your fault," she says.

BY THE TIME I REACH DENVER, THE SUN IS COMING OVER THE horizon. I've only slept two of the past twenty-four hours, but I feel curiously alert, and curiously empty, all at once.

I enter St. Joseph's, a hospital I've never set foot in before, but it seems familiar—maybe because I've pictured this exact scenario so many times. I'm led by a somber nurse to my father, and he looks so changed that for a moment I think she's brought me to the wrong room. His lips are thin, bleached of color, and his skin is so white it has a blue sheen to it. The veins on his hands stand out like rocky outcroppings across a desert plain. My throat feels swollen, but before I can give into my grief, my mom begins sobbing, as helpless and childlike as ever. For a moment I hate her. I hate her for staying with him for so long, for letting him get to this point, for sitting there blubbering like a lost five-year-old who needs me to come in and fix everything.

Just once, I would like to have been the lost five-year-old who got saved.

I pinch my lips tighter, though, and go to her side, taking the seat next to her and letting her collapse on my shoulder. She tells me he ran into a telephone pole. She doesn't mention that he'd been drinking—that part goes without saying, I suppose.

"I don't know what's going on," she says, continuing to weep. "The doctors keep talking about the bleeding and cirrhosis, and it doesn't even make sense. Why didn't you answer your phone? I called and called."

I'm not getting into this with her right now. Yes, I blame myself, but I also blame her. She's never lifted one finger to solve this problem the whole time they've been together. Surely all the fault can't rest with me.

I ask the triage nurse to have the doctor stop by our room. It takes over an hour, and when he does walk in, he looks relieved. I imagine he's glad to find an actual adult in the room, as opposed to my mother, who keeps saying "please just fix him" as if my dad's a broken toy.

The doctor tells me my father has a subdural hematoma— bleeding in his brain. Right now they're watching it, but he's certain my dad will need surgery.

"So can we get that scheduled?" I ask.

"We'd like to wait, if possible," he says. "Your father has moderate cirrhosis, which is causing some internal bleeding. The odds of him making it through the surgery, in his current condition, are poor."

I feel like I've been hit. My mother cries harder, so I clench my jaw and persist. "How poor?" I ask. "Fifty percent?"

"Fifty percent," he replies, "would be extremely optimistic."

When he leaves, my mother continues to cry and asks me to get a second opinion. I tell her I'll handle it, and I convince her to go home to sleep for a while. "Can you call Sean?" she asks. "I tried him, but it said his number was out of order."

She leaves and I bury my head in my hands, at a complete loss.

Each time I think I've hit rock bottom, I find out I can go lower. I thought my life couldn't be any worse this time yesterday: unemployed and homeless and broken-hearted. But now my father is dying, my brother is missing, my mother is as helpless and grief-stricken as a child, and it's on me to fix all of it.

When I clearly can't even take care of myself.

I*T'S JUST AFTER DINNER WHEN MY FATHER FINALLY OPENS HIS* eyes. He's so happy to see me, and also so sad that I can feel my heart cracking in my chest. I'd like to be the one person in this room capable of holding it together, but I can't do it.

"I'm sorry, Erin," he says when I take his hand. "It was just a stupid mistake."

"It's okay," I tell him. But it's not okay, of course. He did this to himself, all of it, and it's not okay.

"I just want to know you're taken care of," he whispers. "I just want to know that if I'm going, I don't need to worry about all of you."

"You don't need to worry about any of us," I promise him. I know as I say it that as soon as this is over, I'll be taking any shitty marketing job I can find. Sean and my mother will be more my responsibility than ever if he doesn't survive.

"I'm so glad you found Rob," he says. "He's a good man. He'll make sure you're all cared for. I just wish I could be there to see you married."

I flinch. I never even told them we broke up. I should have...I was just scared of tipping the apple cart. Scared it would be the last straw and send my father over the edge. But he went over anyway.

My mother bounces out of her seat. "You could, Erin! We could find a priest. Maybe Father Duncan or even the hospital chaplain. You could do it right here."

I blink, unable to tell them the truth at this horrible moment but unwilling to lie either.

"Would you consider it?" my father asks, squeezing my hand. "I'm sorry. I know it's not the big fancy thing you probably want, but you could still have that too, later."

I swallow hard on the lump in my throat. "We'll see, Daddy. Rob's not even in the country right now. Let's talk about it later."

"I'm going to hang on until I can see it," he says, squeezing my hand. "Is Sean on his way?"

Once again, the lies pour from my mouth. "Yes," I say. "He'll be here soon."

I am incapable of telling the truth, just like Brendan said, but maybe that's for the best—the only person who ever knew the truth was him, and look how that turned out.

THAT NIGHT, AFTER MY FATHER FALLS BACK ASLEEP, I LET MY mother have the pull-out chair and leave. I've been up for nearly forty-eight hours, and as I walk carefully down the white-tiled hall-way, exhaustion and grief make me feel lost and small and cold.

I think I'm dreaming when I hear Brendan's voice, calling my name. I turn, astonished to find him crossing the waiting room to reach me.

He pulls me tight to his chest, and being in his arms again is like finding solid ground after months adrift at sea. I thought I was too tired to cry, too cried-out to cry, but I find that I'm not. I can feel it inside me, rising like the tide.

"Olivia told me," he says. "They wouldn't let me come back to see you, though. Are you going home?"

I shake my head. "My parents' place," I say, my voice growing choked. In a few days, I may never be able to say those words again. "I want to be nearby."

"I'll drive you there." My mouth opens to object, but before I can he stops me. "You're not driving there alone, and you're not staying there alone. You decide you want me gone, I'll go. But not until someone else is there with you."

I mean to argue with him, but instead my shoulders begin to shake, and I cry silently against his chest.

"I didn't answer the phone last night," I whisper, finally admitting it aloud. In spite of everything that's happened, he's still the only person alive I can tell this to. "I saw that my mom was calling, and I was so busy feeling sorry for myself that I let it go to voicemail."

He pulls me tighter. "You were right to do it. You should have done it a long time ago. This isn't on you."

For some reason that just makes me cry harder.

I don't remember walking to Brendan's car or riding to my parents' condo. I don't remember any aspect of it until we arrive in the guest room and he lies down, pulling me onto his chest as he drags the quilt over both of us.

I'm no longer crying, but I'm also not ready to sleep. "Why are you here?" I whisper. "I know what you said at the hospital but...the second Rob came back, you treated me like some one-time thing. Like you didn't even know my name, and it never mattered. So why are you acting like you care now?"

He pushes my hair off my face, pressing a thumb to the tear under my eye and wiping it away. "I'm sorry," he says. "I'm so fucking sorry. It just seemed easier that way. I wasn't going to ask you to sneak around behind his back. And if I can't give you the things you want, someone should."

"Why didn't you at least tell me that? You acted so ambivalent about it."

"I acted ambivalent because I was *pissed*," he says. "You think this is easy for me? Every time I hear from Rob, it sounds like you're back together, or on your way to it. One minute you're naked in my bed and a few hours later he's calling to tell me you agreed to go out with him. I just didn't know what to do, and I still don't know what to do, but I'm sorry."

Suddenly the way he acted sort of makes sense. Whether he'll admit it or not, he was jealous, and a part of him still wanted me. That shouldn't be enough for me, and it isn't enough, but it takes a little of that shattered thing in my chest and pieces it back together.

"What about the girl?" I ask. "Crystal. Rob said she was at your place when he came by."

Brendan gives a low laugh. "I'm not dating anyone. I had to say something to keep him from walking in. You never came back for any of your stuff. It's all over my apartment."

I sigh. "I thought it would be too hard, seeing your place. I was hoping you'd just drop it off."

"And I never dropped it off," he says, "because then you'd never have a reason to come back."

"You put your arm around her," I say, and my voice breaks all over again. "You were willing to let everyone know you were together last night, but you never did that with me."

He pulls me closer. "If I'd ever been like that with you, odds are that it'd eventually get back to Rob. I was doing it for you, and believe me, it pissed me off every time."

Everything he says makes sense. Everything he says stitches me back together. I still have a million questions though. Mostly I want to know why he can care as much as he seems to, but not choose me. My mouth opens and he laughs softly.

"Baby, go to sleep," he says. "Tomorrow's going to be a long day."

"One more thing," I say. "Who keeps calling you at night? Is it Gabi?"

He pauses. The silence stretches so long that it seems like a confirmation in and of itself.

"No," he finally says. "It's her mom."

❧ 64 ❧

BRENDAN
Present

Erin is the last person I want to tell about Gabi, but at this point I don't have much of a choice. And while I hate what this story says about me, I can't go on letting her believe that my inability to be in a relationship is somehow her fault.

So I start at the beginning. I tell her I was mad after the wedding, mostly at myself. That I couldn't stand to see her with Rob, so I finally just left.

I tell her how hard it was, hearing about her and Rob as they got serious. And how, for a while, Gabi seemed like she could fix me. That I led her to believe we were something we were not, simply because I was hoping she could be *someone* she was not. And I let her keep believing it because it was easier than telling her I'd made a mistake.

And then I tell Erin how it ended.

By the time I got to the apartment, the police had already kicked in the door and pulled Gabi out of the bathtub. When I came in, she was lying there on our floor, covered in blood, and in that moment I wanted nothing more than for her to be alive.

Now I wish she hadn't been.

There's not a day that goes by when I don't think of her parents. What it must be like for them to see their brilliant, beautiful daughter—the one who once biked fifty miles a day, the one who was going to medical school—and know she no longer recognizes them, can't even feed herself.

That's why, when her mother calls at night, screaming at me, telling me I killed their child, I don't argue.

How can I? I didn't put Gabi in that tub, and I didn't cut her wrists. But that doesn't make me innocent. If she hadn't met me, it never would have happened.

ꕥ 65 ꕥ

ERIN

"She was under the water too long," he says, and right then I think I know the story's outcome. I can't even imagine a worse ending is possible, but it is.

His sympathy lies with Gabi's parents, but mine lies with him. I've seen the way that guilt eats at him and derails him. I just could never put a finger on its source.

"If I thought I could be with someone again, it would be you," he says. "Before you got together with Rob, even while I was with Gabi, it was always you I wanted. It's never stopped being you. But I can't."

My chest feels so tight it hurts. I want to persuade him he's wrong, and not just for myself. He thinks of what happened to Gabi as something he *did*, the culmination of a pattern that had long been in play. He thinks by shutting himself off he can make sure it never happens again. But that's not who he is. I know it in my bones, and I just want him to know it too.

"Brendan, she was unstable. The things she did even before you broke up with her—that wasn't the behavior of a rational person.

If what happened to my dad isn't my fault, by that same logic this can't be your fault either."

He listens. For a single, hopeful moment there is something in his eyes that makes me think I might have convinced him. But then it vanishes, replaced by pain and a grim sort of certainty. I don't know what it will take for him to believe he isn't at fault. I just know that I don't have it.

∽

WHEN I WAKE THE NEXT MORNING, I REALIZE TWO THINGS simultaneously: my father is dying, and Brendan will really never be mine. He'll never be anyone's. What he said last night soothed my sense of rejection—and finally sorted out his behavior for me a little—but it doesn't change anything.

"Do I have makeup everywhere?" I ask as I lift myself off his chest.

He smiles. "I'm pretty sure you cried it all off yesterday. I like you better without it anyway."

The way he's looking at me hurts. I've seen that look before, and I made it mean so much. But just because he looks at me like that doesn't mean he loves me. It doesn't mean anything. Or maybe it does, but it won't make a difference in the end.

I take a quick shower and check my phone when I get out. There are multiple texts, including three from Rob, who somehow heard about my dad. He was boarding a flight home when he texted and will be here this afternoon.

I should be relieved that he's coming, because Rob is competent in ways other people are not. If there's anything my parents need, he will find a way to get it. Whether my father lives or dies, he will know what to do. But I'm not relieved at all, because his arrival means Brendan will leave.

When I get to the kitchen, Brendan hands me a travel mug. "I looked for coffee, but I could only find instant," he says.

"My dad likes instant better," I reply, suddenly finding it hard to speak.

There are so many stupid, trivial things about the people we love. Things you never care about until they're gone. And then all those things—the sound of a heavy tread at the side door, instant coffee, creaky knees heading upstairs—become things you miss, when they're things you never knew you loved in the first place.

As we drive to the hospital, Brendan asks if Sean is on the way, and my whole body sags. I woke feeling like I was capable of handling this, and now I remember why I'm not. My brother is missing, and I can't give my dying father a single thing he wants.

"I can't find him," I reply, my voice breaking once more. "His phone's been disconnected."

"Hey," he says, turning my face to look at him. "It's going to be all right, okay? Let's just worry about your dad for now."

He pulls up to the front entrance. "I'll park and meet you inside."

"You don't have to—"

"Yeah, blah blah blah. I know," he says. "But I am." His mouth curves slightly to one side, and he looks at me in a way no one else ever has: as if he knows me. As if he knows everything I'm thinking, everything I fear, everything I need. What would it be like, going through life with someone who knows you that well, someone with whom you don't have to pretend? It would feel like a miracle.

"If you're coming up," I say, "I need to tell you two things—first, Rob is on his way back from Amsterdam. Second, my parents still think Rob and I are engaged."

His jaw tightens. "You broke up him with him two months ago. How can they not know?"

I try to speak, and my mouth twists with the effort not to dissolve into tears. "My dad wanted to see me married so badly. He still does. I figured he'd drink more if he knew it wasn't happening. And now...I can't tell him the truth. I just can't."

Brendan frowns, but in this, his opinion doesn't matter. The chances of my dad living through the surgery are so poor. If he's going to leave the world, I want him to do it feeling like it's safe for him to go, and I'll tell whatever lie I have to in order for that to happen.

～

I ENTER MY DAD'S ROOM HOLDING MY BREATH, BOTH EXPECTING the best—my dad awake, laughing—and the worst—my mother weeping, all the monitors unplugged. It's neither one, really. My dad is asleep, and my mom sits, looking older and more rumpled than I've ever seen her. I tell her to go home and she objects.

"I shouldn't leave you here alone," she says. "What if you need to leave and he wakes up?"

"Oh...um..." I stutter. "I won't be alone. Uh, Brendan is here."

My mother's mouth pinches. "Is *he* the reason you were too *busy* to answer your phone on Saturday?"

I finally snap. "Oh right," I reply with a bitter laugh. "Because Dad getting drunk and hitting a telephone pole is my fault."

"You could have prevented it."

"Don't," I say, pointing at her. "Don't you dare blame me. It wasn't my job to prevent this. It was Dad's, and it was yours, and you never lifted a finger. You yelled at me when I tried to get Dad to go to rehab. So if you're hell-bent on finding a culprit, start with yourself."

Her mouth opens, but no words emerge. And then, predictably, her eyes well. "I can't believe you chose right now to attack me."

"I'm not attacking you. I'm telling you the truth. Grow up and listen to it for once."

When Brendan enters a few minutes later, we're sitting in stony silence. She's drawn herself up, shoulders back.

"I think I'll go home for a while," she announces, looking at neither of us. "Make sure to let me know when your *fiancé* arrives."

After she leaves, Brendan takes the seat beside me and squeezes my hand. He knows. He knows exactly what I'm feeling:

that I'm so tired of supporting my mother and taking the blame, but that part of me agrees with her assessment. He just knows.

He walks to my father's bedside, and I join him.

"All he wanted was to see me married, Brendan," I whisper. "And now he won't, all because I was scared he'd make a fool of himself at the wedding and because I didn't want him to drink more leading up to it."

He squeezes my hand. "You can't blame yourself for that."

"Yes, I can. Why did I dance around the whole thing? I should have made him stop drinking. I should have forced him to go to rehab. Instead I did everything I could to smooth the way."

"You *did* try to get him to rehab, remember?" he asks. "He's a grown man. There's nothing you could have done, especially without your mother's support. Don't start finding ways to blame yourself, Erin. This was your father's problem, and you about killed yourself trying to be a good daughter to him."

He pulls me back to our chairs and I bury my head in my hands. "He thinks Sean's coming. He asked if Rob and I could get married here, and I lied and said maybe. What am I going to say when he wakes up?"

In a single swift move, Brendan picks me up and deposits me in his lap.

"Tell me what to do," he says. "I hate seeing you like this. Anything. Name anything."

If I were my mother, I'd keep crying and ask him to fix this. To make it go away. To find my brother, to make my father not care about seeing me married, to make it all better.

You could stay, Brendan. You could be the person I lean on, and you could never leave. That's what you could do.

Perhaps I'm more like my mother than I thought. No matter how many times I'm rebuffed, I can't stop hoping for things another person can't give.

❧ 66 ❧

BRENDAN

E rin is in my lap, as fragile as a child.

I tell her I'll do anything, and I mean it, but she doesn't reply.

"I'm sorry," she whispers. "I destroyed your shirt."

"You can destroy all of my shirts, Erin. Every last one."

She removes herself from me and returns to her chair. I wish she hadn't. I miss her weight and her smell and the feel of her, the way her cheek rests just about my collarbone, the way her lashes brush my neck when she opens her eyes. I miss everything. I've been missing all of it for a very long time.

ROB ARRIVES MID-AFTERNOON, IN A FRESH SUIT. DID THE douchebag actually drive home and change to come here?

His eyes narrow when he sees me beside her. He must know something happened between us—even that girl I brought to the vineyard accused me of it on the way home that night. And if she could figure it out, anyone could.

I stabbed him in the back, but I can't bring myself to regret it. Those weeks with Erin were the best of my life, and Rob and I were never going to be friends again anyway. Not after I realized how he'd bullied her into giving up the things she loved. I left for Italy because I couldn't stand seeing them together, but I left believing she'd be better off with him, and I was wrong.

Erin stands and walks over to him. It seems to me that she rises reluctantly, but perhaps that's wishful thinking. He hugs her, a hug that lasts way too fucking long.

Rob turns to me. "I'll walk you out," he says.

It's impossible to miss his meaning. *Time for you to leave, asshole.*

I want to stay, but I no longer have a place here. I wish I did. I wish it was my job to be the one comforting her.

Once we're halfway down the hall, he stops walking. His hands are in his pockets, and he's staring at the floor.

"It was you, wasn't it?" he asks. "You're the one she was with while I was gone."

He isn't actually asking. For Erin's sake, I'd have denied it, but it's clear he already knows.

I meet his eye. "Yeah, and I don't regret it. I walked away a long time ago because I thought she was better off with you, and she wasn't."

"Oh, but you think she'd be better off with *you?*" he demands. "You can't stay with any girl for more than an hour, and that's about how long you can keep a job. All those years you spent trying to talk me out of shit—telling me I shouldn't ask her out, telling me we shouldn't move in together, and I shouldn't propose —that was all just you wanting to take your shot."

Maybe he's right, to some extent. But that's not entirely it. If I'd truly believed he could make her happy, I'd have left it alone. There was always a part of me that knew he couldn't, though.

"I didn't want you with her because you don't deserve her," I reply, "and I knew you couldn't make her happy. You still can't. Which you proved when you started fucking around with

Christina. I don't care if Erin believes your little story about how innocent it was. I know there was more to it than that."

He rolls his eyes. "Even if there was, I'm not going to take shit about it from you. Let's see you date someone for a week before you start criticizing me."

"This isn't about me. It's about you. And if you were a better person, you'd admit you can't make her happy and walk away."

He wants to hit me. I can see it. And I want him to do it, because God knows I'd like to hit him back. I've never wanted to hit someone more. But neither of us will go there, not with Erin just down the hall.

"Well, I'm not walking away. I'm going to marry her," he says calmly. Too calmly, as if he knows something I don't. There's certainty behind his words.

"She doesn't want to marry you. I think she's made that clear."

"But she will," he says, with a hint of smug triumph surfacing in his eyes. "Just watch."

He turns and walks back to the room. Every bone in my body wants to beg her not to listen, to turn down anything he suggests.

Except I've got nothing to offer in its place.

❧ 67 ❧

ERIN

Rob settles into the chair Brendan just vacated, grabs the same hand Brendan just held. It's not the same, but chocolate isn't the same as broccoli, and that doesn't mean you're only meant to eat the first.

"How's he been?" he asks. "Has he woken up since yesterday?"

I tilt my head. "How did you know he woke up yesterday?"

"Your mom called me. She didn't appear to know we'd broken up." My eyes fly open in alarm, and he squeezes my hand. "I didn't tell her. It was pretty clear from what she said that you didn't want them to know. My question is why you didn't."

It's an opening. If this were a movie, it would be the point where I tell him my father is an alcoholic, and my mother and I have danced around it my entire life. Except this isn't a movie, and that's not who the two of us are.

"I didn't want to upset them," I reply.

"I brought your ring," he says, pulling it out of his bag. "I thought it might help, under the circumstances."

I hesitate, but decide it'll make my dad feel better if he sees it. Just one diamond in that ring could pay someone's mortgage for a year. I look at it and think *showy*, but my dad looks at it and thinks *secure*. And what he thinks matters far more right now. I slide it back on my left hand and move the emerald to my right.

"She told me something else," he adds. "She said your dad asked if we could get married here, and you said maybe?"

I sigh heavily. *Fuck if my mom doesn't seem to go out of her way to make every aspect of my life harder.* "I didn't know what to say. I just couldn't say no right then."

"We could, you know." He recaptures my hand. "The hospital chaplain could do it."

My jaw drops. "That's crazy. We aren't even dating."

"We were a couple for four years," he says, squeezing my hand. "It's just a matter of time before we get back together. Why wait when we could do it now and give your dad what he wants?"

I suddenly feel so, so tired. More tired than I knew it was possible to feel. Though it's insane to even consider what Rob is offering, maybe it's also insane not to.

I could end all the chaos. I could give my parents something positive to focus on now and a little peace going forward. I could go back to the life I had—the nice house and the security of all of it. And maybe, when things with Brendan grow more distant, I could go back to feeling numb again. I want that, because being here, being me, missing Brendan—it feels like too much to bear.

I can grant my father's dying wish. One of them at least. But in granting it, I also know a piece of me will die too.

❧ 68 ❧

BRENDAN

I t takes a full day to find Sean. His boss refused to tell me anything at first, and it was only after I wore him down that he directed me to the people on staff who might know where Sean went.

I hate that it's taken so long to find him—Erin must be worried sick, and I guess I am too, but for different reasons. That sense of foreboding I felt yesterday is still with me, as if there's an hourglass somewhere, its sand spilling quickly. I don't even know what happens when it reaches its end—I only know the result will be one I can't live with.

He's holed up above a strip club north of Denver. I knock on the door and a girl answers, peering at me through the tiny opening allowed by the door chain. I tell her I'm Will's younger brother, and she slams the door and deadbolts it again. It occurs to me, too late, that maybe I shouldn't have led with Will's name since Sean got busted for possession while Olivia was staying at his apartment.

I knock again. A minute later I hear the slide of the chain. Sean opens the door and lets me in. He looks jittery and strung out, but given that I'd expected to find him with his arm tied off and not knowing his own name, he's surprisingly cogent.

"You don't know me..." I begin.

He laughs unhappily, derisively, still refastening the locks. "I know you."

He says it like he knows I've done something wrong, but I'm not sure how he would. Erin hasn't spoken to him in weeks. I want to ask him if she said something about me, like a fucking lovesick tween. I run a hand over my head. It's not what matters now.

"Erin's been trying to get ahold of you," I tell him. "Your dad is in the hospital. And it's pretty bad."

He stiffens. "How bad?"

I blow out a breath. I don't like this guy. I think he's made Erin's life hard, and he'll probably continue to do so for the rest of his existence, but I'll never forget the moment I heard my father was going to die. In spite of everything, I feel a shred of sympathy. "He needs surgery, but they don't think he'll survive. They're holding off on it until you get there."

Sean fastens the final lock and sinks into a chair, burying his face in his hands. Sweat beads at his hairline. "I can't," he says. "I can't leave."

I stare at him. *What kind of selfish prick won't go see his dying father?* Any sympathy I felt for him is absolutely gone. "Even if you don't give a shit about your dad, you owe this to Erin. For once in her life, she shouldn't have to deal with all this alone. So pull your shit together and be there for her."

"I can't leave, okay?" he shouts, throwing out his hands. "She and Rob broke up so I was trying to get her money back. I thought if I ran a few big deals for this guy, I could at least get some of it for her, but I got robbed. So now I owe this guy fifteen grand I don't have. I walk out of here, and I'm a dead man."

I flinch. I've smoked more than my share of various things, but I'm out of my element with something like this. "You can't ask him to give you time?"

He laughs unhappily. "This isn't the IRS. A guy like Danny isn't going to fucking garnish my wages until I've paid it back. And if you found me, they probably can too."

"Exactly," I reply. "So go to the cops. Give them information on this guy in exchange for immunity."

He shakes his head. "Even if that worked, they're not going to let me just saunter off to the hospital. I'd need to make bail. And believe me, no one I know has that kind of money."

I don't care if he rots in jail, or worse, but Erin does. She would rather die than see him hiding here or locked up for life, and if she learns what's going on, she'll somehow get the money together to pay this dealer off—probably by going back to the shitty job that made her miserable. Or worse, by getting it from Rob, leaving her beholden to him.

I'd rather lose my whole business than see that happen.

"I have that kind of money," I tell him.

THE POLICE STATION EATS UP MOST OF THE DAY, AND BAIL EATS up every penny of the money I need to keep my business running this winter. If Sean doesn't return when this is over, my company is done.

"Why are you doing this?" he asks as we drive to the hospital. He's said little to me all day, acting more like a resentful teenager than a grown man who just got his ass bailed out by a stranger.

"Because your sister needs you," I tell him. "And because she's been through too much shit to have to deal with your shit too."

The sky is the brightest blue, the color of the Caribbean as your plane dips beneath the clouds. Cool outside today, too. A perfect day for biking. I hope when this is done I can hang on to my business, but there's not a doubt in my mind I made the right decision. If her father were to die without seeing Sean, Erin would never forgive herself.

"Erin told me all about you," Sean says with disgust.

I glance over at him. "Is that why you're still acting like I'm a piece of shit even though I bailed you out?"

"I appreciate what you're doing. That doesn't mean I trust you with my sister," he replies. "Rob's an asshole, but he wouldn't fuck her up. I could tell from the moment she started describing you that you would. It was like she was happy, but upset too, like she knew you were going to hurt her."

Which is exactly what I did.

~

I DELIVER HIM OUTSIDE THE SAME HOSPITAL DOORS WHERE I dropped Erin yesterday morning.

"Room 1108," I tell him.

"You really don't want me to tell her it was you who bailed me out?" he asks, his hand on the door.

I shake my head. "Let her believe you came on your own. She doesn't need to know the rest."

She's better off thinking of me as the guy who didn't care enough than the guy who cared a little too much all along, but dissatisfaction gnaws at me as I drive away.

For no reason I can explain, I call my brother. We've barely spoken since I started hooking up with Erin. But like every other fight we've ever had, this one will end when one of us is struggling. And right now, I'm definitely struggling.

"You did all this for Erin?" he asks, once I tell him what happened. "You just risked your entire business for a girl you claim you don't want a relationship with?"

"Yeah."

He's silent for a moment, and then he laughs—mostly to himself. "Don't you get it yet? When you love someone so much you're willing to give up everything on her behalf, committing is the easy part."

"It's more complicated than that," I argue.

"No, it's not. You're just fucking scared. That's all this is."

I'm pissed when I hang up the phone. But when I reach the interstate, I turn north instead of south. As angry as I am, I know he's right. And there's something I need to face if I'm ever going to move forward.

🦋 69 🦋

ERIN

I need to tell my parents that I can't find Sean. I just don't know how. I've called every friend of his I know of. But "know of" is the key phrase. And the people I don't know are the ones he's with when he's using. Which is obviously why he can't be located.

Like a child, I'm sitting here, waiting on a miracle. A last-minute reprieve, a Hail Mary. Except the hours are passing quickly. The attending informs us that they've scheduled the surgery for late this afternoon, at which point I stop counting hours and switch to minutes instead.

There are 202 left.

But Rob promised he'd look for Sean, and while I seem to fail at almost everything I do these days, Rob does not. He's already begun to turn things around—we've now got the area's best neurosurgeon performing my dad's surgery, thanks to him, and he took care of my parents' mortgage payment for the next few months.

It's hard not to see the pattern here: life falls apart without Rob, and it comes back together with him. Rob never hurt me the way Brendan has. Maybe he isn't perfect, but there's a lot to be said for the absence of pain.

Two hours before surgery, my father wakes and asks if Sean is almost here. I tell him I think so, part of me hoping he just falls asleep before the surgery so he never learns the truth.

After a while, my dad stops asking. He just watches the door. And when Rob walks into the room with Sean behind him, it feels like a miracle.

We all burst into tears—me, my mother, my father. All of us relieved and sick with grief, knowing this may very well be the last time we're all in the same room.

Sean and my mother go to my father's side, and Rob comes to sit next to me. I hear my dad telling Sean he's a good son and he's proud of him. I guess my mother and I aren't the only liars in the family.

"How did you find him?" I ask.

He wraps his arm around my shoulders. "I'd do anything for you, Erin. You should know that by now."

I do know that. I can't begin to thank him. We were broken—I was broken—and now things feel like they might come together again. All because of him.

"I want you to move back home," he says. "Harper's roommate must be due back any day now. I just want to take care of you."

I hesitate. It feels wrong, but when has making a decision based on what I *feel* ever proven helpful? Brendan's the only person who's ever felt right, and he was never even a real option. That verse from the Bible comes to mind: *When I was a child, I spoke as a child...but when I became a man, I put away childish things.*

It's time for me to put away childish things. To admit that I wanted more from life than I'm ever going to get, and that I need Rob. I'm overwhelmed and incompetent on my own—look at what a mess I made of my life in the short time he was away—but he came back and fixed everything. He is what will keep me from ending up like my parents and Sean. He is the thing that will stand between all of us and disaster.

"Okay," I tell him. My voice is barely a whisper but he hears it.

~

MY FATHER IS WHEELED FROM THE ROOM TO GO TO THE OR, and my mother weeps. The hours pass, and she continues to weep, aside from the time she spends blaming me for all of it. She doesn't say it aloud. She just says, "I wish this hadn't happened," and looks directly at me.

Sean is using again. He's too pale, too restless. For the first time in my life, I'm beyond caring. I'm glad he's alive. I'm glad my dad got to see him. It feels like little else matters at the moment.

"I can go talk to the chaplain if you want," Rob suggests. "I'm sure he could marry us here after your dad's surgery."

I blink. I'd forgotten that was even under discussion. I shake my head. "We're not ready for that, Rob. And it feels like tempting fate, planning something that depends on my dad making it." What I don't say is that the very thought only adds to my grief, and I already have plenty.

He squeezes my hand. "Sorry. I just thought it might help if you had something to focus on."

A short time later, the doctor arrives to tell us my dad survived. I silently thank God for saving my father, which is easy to do, and then I say another prayer of thanks for Rob. That one, oddly, is more difficult.

Part of me still desperately wishes things had gone a different way.

❧ 70 ❧

BRENDAN

The assisted living facility sits in an enviable location. When I arrive, the sun is in its last moments of fullness, hanging heavy before it descends behind the mountains. It's the kind of view that makes you stop in place for a moment, and Gabi is never really going to see anything like it again. The guilt I feel about what happened with her is a constant in my life, but right now it's so amplified I can't feel anything else.

The woman at the registration desk tells me Gabi is probably in the art room. They use a lot of euphemisms here. They label the rooms—music room, art room, game room, library—not for the residents, but for the people who love them. It's a way of pretending anyone here has a normal life.

I walk into the room, seeking one blank face among many, and I find it. Gabi's hair is short now, but I would know her face anywhere, even with eyes that no longer flash or let me see inside her soul. Immediately I wish I hadn't come. She won't understand my apology. I'm not even sure if I came here for her or just to make myself feel better—which is something I don't deserve.

A man approaches me from the other side of the room. It takes me a minute to place him because he's aged a decade in the three years since I last saw him: Gabi's father, a man who must hate me above all living beings.

My chest tightens. We haven't spoken since he came to my apartment in Italy to retrieve her stuff. Another hard memory. He'd wanted to see the bathtub, which I hadn't even seen myself, since the place was still considered a crime scene. The look on his face when I opened the bathroom door to her blood still glazing the tub made me wish I'd refused.

"Hello, Brendan," he says. He extends a hand, which I did not expect. His wife certainly wouldn't have done it.

"I'm sorry..." I hesitate. "I can come back."

"No," he says, indicating the table where Gabi sits, staring vacantly at the wall. "I'm glad you're here."

I take the seat on one side of Gabi, and he takes the other. It's been a long time since I was this near her, and I have the same desire I did the last time: to shake her, tell her to wake up, to come back, to stop doing this to all of us.

"It gets easier," he says softly, looking from my face to Gabi's. "You get used to it."

I nod. There's a lump in my throat, as much for him as for his daughter. I can't imagine living with this kind of pain, and it's pain I caused. Gabi is his only child. I think about this every time I hold Caroline—how unbelievably awful it must be to have a lifetime of memories with your little girl, only to lose her. To know you'll never chat with her at breakfast again or watch her open birthday presents. To know she had so many big moments taken from her, and that all that potential is gone.

"I've been wanting to talk to you," he says. "About my wife. I'm sorry about the calls. I've tried to stop her, but she waits until I'm asleep."

My gaze rises. The last thing I ever expected from him, or wanted from him, was an apology.

I swallow hard. "I don't blame her for calling. I deserve it."

He looks surprised. "I hope you don't mean that."

I stare at my hands as they clench and unclench, and then at Gabi's hands, now incapable of action or intent.

"What happened..." I say, my jaw tight, "happened because of me."

"I loved my daughter," he says. His eyes tear up a little, making this so much harder to watch. "I will always love my daughter. But she had problems. It's something my wife never wanted to admit and still won't admit. She was always dramatic and high strung. You told her no when she was little, and she'd either fly into a rage or weep like her heart was broken." His small smile at the memory twists. "It was cute at the time. But as she got older it was...less controllable. She was diagnosed as bipolar her freshman year in high school, but I don't think either of us really knew how bad it was until the first time she tried to commit suicide."

He must see the utter shock on my face. "You didn't know?" he asks.

I shake my head. I had no idea. The only unhappiness I ever saw in Gabi was the unhappiness I caused.

"Several times, beginning in high school. Sometimes it was over a break-up, but once over a bad grade. I didn't want her to go pre-med. I didn't think she could handle the pressure. I didn't want her going to Italy, either, without one of us with her. My wife, though —she just wanted Gabi to be normal, wanted to believe she was better. She told me your boss knew about Gabi's history and was going to keep an eye on her. I didn't learn until much later that was not the case."

I look at Gabi's face. She's still beautiful, but she's *gone*. I don't know how he stands it.

"I'm still the one who drove her to it."

"Brendan, you were a kid. You're still a kid. People change their minds about a significant other all the time. I can't tell you how many of my friends are divorced because someone changed their mind twenty or thirty years in. It's hard, but people are allowed to do that. So for you to take responsibility for all this when you only knew her a few months is insane."

"I still shouldn't have—"

He cuts me off. "Stop trying to convince me you're at fault. If this hadn't happened with you, it would have happened soon enough. The first year of medical school? I can't imagine she'd have made it all the way through. My wife calls you because it's easier for her to blame you than blame herself."

I'm speechless, awed by this man's ability to forgive. I don't think I'd be capable of the same. I sit with the two of them, letting everything he told me sink in.

Maybe it really wasn't my fault. Maybe it's just who she was.

Something begins to loosen inside me, something that's been strung tight for a long time. And as it starts to spin free, all I can think about is Erin.

I WAKE IN MY APARTMENT THE NEXT MORNING TO FIND reminders of Erin everywhere—the running shoes she never picked up by the door, her moisturizer on my bathroom sink, the holes I've put in my wall.

In my closet is the box of mementos Gabi once dumped on the floor. I hate that box, and I hate the moisturizer and all the other shit. I hate them because they remind me Erin's gone, and that I was so fucking happy when she was here. How could I have ever thought history might repeat itself with her? Erin isn't Gabi. Hell, of the two of us, I'm the one close to losing it right now, not her.

When I get home the box is still sitting there, and what Will said yesterday finally sinks in: committing to Erin would be easy. It doesn't scare me in the least, because there's nothing I wouldn't give up to have her, and because I know I'm not going to change my mind.

Now I just have to hope that Erin hasn't changed hers.

❧ 71 ❧

ERIN

My father is released from the ICU the day after his surgery, and while the cirrhosis is not something we can cure, we are told he's "out of the woods" for now.

Later that afternoon, I get a voicemail from the chancellor at ECU, asking if we can meet to discuss job opportunities. I can't imagine any way in which I could gracefully return to my old position, but I would not be surprised if that's what he wants me to do. I've heard quite a bit from Harper about the state of the marketing department since I left, and apparently Tim hasn't fared too well without me there to do his job.

So it's a day full of miracles. I just wish a day full of miracles was enough for me. Everything has turned around, but I'm still miserable.

With the surgery behind them, my parents begin planning for the future, their own and mine alike. "Did you talk to Rob about getting married at our church?" my mother asks me. The question is entirely for Rob's benefit, as she knows I have not.

Rob raises a brow. "Church?"

"You need to be married in the church," my father explains, his voice raw from being intubated, "so you're married in the eyes of God."

"It's a Catholic thing," I whisper, praying he will at least wait until we're alone to object. "We can talk about it later."

"Of course," says Rob to my mom, as if *she* is the bride. Or as if I'd actually agreed to marry him. "Whatever you want."

It's a relief when I get paged to the nurse's station. The talk of weddings—talk Rob participates in happily—is giving me a headache, and my mother's happy tears are even more annoying than her sad ones.

I'm almost to the desk when Brendan steps into my path. He's unshaven, with circles under his eyes, but he's still so beautiful it breaks my heart. He holds out his arms, and I walk straight into them, even though I shouldn't. I bury my nose in his chest, wishing we could stay exactly like this forever.

"I heard your dad made it through surgery," he says, his voice low against my ear.

His voice, the smell of his skin, the feel of his chest beneath my cheek. These are things I have lost. These are all things I will never have again. How am I going to stand living in a world where these things are no longer mine?

"Rob got this amazing neurosurgeon," I tell him. "It's a miracle."

He stiffens at the mention of Rob's name. "Can we talk?"

I agree, and he leads me down the hall, turning in to the first empty room he finds.

He reaches for my hands, linking our fingers, and then goes absolutely still. His gaze on the engagement ring on my finger.

"Why are you wearing that?" he asks, his hands tightening on mine so I can't pull away. "Why the fuck are you wearing that ring?"

I could explain why I'm wearing the ring, but I suppose it's no longer all for show the way it was a few days ago. If I'm moving in with Rob, of course we're going to get married. And Brendan has no right to question me either way.

"Don't make this harder," I tell him. "You didn't want me, Brendan. So you can't come in here now and make it all worse."

"I did want you," he says adamantly. He lets go of my hands and cradles my jaw, forcing me to meet his eyes. "I wanted you so much, and I was so fucked up over the thing with Gabi I wouldn't let myself try. But I'm ready now."

"Why?" I demand. "Because I'm taken? Does that suddenly make it feel safe enough for you?"

He bites his lip. "I talked to Gabi's dad yesterday," he says. "And he said some things that made it finally sink in—what you've been telling me all along. That wasn't her first suicide attempt. She'd been really unstable for a long time before she met me. And yeah, I'm still scared, but I know you're not her. Look at everything you've dealt with over the past few weeks. I want this. I'm ready for it to be anything you want it to be."

His words—they'd have meant everything to me a week ago. They still mean everything, but now they make my chest ache. I can't go back on things with Rob again. Not after everything he's done for us. "You're too late, Brendan," I whisper.

"No. No, I'm fucking not. You aren't married. There's nothing here you can't undo. You don't even love him."

I blink back tears. Every bone in my body wants to agree with him, but I can't. "It's not the same as with you, but I do love him. It's just different."

"You love him like a *friend*, Erin. You don't marry someone you love as a friend. You don't belong with someone you only love as a friend. You want more, and you've wanted it for a long time or you'd already have married him."

I did want more. But sometimes you have to choose what's merely *enough*, and there's relief in knowing that you'll at least be able to survive it if it fails. "I'm just better off with Rob. Around him, things go the way they're supposed to."

"But around me you're *real*. You get to be the person you actually are, the good and the bad. I love that girl, and he doesn't even know her."

My throat is so clogged I can hardly swallow. "He knows about my dad. I told him. He's going to help me get him into rehab."

"Yeah, because you were forced to tell him," he hisses. "But does he know the rest? Does he know the things you love? That you hate listening to NPR and that those bluegrass interludes they play make you want to put a knife in your eye? That you'd rather sit outside or hear a band than go to some fancy fucking dinner? That you test drive a Ducati every time you're here?"

I flinch. "No, but—"

"Are you ever going to dance with him in the middle of the night wearing nothing but a T-shirt? No, because he won't even dance. Because he wouldn't even understand why you'd want to. Are you ever going to strip off all of your clothes and spread out on his couch when you want to get laid? Are you going to bake for him and sing at the top of your lungs while you do it? Let me answer for you: No, Erin, you won't. That's not who he is or what he wants, and you won't. And those things aren't peripheral. They're *you*."

I bury my face in my hands. Every single thing he's saying is true, and I feel how badly I want those moments back with him. How much I'm going to miss being myself, and being myself with *him*. But my family is sinking, and that's what's important here, not whether I ever dance half-naked again. As much as I might want Brendan, what I need most is to know that we—me, my parents, Sean—are safe. And even if I could afford to risk it, there's no guarantee Brendan won't change his mind. The past few weeks have been awful, but to lose him when I'd really thought we had a chance would be so much worse.

"I was happy until you showed up," I cry. "Before you came back from Italy, I was fine. I was happy then, and I'll be happy again."

"You weren't happy, Erin. You still aren't or you wouldn't be in here with me crying. And I don't want to make you cry, but I'm in

love with a girl you want to kill off, and I don't know what else
to do."

He pulls my hands from my face and leans in, capturing my
mouth. I let him. I let myself have this one last time, his mouth
and his heat and my tears slipping between our skin. And then I
pull back, and I leave him behind for good.

72

ERIN

By the following day, my father's condition is considered stable. The doctor requests a meeting with all of us, and I'm relieved that Rob is back at work and will miss it. I have no idea what will be said at this meeting, but it feels like our secrets are on the move now, that the trap door they hide under has begun to lift, and things that are meant to stay hidden may be about to slip free. Rob sort of knows about my dad, but he doesn't know the rest of us are just as sick in our own ways, and it's something I'd prefer he not find out.

My parents are back to performing The Doyle Show when the doctor walks in: my dad the gruff but lovable patriarch, my mother giggling and giddy. I'd almost stopped noticing it, but now I can see nothing else. The falseness of it sickens me.

The doctor's smile is patient, but small. It's obvious he's here to discuss something serious, something neither of my parents wants to hear.

"Before Mr. Doyle goes home," he says, "there are a couple of issues we need to address."

"We can't wait to get home," my mother says briskly. "We're

having a big celebration dinner tomorrow night." Her eyes widen as if she's just had the most brilliant idea, so brilliant it startles her. "You should come! You've never had chicken parm like mine, I promise you."

I flinch, embarrassed for her, and Sean looks away. She is the only person in the room who doesn't realize how insane she sounds.

Dr. Taylor doesn't even smile in response. He's not one of those doctors who makes friends with his patients, and in this case that may be a good thing. He's unlikely to be bringing good news.

"I've gone over your labs and your biopsy report," he tells my father. "As you know, cirrhosis is irreversible, but you still have the possibility of ten good years, maybe more, if you can manage not to drive into any more telephone poles."

My father nods. "I won't. I just need to learn not to stay out so late."

My mother squeezes his hand. "We're getting older. I think we both need to remember to take better care of ourselves."

I feel like I'm choking. My father is dying from cirrhosis and he could have killed someone last week. I can't believe they still refuse to see this. I've given up every piece of happiness in my life to make sure they're safe, and I'm not playing this game with them for one more second.

"No." My voice is like breaking glass, making every other action in the room cease, every head turn toward me. "No, this wasn't lack of sleep. You don't get to pretend this was lack of sleep."

"Erin, stop," my mother scolds. Her voice is mild, but in her eyes I see a warning, the same one she gave me as a child when someone asked why my father was absent at a school concert or an award ceremony.

Except I'm an adult now. She's no longer a foot taller, and I'm no longer the little girl who needs her to survive.

"He could have killed someone," I reply. "That telephone pole could have been a *child*, Mom. That could have been *me*. Would you still be pretending then?"

"We can discuss this later," she says, her eyes narrowed.

"Mr. Doyle had a blood alcohol content of .25 when he arrived here that night," says Dr. Taylor. "I think he should consider attending a rehab program."

"Everyone has a few too many once in a while, doc," my dad says. His tone is jovial. It's his "come on, boys will be boys" schtick. I've heard it way too many times before.

"Your cirrhosis didn't happen on its own," the doctor replies. "If none of that persuades you, I'd encourage you to consider the fact that you're also facing a DUI charge. Given how high your blood alcohol content was and that this wasn't your first DUI, rehab may be the only thing that keeps you out of jail."

He leaves, and my parents bluster, completely outraged. As if the doctor just accused them of child pornography or human trafficking, something so far out of left field they can't begin to imagine how he came up with it.

"He's crazy," my mother insists, turning to my dad. "Rob will find us a lawyer—the *best* lawyer. We'll get you out of this."

I laugh, but it's not a happy sound. I've wondered when I might hit the point of *enough*—the moment when my debt to them is paid, when I abandon responsibility. And here it is: with my father in the hospital, dying of cirrhosis, facing jail time.

Enough.

I stand. "Dad needs *help*, not a lawyer. Not a penny of my money, or Rob's, will go toward defending him unless he's gone to rehab first."

"Erin," my mother gasps, ready to scold.

I stop her before she can start. "Mom, shut up, for once in your life. You're as big a problem as he is." I turn toward my father. "Five days ago, I thought you were going to die. And if you had, it would have been my fault, and Mom's, for letting you do this. You're still going to die. Maybe it'll take a few years and maybe it won't, but I'm done being a part of it. When it happens, I'm not willing to feel the way I've felt over the past week. You know what your drinking is? It's cowardice. And Mom, every single time you let him do it without comment, you're just as bad. And I've been bad too. I *shouldn't* have been answering your calls. I *shouldn't* have been in bars looking for you at three AM when I had to be up for work in a few hours. So Dad, here's the deal: go to rehab, or this is the last time you'll see me, either of you. I'm not going to be a part of this anymore."

All three of them look shocked, but it's my mother whose shock turns to rage in a heartbeat. "How dare you make this about yourself right now, of all times? Why is it so hard for you to be—"

"Stop, Mom," Sean says. "She's right. We're all fucking cowards. She's right. I'm going back to rehab. Dad needs to go too. If he doesn't go, I don't want to hear from you again either."

My mother starts carrying on about how she raised us, reminding Sean of all the times she's supported him. It's my father who stops her.

"Okay," he says, his voice low and gravelly. "I'll go."

"You don't have to do this," my mother insists.

"I think," he says quietly, closing his eyes, "that I probably do."

❧ 73 ☙

ERIN

Rob arranges everything. He gets my dad into the best treatment program in the area, and he says he knows a lawyer who "always wins."

"And I got you an interview with my firm," he adds.

My heart sinks. I was willing to take any job a few days ago, and I still will be if nothing else works out, but the idea of working at his company is just too much.

"Oh," I stammer. "I appreciate that, but I got a call from the chancellor at ECU. It's possible they're going to offer me something there."

He smiles wide, as if I'm a child who's just said something ridiculous but cute. "Babe, you can make thirty percent more at my company. And the bullshit you went through with HR would never happen in the private sector."

"Maybe," I reply. "But I still want to hear what they have to say. Aside from Timothy, I really liked working there."

"I can't imagine it's about a job anyway," he argues. "Not given the way you left. He probably just wants you to call in a favor with Olivia."

I exhale heavily. He's probably right. Just because the truth sucks doesn't mean you ignore it. "Fine," I sigh. "I'll go to the interview."

We're lucky to have Rob. I just wish I could think that without this feeling of resignation. Everything is fixed, and everyone is saved, but I still cry myself to sleep back at my parents' place that night.

So I guess not everyone is fixed. I secretly wonder if I'm broken beyond repair.

SEAN SPENDS THE NEXT MORNING AT THE POLICE STATION—I don't ask why because I don't want to know—and when he returns, I drive him back to rehab.

"I'm sorry about summer semester," he says. "I'll figure out a way to get those credits. And I'll pay you back, I promise."

I've heard Sean's promises so many times. He could have said nothing at all and it would hold more weight. But he's trying, and I'm not going to make all of this harder for him by arguing. Very little feels worth fighting over at the moment.

"You think Dad will make it?" he asks.

I glance at him. Given that he's now entering rehab for the eighth time, I can't say I have a lot of faith in the process. I tell him I don't know, and I can hear the apathy in my voice. This week, it seems, has used up my ability to care about pretty much everything.

Sean doesn't speak again until we pull up to the rehab center. "The last time I saw you—when we went to lunch? You glowed, like you did when you were a kid," he says. "I'd forgotten that about you. I'd forgotten you could even *be* happy like that. You're back to faking it now, though."

I take the first available parking space and climb out of the car. "I'm not faking anything, Sean." I slam the door harder than I should. "Our father is dying, and I'm unemployed. Who would be happy right now?"

"I don't think that has anything to do with it, though," he says, reaching into the trunk for his bag. "It was Brendan."

"If I seemed happy, it had nothing to do with him."

"If you say so," he replies. "Or maybe being scared of shit runs in the family." Without a backward glance, he walks away.

I spend the return trip to the hospital fuming. *What an asshole.* He took my entire life savings and is back at rehab for the eighth time. Why would I listen to his opinion about *anything*?

Besides, what he said didn't even make sense—happiness and bravery are completely different things. And I'm not a coward. I've gone into the seediest bars known to man to find my father. I kept running when I wanted to give up. I've held my family together in my most broken moments. I stood up to my boss and ended a relationship when it wasn't working, although I guess I can't take much credit for that now that we're back together.

"I'm not scared of anything," I say aloud, as if I can prove it to myself. Except I don't sound brave, or fearless. I sound like a child arguing against the most obvious truth.

It's my father's turn to go to rehab later in the afternoon. Rob insists on driving us, although I wish he wouldn't. Somewhere inside, I know he finds this situation distasteful. We are like a dirty guest room he's forced to stay in for a weekend. He smiles and struggles to control his disgust the entire time.

My mother climbs in the backseat of Rob's Range Rover with my father, filling the air with false good cheer. It reminds me of bug spray—the scent not quite sweet enough to disguise what is toxic.

"I spoke to Father Duncan," she says. "He said he'd be happy to marry you in the church, despite the situation. We could probably get a date within the month, as long as you aren't going to insist on bridesmaids and..." Her voice grinds to a halt.

Rob's hand, holding mine, feels leaden.

"Yeah," he says. "Just family. No one else."

My mother starts prattling on about the morning weddings she's attended, places we can go for a nice brunch afterward. She asks if we'll have a honeymoon, and I finally snap.

"Mom, can we please stop discussing this? Let's just get through one thing at a time."

She's probably mad, but I don't really care. I turn on the radio, and Rob immediately hits the preset for NPR. I think of Brendan again, although I never actually seem to *stop* thinking of Brendan. Everything he said was correct. I don't want to listen to this, but I'm not going to ask Rob to change the station. I'm not going to ask Rob for anything I want, ever. I want so many things I wouldn't even know where to start, and I don't think I'd ever be able to stop.

One of their annoying little bluegrass interludes comes on, and I want to laugh and cry at the same time. Even the stupidest, smallest things make me think of Brendan, and every one of them hurts.

My head begins to throb. The bluegrass continues. My mother, behind me, is talking too loudly, her false enthusiasm grating on my ear as she comments on every fucking thing we pass. Every building, every road sign, every billboard. Pretending all is well, even with half the family in rehab.

But I guess I'm doing a lot of pretending too.

Rob catches my eye and smiles, though it doesn't meet his eyes. "Let's try to get dinner back home tonight. Why don't you see if we can get a table at De La Mer around eight?"

De La Mer is quiet and expensive and sterile, the kind of place I hate. I bite my lip. *Brendan, get out of my head.*

"I'm pretty wiped," I venture. "Do you think we could go somewhere low-key? That place with the patio on Edgemont always looks relaxed. And they have bands sometimes."

He frowns. "I was kind of craving some ahi tuna. And if there's a band, we won't be able to talk."

It's not worth fighting over. Very few things in life are. I go online to reserve our table, ignoring the odd dread I feel about the night I've just planned. What is there to dread about a nice dinner at a good restaurant? Nothing.

We check my father in, and the sick feeling in the pit of my stomach remains. The truth is that it's been here, to some extent, ever since I agreed to get back together with Rob. I'm beginning to worry it's permanent.

My mother decides to stay for that night's family therapy session, so Rob and head back alone. We reach the highway, and he rests his hand on my thigh.

"It'll be good to have you home," he says.

Oh, God. I'm not sure how I'm just realizing this now, but tonight will be our first night alone since we got back together. And there are things he'll expect. I've slept with him a thousand times, but the idea of doing it tonight sickens me.

I stare out the window. No place is more beautiful than Colorado in August, but right now all I can see is what's bleak— the grass that's parched and the dry ground and the ugly highway. Everything looks dead to me, looks like nothing, and that's what I feel inside.

Maybe because I've just chosen a lifetime of things I don't want —NPR and fancy dinners and boring sex. This life is the safest course. But what's the point in living a life you hate?

I squeeze my eyes shut to stop thinking, but I only hear Brendan and Sean in my head, and they're both saying the same thing. They're telling me I'm giving up everything I love because I think it will keep me safe—from pain, from worry, from the sick parts of myself. But safety is meaningless if you gain it by giving away what matters.

I've been confusing comfort with happiness, apathy with freedom. Just like my parents, I'm missing my real life every single day by choosing things that are empty, by choosing to pretend.

I don't want to give up dinner outside, or music. I don't want to give up sex in a hammock, or on a picnic blanket. Or late nights with someone who will stay awake with me when my whole life is turning to shit, who knows everything ugly inside of me and wants me in spite of it. What am I getting in exchange for all of those things I've pushed away? Less pain, maybe. Fewer demons to fight and resist.

Sean is right. I'm as big a coward as anyone in my family.

He turns the radio on. Bluegrass music again. I reach out and turn it off so I can say brave words at last, really meaning them this time.

"I'm sorry, Rob," I tell him, "but this isn't going to work."

❧ 74 ❧

BRENDAN

"How long you plan to keep doing this?" Beck asks, sliding me a beer.

We've been friends for a long time, but that doesn't mean I feel like answering his questions, even if he does let me drink for free. I wrap my hand around the bottle, looking at it as if it holds answers. "Doing what?"

"Sitting in here alone and pissed off, drinking to forget about Erin."

I roll my eyes, though the mention of her name has made my stomach drop. "What makes you think this has anything to do with Erin?"

He raises a brow. "Do I really look that stupid to you?"

It's been three days since she walked away from me at the hospital. Three days since I realized getting serious with Gabi *wasn't* the biggest mistake of my life. Refusing to get serious with Erin was.

"It doesn't matter," I reply, resting my head in my hands. "It's over. She's marrying someone else."

Beck hesitates, like he wants to argue, and finally decides

against it. "Then you've got to move on, man. I'm tired of watching you sulk and go home alone."

I look around. There are girls here, girls I'd have taken home once upon a time. I don't have much interest in being that guy again, but who am I otherwise? I'm *this*, the guy who didn't pull his head out of his ass until it was too late. The guy too damn miserable to care about anything right now, even the business he once wanted so badly.

"Something's got to change, bro," says Beck.

Yeah, I guess it does. I haven't been with anyone since the morning Erin left my apartment, but I can't keep going the way I am. Alone, kicking myself for my mistakes, missing Erin while she's planning a wedding to Rob...or already married to him.

Jesus, the next few months are going to be so fucking hard. I'm going to need something more than what I've got at the moment to survive.

I look around the room. No one appeals to me. Doesn't mean I shouldn't at least try.

75

ERIN

The conversation with Rob on the way back to my parents' place was ugly, as I suspected it would be. He called me words I've never heard him utter before.

"I guess this is really about Brendan," he said, his lip curling, "and if it is, you're even stupider than I thought."

"It has nothing to do with him," I said, and it was sort of the truth. I have no idea what's going to happen with Brendan—maybe his pleas at the hospital were some temporary thing he regretted an hour later, and maybe they weren't. But if I want to be different from my family, I need to make brave choices. I need to stop confusing comfort and happiness. My happiness with Brendan is not certain, but my unhappiness with Rob is, and that's all I need to know.

Except now, sitting outside Brendan's place, I feel anything but brave.

A part of me would like to stay in the car for another hour, drumming up my courage. I don't, though, because Brendan is inside, feet away from me, and I have missed him so desperately that I can't stand to wait another minute.

I climb the stairs and knock. For a moment I think I hear voices inside, and when he opens the door, half-dressed, I know immediately that I've interrupted something.

And then, in the other room, I hear a voice. A female voice.

"Oh." The word bursts from my mouth, along with every ounce of free oxygen in my body. If he'd punched me, I'd be more steady on my feet than I am at the moment. The disappointment, the pain of it... it's too much to cope with in such a short span of time. *I should have known. I should have known. I was stupid. Again.*

I should probably still tell him what I came here to say, but I don't have it in me. All I want to do is get away as fast as I possibly can. I turn to leave, but he grabs my elbow before I reach the stairs.

"Erin," he says, not allowing me to pull away. "Wait."

When I don't come back, he reaches a single arm around my waist and lifts me against him, holding me tight to his chest, his arm an immovable band. I feel his breath brush my ear as he speaks.

"Why are you here, and why are you running off?"

"Please just let me go. I shouldn't have come. You've already got someone here, and I should have known you'd—"

"There's no one here."

My throat constricts and words barely edge their way out. "I heard her."

"You heard the TV."

My heart beats so hard I can hear it pounding in my ears. Part of me doesn't want to believe him. The frightened, cowardly part that knows I'm safest by leaving here, by hating him, by protecting myself from everything that comes if I remain. I've been this person with him so many times it feels natural. But I'm not going to be that girl anymore, so I do the brave thing, the scariest thing, the thing I most want to do in the world: I stay. Instead of running, I lean into him, pressing my face to his chest.

"Please be here because you broke up with Rob," he says, his shaky exhale ruffling my hair.

"I did," I whisper. "Do you still want this?"

He tips my chin upward. "More," he says, "than I've ever wanted anything."

His hands go to my face, holding it like something he treasures, and then his lips are on mine. A soft kiss, restrained and sweet.

After the drama of the past few weeks, it's a little surreal to suddenly discover our story might have a happy ending after all. "Is this really happening?"

"It'd better be," he replies, "because I don't know what I'll do if it's not. I've already put way too many holes in the wall to ever get my deposit back."

I look around as he pulls me inside the door. His apartment *does* look destroyed. "Those were because of me?"

"One every time we spoke, and one every time I had to hear from Rob about you guys getting back together." He slides his hands through my hair, pressing his fingertips to my scalp. "I can't believe you're here."

He finds my mouth again, less soft this time, and from the moment he touches me, I want everything. I lean into him and he hardens against me...a single sharp inhale and I find myself pressed to the wall with his hands on my hips.

His urgency makes me forget anything I meant to discuss. I decide that whatever it was, it probably didn't matter all that much, but he pulls away again.

"Why are you stopping?" I ask breathlessly.

He flinches. "I'm trying to behave myself here, but it's easier said than done. I haven't had sex since you left."

My mouth falls open. "At all?"

He gives a somewhat pained laugh. "I haven't slept with anyone but you since *Tahoe*, Erin. Before that, even."

That can't be true. There were so many nights I didn't see him even when we were sleeping together. And all those weeks where he was off with girls like Crystal.

"But...all those nights when you just disappeared..."

"I wanted to be with you every fucking second and occasionally it freaked me out," he admits, staring at the floor between us. "I was trying to pull back. I just could never do it long enough."

That last shattered piece of me stitches itself back together. All those nights I made myself sick, imagining him with other girls, and he was actually alone, trying to get over me. I wish I'd known, but it doesn't matter now. Nothing matters except that we're together and this is really happening.

My hands go to the waistband of his shorts. "Well I haven't been with anyone but you since before Tahoe either," I tell him, "so I don't want you to behave."

He looks shocked for a second and then something fiercer, more possessive, takes over. In a second he's pinning me to the wall, his hands making quick work of my jeans before he lifts me up and carries me to the couch.

He lays me down and moves above me, his mouth on my neck, and then sliding lower. His hand slips under the elastic of my panties, his touch unbearably light, a whisper and nothing more. I writhe beneath him, waiting for him to increase the pressure, to move things further, but he doesn't. He just tortures me with his gentle fingers until my entire body is strung tight.

"Brendan, I need—"

"I know what you need," he says, his voice husky. "But I've thought about nothing else for weeks, so I think I'll take my time and wait until you're begging."

I arch toward his hand. "I'm already begging." My voice is reed thin and breathless.

He laughs, his tongue following the trail his fingers just made, but just as light.

"*Please*," I say, and he finally relents, sliding the panties off and pushing my legs apart before he moves up, filling me with a single roll of his hips.

"That's so good," he says, squeezing his eyes shut. "Give me a minute. Don't move."

Something about being told not to move makes me want to do it more than I ever have before. "Please, Brendan."

"Christ," he groans. "Don't move and don't beg. Either one of those will end this quickly."

Slowly he withdraws and enters me again. My nails dig into his skin.

"More," I demand.

"I don't remember you being so bossy," he says with a grin, but he complies—for a minute. And then he slows again.

"Faster. I'm not going to finish at that pace," I breathe.

"Lucky for you," he replies, "the night is young."

Much later, after we've made good use of the couch, and the kitchen table, and the floor, we make our way to bed, and finally talk.

"I still don't understand why you got back together with Rob," he says, rolling onto his back. "He never made you happy. Even if I wasn't in the picture, I don't know why you were willing to settle for him again."

I sigh. "It was weak. But he'd done so much for us, and then when he found Sean it just felt like we needed him. Like my family and I were too incompetent on our own."

Brendan stills for a moment, and then rolls toward me. "Did Rob tell you he found Sean?" he asks, his jaw clenched.

I shrug. "Yeah. More or less."

Brendan sits up. "That son of a bitch," he says between his teeth. "He didn't find Sean. *I* did. I stayed up all night tracking him down and paid his fucking bail."

I sit up too, pulling the sheet to my chest. "Why didn't you tell me?"

He frowns. "I figured you were better off thinking Sean had done the right thing on his own."

"But the bail...I mean, was it a lot? Where'd you get the money?"

"I used the money I set aside for leading heli-skiing tours this winter," he says. "It's fine. I'm getting it back."

My heart seems to swell in my chest—he risked his entire business on my behalf and wasn't even going to let me know. I press a kiss to his cheek.

"I wiped out the last of my savings paying Rob back for my parents' rent," I sigh. "I'm meeting with the chancellor at ECU tomorrow. Once I've got a paycheck again I can—"

The smile leaves his face. "You're not going back to work for Timothy," he says. "I'll end up getting arrested for assault if you do."

"Definitely not," I agree. "But until I find something and you get your money back we're both broke. It's a good thing we never leave your apartment anyway."

"It's not forever," he promises, cradling my face in his hands. "We'll figure it out."

I'm pretty sure we already have.

WHEN WE WAKE I CAN'T SEE THE CLOCK, BUT I CAN TELL BY THE full sunlight blazing in through the French doors that it's not early —which isn't all that surprising given how late Brendan kept me up. As much as I want to snuggle against him, I don't. Harper's roommate gets back today, and I have to get my stuff out of her room before I meet with the chancellor. Reluctantly, I slide one leg forward to climb out of bed when a hand lands on my hip like a vise.

"Where do you think you're going?" Brendan asks, rolling over and dragging my hips against him. His erection presses into my back, and I feel that familiar longing in my gut, which is just ridiculous. Surely there's some limit to the number of times you can have sex in a twelve-hour period.

"I told Harper I'd be over there this morning to move my stuff into her room. I'm already late."

"Move it here," he says.

I smile. "That's nice of you, but I have no idea if I'll get a job offer today. It's entirely possible I won't have my own place for months."

"I don't want you to get your own place," he says, rolling me to face him. "I want you here."

I feel joy flutter in my chest. I never thought I'd see the day when I'd accuse Brendan of moving too fast.

"Baby steps," I tell him with a laugh. "Let's see if you can get through a full day without feeling trapped."

"I assure you that won't be an issue. Come on, Erin. We were practically living together before Rob got back anyway. And I've spent weeks feeling sick every time I came home, knowing you wouldn't be here. I never want to feel that way again."

"I'll bring a *few* of my things here."

"All of them."

I laugh. "Brendan, this is a negotiation. You're supposed to move toward the center."

"It's not a negotiation," he says, pulling me tighter. "Bring everything."

AN HOUR LATER, WE APPEAR AT HARPER'S PLACE TOGETHER. Harper, who took her lunch early to help, looks at our joined hands and raises a brow.

"You sure you want to do that, Brendan?" she asks. "Someone might see."

He gives her half a grin. "Yeah, Harper, I'm sure. Thanks for your concern."

We go to the bedroom, where I've stacked boxes along the wall on one side. It worked fine in here, but I can't just leave all this in Harper's room.

"I'll move what I can into the car and leave the rest here for now," I tell her. "Just give me a day to figure things out. I can probably store it at my parents'."

"No, you won't," says Brendan. "It's going to my place."

"*Some* is going to your place," I reply. "That's what we agreed."

"That is not what we agreed." He grabs two boxes and moves toward the door.

Harper frowns.

"You're not moving in with him," she says. "You've only been single for, like, a day! You need to keep your options open."

"She's not keeping her options open, Harper!" shouts Brendan over his shoulder. "She has no options."

"Erin," she says quietly, her voice full of doom.

I smile. While I have no intention of moving all of my stuff to his place just yet, he's really sort of right.

"I don't want options," I tell her. "I've got exactly what I want."

THAT AFTERNOON I GO TO THE CHANCELLOR'S OFFICE, TRYING to keep my expectations low. Rob was right about one thing: working for a nonprofit has not done me a lot of favors so far. If the chancellor is going to offer me my old job back, or a crappy job in another department, I'm determined to say no.

I enter his office feeling hopeful and sick with nerves at the same time. And when his first question is about Olivia, all that hope flutters away and I just feel sick. Rob said this was probably just about the chancellor wanting me to call in a favor with Olivia, and he was right.

"You said she just had a baby, too?" he asks. "But she's still racing?"

I nod, forcing a smile on my face. "She is. She just took first at Western States."

"Do you think she might be willing to let us photograph her for the alumni magazine?" he asks, and I want to bury my face in my hands. I can't believe I put on a suit for this. I can't believe I really hoped he'd want to hire me after I stormed out of my job.

"Yes," I reply. "I'm sure she'd be happy to do it." Which is a lie. Olivia will have no interest in doing it, but that's a problem for later. I just want to say whatever is necessary to get out of here.

He leans forward. "I'm not sure if you're aware of this," he says, "but the marketing department has been in shambles since you left. I'm wondering how you'd feel about taking it over. They've fallen so far behind in the past month that we need someone who can hit the ground running."

My jaw drops. I thought my best-case scenario was a job in another department. Taking Tim's job never even occurred to me.

"I'd love it," I reply, wide-eyed. "I just can't believe Timothy quit."

The chancellor shrugs. "He hasn't exactly quit," he says. "But it's become clear of late that he's not up to the job. I'm meeting with him after this to let him know."

I nod, speechless. If I were a better person, it would be enough for me that I'm being offered a job, particularly one with a starting salary nearly double what I made before. The fact that it's Timothy's job, though, makes it infinitely sweeter.

He tells me he'll email the offer letter this evening and I leave in a daze. A week ago, I'd lost everything, and now I've got all of it back, only better. And maybe a month or a year from now I'll realize everything isn't what it seemed, but right now, my life seems pretty close to perfect.

My happy thoughts are punctured by the unwelcome appearance of Timothy, standing directly in my path as I head to the parking lot. I was almost inclined to feel sorry for him, but the moment I see his smirk I just want to rub the news in his face.

"I'd ask you how the job hunt was going," he says, "but given that you're on campus on a Tuesday afternoon, I guess I know the answer."

I reply with a smirk of my own. "I'm actually not too worried about it."

"You should be," he says. "Anyone who calls me for a referral is going to get an earful."

I laugh, which he clearly was not expecting. Why was I ever intimidated by this man? He's a thirteen-year-old bully in a man's body, and not much of one at that.

"I'm still not worried. You never know what's in store, Timothy," I tell him. I glance back in the direction of the chancellor's office. "Maybe even right around the corner."

ON THE WAY HOME I CALL BRENDAN TO TELL HIM THE GOOD news.

"I'm still at the office," he says. "Meet me here and we'll go celebrate."

The suggestion thrills me and makes me uncertain again all at once. It's the first time he's ever suggested I come by. "Really?" I tease. "This doesn't cross some work/private life divide of yours?"

"It would," he says, "if there were a divide. But there isn't anymore."

I arrive to find his office is laid out very similarly to the one in which we first worked. I shout to him that I'm here and jump up on the tour desk, the way I always did that summer we worked together.

When he walks out, he comes to a dead stop.

"What?" I ask.

"You," he says. "It just hit me, seeing you sitting like that, how you tortured me that summer we worked together."

"I tortured *you*?" I guffaw. "I had such a crush on you, and you were so mean to me."

"I spent that entire summer fantasizing about you until I thought I was gonna go out of my mind," he says. "It was terrible."

My mouth curves into a smile. "And what were you imagining us doing?" I ask.

"Sometimes it was you, just like that," he says. "You swinging those legs over the tour desk."

"That's it?"

He creeps closer, pushing my knees apart until he's standing between them and our chests are touching.

"Not even close," he says, cupping my jaw. "But I'd start like this."

He kisses me, and for some reason—in this place, in this moment—I become my twenty-two-year-old self, the one so consumed with lust, so obsessed that even the sight of the back of his head could make my legs weak.

"And then," he says, unbuttoning my blouse, "I'd do this."

He pushes my skirt around my waist. "Now lay back," he whispers, "and I'll show you the rest."

76

ERIN
Two Months Later

As I'm apt to do, I start yawning the moment Brendan and I board the flight to Seattle, where we will celebrate Will and Olivia's anniversary as well as our goddaughter's baptism. It's been a busy couple of months, but the best possible kind of busy—I love my job and Brendan's tour company is thriving. Because of our schedules, we really only see each other at night, but we make the most of it.

Brendan once worried that he'd drag me down, the way he thought he did Gabi. But the truth is that I was already drowning —suffocated by the demands placed on me by my family and Rob —and Brendan gave me just enough air to realize it was happening at all, and to make it stop.

There are no more two AM calls for either of us. Brendan finally blocked Gabi's mother, and my father and Sean successfully completed rehab. I have no idea if they'll stay clean, but I know I'm done covering for both of them.

"You know what would make a good anniversary present?" he asks me now, sliding his fingers through mine and glancing back toward the bathrooms.

"A, we are not attempting to join the mile-high club in the middle of the day when every single person will watch us both entering and leaving the bathroom."

"And what's B?"

"B is that it's not even our anniversary. It's Will and Olivia's. And before you start bitching, keep in mind this *could* be our four-year anniversary too if you hadn't taken off with the wedding coordinator that night."

I'd convinced myself it no longer bothers me, but the irritation in my tone suggests otherwise.

He turns toward me. "I never laid a finger on the wedding coordinator," he says. "Where'd you get that idea?"

I swallow. "Rob told me. And I was completely devastated. I went to my room afterward and cried myself to sleep."

His jaw clenches. "Erin, I waited. I waited and waited, feeling like an asshole, until I got a text from Rob saying he'd finally gotten you to come to his room."

My chest tightens. Rob played us both. He knew, even back then, that there was something between us, and he went out of his way to make sure nothing came of it. Obviously it all worked out anyway, but I'm sad for the version of me that spent that night and the weeks and *years* after it a little broken.

What might have happened if it had gone another way? Where would we be right now?

Brendan shrugs. "He did us a favor."

"*What?*" I demand. "How can you say that? He lied to both of us."

"I was too young, and you were definitely too young. It wouldn't have lasted."

I open my mouth to argue and he stops me. "It's all worked out for the best," he says. "I'd gladly give up a couple of years with you, if I'm getting forever in exchange."

"Forever, huh?" I tease, leaning against his shoulder.

"Yeah, smart ass," he says. "You got a problem with that?"

I laugh. "Nope. Forever sounds just about right."

TWO DAYS LATER, I'M STANDING IN FRONT OF THE ENTIRE church with Brendan by my side. He's giving me that look, the one he should not have on his face in church—especially not now, with everyone watching.

"Pay attention," I chide, bumping him with my hip. "This is serious."

"I *am* paying attention," he says, his eyes dipping to my mouth. He leans close so only I can hear. "But I'm going to do such bad things to you when we get home tonight."

I'm okay with that, obviously.

The prayers end. Our goddaughter is handed to the priest to be anointed and begins screaming bloody murder. She might look like Will, but she's got Olivia's temper. After Will and Olivia say their part, and Brendan and I say ours, communion begins. I open the missalette for both of us, though I know for a fact Brendan will refuse to sing.

He leans down to my ear again instead. "Will told me this morning that the next baptism had better be our kid."

I try not to smile and fail. I'm willing to be patient with him, but I still want the whole package. I want it to be us here someday, with our child. "Yeah? And what did you say?"

"I said the wedding probably ought to come first."

I'm smiling so broadly that I'm embarrassed for myself. "That's usually how it works."

"He also said I should start asking now, since you'll probably turn me down five times like Olivia did him."

My eyes flicker to his. "I think you're safe."

His hand slides to my back and he leans down to my ear once

more. "Will you drag out the planning until we're a million years old? There are some rumors that you do that."

I elbow him. "No."

"Are you going to refuse to put out the night before, like you did last night?"

I roll my eyes. "Your mother and Peter were in the next room. And I can't believe you're worrying about not getting laid on *one* night so far in the future."

He turns to me, his face suddenly earnest. My heart begins to beat a little faster. "It's not that far in the future, Erin. You scared?"

"Not anymore," I tell him, nestling against his side. "Not in the least."

THE END

Want a peek at Erin and Brendan's wedding?
Sign up for Elizabeth's newsletter at elizabethoroark.com

ALSO BY ELIZABETH O'ROARK

What if you discovered you were living your life for the second time--and you were still in love with someone from the first?

"Seriously one of my top, top reads--not of just 2019, but ever."- **Amazon Bestselling Author Maria Luis**

Turn the page for a sneak peek!

PARALLEL

I had a nightmare as a child. A nightmare that visited me again and again. I've never forgotten it, not a single detail, although if my parents hadn't kept the psychologist's report, I'd probably assume the years had added and detracted from it in various ways. But they didn't. It's all in writing, exactly as it rests in my head.

Quinn, age four, was brought into our clinic due to recurrent nightmares. Parents report that patient wakes several times a week, crying for her "husband" ("Nick"), and claiming they've been separated by someone. Patient insists she "isn't supposed to be here" for hours and sometimes days afterward. There are no further signs of psychosis.

At first those nightmares—their weirdness, their specificity—made my mother scared for me. Over time though, she also became scared *of* me, and that taught me a lesson I'd continue to find true over the coming years: the things I knew, *real* things, were safest kept to myself.

∾

QUINN
2018

Déjà vu.

It translates to *already seen*, but really it sort of means the opposite: that you *haven't* already seen the thing, but feel like you have. I once asked Jeff if he thought they actually call it *déjà vu* in France or perhaps keep a better, more accurate expression for themselves. He laughed and said, "you think about the weirdest shit sometimes."

Which is so much truer than he knows.

"Everything okay?" he asks now, as we follow my mother and his into the inn where we will marry in seven short weeks. I've been *off*, somehow, since the moment we pulled into town, and I guess it shows.

"Yeah. Sorry. I've got the start of a headache." It's not entirely true, but I don't know how to explain this thing in my head, this irritating low hum. It makes me feel as if I'm only half here.

We step into the lobby and my mother extends her arms like a game show hostess. "Isn't it cute?" she asks without waiting for an answer. "I know it's an hour from D.C., but at this late date it's the best we're going to do." In truth, the lobby reminds me of an upscale retirement community—baby blue walls, baby blue carpet, Chippendale chairs—but the actual wedding and reception will take place on the lawn. And as my mother pointed out, we can no longer afford to be picky.

Jeff's mother, Abby, steps beside me, running a hand over my head, the way she might a prize stallion. "You're being so calm about this. Any other bride would be in a panic."

It's posed as a compliment, but I'm not sure it is. Losing our venue two months before the wedding *should* have made me panic, but I try not to get too attached to things. Caring too much about anything makes perfectly reasonable people go insane—just ask the girl who burned down the reception hall her ex was about to get married in...which happened to be the reception hall *we* were getting married in too.

My mother claps her hands together. "Well, our appointment with the hotel's events coordinator isn't for another hour. Shall we get some lunch while we wait?"

Jeff and I exchange a quick look. On this point we are both of one mind. "We really need to get back to D.C. before rush hour." *Are my words coming out as slowly as they feel?* It's as if I'm on delay somehow, two steps behind. "Maybe you could just show us around?"

My mother's smile fades to something far less genuine. She wants giddy participation from me and has been consistently disappointed with my inability to provide it.

She and Abby lead the way, back to the porch where we entered. "We've already been discussing it a bit," Abby says to me over her shoulder. "We were thinking you could walk down the stairs and out to the porch, where your fa— *uncle*, I mean, will wait." She pauses for a moment, blushing at the error. It shouldn't be a big deal at this point—my dad's been gone almost eight years —but I feel that pinch deep in my chest anyway. That hint of sadness that never quite leaves. "And then we'll do a red carpet out to the tent."

Together we step outside. It's a gruelingly hot day, as are most summer days anywhere near D.C., and this thing in my head only gets worse. I vaguely notice my surroundings—blinding sun, a technicolor blue sky, the rose bushes my mother is commenting on, but all the while I feel displaced, like I'm following this from far away. *What the hell is going on?* I could call it déjà vu, but it's not really that. The conversation occurring right now, with this group of people, is wholly new. It's the place that feels familiar. *More* than familiar, actually. It feels important.

They're discussing the lake. I'm not sure what I've missed, but Abby is worried about its proximity. "It would just take one boatful of drunks to create chaos," she says. "And we don't want a bunch of looky-loos either."

"Most boats can't reach this part of the lake," I reply without thinking. "There's too much brush under the water on the way here."

Abby's brow raises. "I didn't realize you'd been here before. And when did you ever sail?"

My pulse begins to race, and I take a quick, panicked breath. They know I haven't been here. They know I don't sail.

I don't know why I let it slip out.

"No," I reply. "I read up a little before I came." The words sound as false to me as they are, and I know they sound false to my mother too. If I were to glance at her right now, I'd see that troubled look on her face, the one I've seen a thousand times before. I learned early in life it bothered her, this strange ability of mine to sometimes know things I should not.

Jeff's phone rings and he turns the other way, while my mother walks ahead, frowning at the ground beneath her. "I hope they're going to water soon," she frets. "If it stays this dry, that carpet will be covered with dust by the time the ceremony starts."

She is right, unfortunately. I can see the soil shift loosely before me, the grass burned and threadbare beneath an unrelenting sun, all the way to the pavilion. If there were even the slightest breeze, we'd be choking on it right now.

We round the corner of the inn, and the lake comes into view, shimmering in the early July heat. It looks like any other lake, yet there's something about it that speaks to me. I stare, trying to place it, and as I do, my gaze is compelled upward, beyond its sapphire depths, to a cottage in the distance.

It's a tap, at first. A small tap between my shoulder blades, like a parent warning a child to pay attention. But then something shifts inside me, invisible anchors sinking into the ground, holding me in place. My stomach seems to drop as they go.

I know that house.

I want to look away. My heart is beating harder, and the fact that people are going to notice makes it beat harder still, but already a picture is forming in my head—a wide deck, a long, grassy slope leading to the water's edge.

"How can the grass be so dry with all this water around?" Abby asks, but her voice is growing dim beneath this sudden ringing in my ears.

And then, her words disappear entirely. There is no ground, no light, nothing to grab. I'm plummeting, and the fall is endless.

When my eyes open, I'm flat on my back. Soil clings to my skin and the sun is beating down so fiercely it drowns out all thought. I'm in some kind of field with a house in the distance, and a woman is leaning over me. Have I met her somewhere before? It feels like I have but I can't place her at all.

"Quinn!" she cries. "Oh, thank God. Are you okay?"

The light is too much. That drumming in my head turns into a gong. I need it to stop, so I squeeze my eyes shut. The smell of parched grass assaults me.

"Why am I here?" I whisper. The words are slurred, the voice barely my own. *God, my head hurts.*

"You fell," she says, "We're at the inn. For your wedding, remember?"

The woman is pleading with me as if I'm a child on the cusp of a tantrum, but nothing she says makes sense. *I* am already married. And since when did London get so *hot*? It's never like this here.

A man comes jogging toward us. His build is similar to Nick's—tall, muscular—but even from a distance, I know he's not Nick, not even close. My eyes flutter closed and for a moment, I feel like I'm with him again—watching the smile that starts slowly before it lifts high to one side, catching the faint scent of chlorine from his morning swim. Where is he? He was *right* next to me a second ago.

The man drops to the ground beside me, and the women scurry out of his way. "She must have tripped," one of them says, "and now she's really out of it. I think she may need to go to the hospital."

I'm not going anywhere with these people, but I feel that first burst of fear in my chest. The throbbing in my head is growing. What if they try to force me to leave with them? I don't even know that I'd be able to fight them off with my head like this.

"Where's Nick?" The words emerge wispy and insufficient, needy rather than commanding.

"The hotel manager is Mark," says another voice. "Maybe she means Mark?"

"Can you sit up?" the guy asks. "Come on, Quinn."

I squint, trying to see him better in the bright sun. *How does he know my name?* There's something familiar about him, but he also just has one of those faces. "Are you a doctor?"

His jaw sags open. "Babe, it's me. *Jeff.*"

What the hell is happening here? Why is this guy acting like we're old friends? I focus on him, trying to make sense of it.

"Your fiancé," he adds.

For a moment I just stare at him in horror. And then I begin scrambling backward, a useless attempt at escape. "No," I gasp, but even as I'm denying it, praying this is a nightmare, some part of my brain has begun to recognize him too, and remembers a different life, one in which Nick does not exist.

Nick does not exist.

I roll face down in the grass and begin to weep.

ABOUT THE AUTHOR

Elizabeth O'Roark lives in Washington, DC with her three children. Drowning Erin is her fourth novel. If you enjoyed this book, please post a review!

ACKNOWLEDGMENTS

The problem with writing a book some people like is that when you try to write the next book in the series, it feels inevitable that people will hate it. That made writing *Drowning Erin* the most torturous experience of my life, and many times over the past 18 months I've given it up completely. Therefore, this book owes its existence to many, many people who are not me:

The wonderful, tireless Katie Meyer, who read all 2000 versions and made finding a title for this book into a part-time occupation.

My editor, Jessica Royer Ocken. You've almost got me onboard with Chicago Style. Thanks for making this so painless.

Natasha Boyd, whose suggestions made this a far better book than it would have been.

Becca Hensley Mysoor, for an invaluable final read-through.

Brooke Castillo, who talked me through my angst and convinced me that "done is better than perfect".

Lori Jackson for a cover I absolutely love

My wonderful beta readers: Shelby Bauer, Karen Metcalf, Lynn Rider, Laura Ward Steuart and Erin Thompson.

And last but not least my family and friends, who've been unbelievable during two very craptastic years. I love you guys.

Printed in Great Britain
by Amazon

81982822R00200